Battle Eagle

A Scottish Dark Ages Romance

The Warrior Brothers of Skye
Book Three

Jayne Castel

Historical Romance by Jayne Castel

DARK AGES BRITAIN

The Kingdom of the East Angles series
Night Shadows (prequel novella)
Dark Under the Cover of Night (Book One)
Nightfall till Daybreak (Book Two)
The Deepening Night (Book Three)
The Kingdom of the East Angles: The Complete Series

The Kingdom of Mercia series
The Breaking Dawn (Book One)
Darkest before Dawn (Book Two)
Dawn of Wolves (Book Three)
The Kingdom of Mercia: The Complete Series

The Kingdom of Northumbria series
The Whispering Wind (Book One)
Wind Song (Book Two)
Lord of the North Wind (Book Three)
The Kingdom of Northumbria: The Complete Series

DARK AGES SCOTLAND

The Warrior Brothers of Skye series
Blood Feud (Book One)
Barbarian Slave (Book Two)
Battle Eagle (Book Three)
The Warrior Brothers of Skye: The Complete Series

The Pict Wars series
Warrior's Heart (Book One)
Warrior's Secret (Book Two)
Warrior's Wrath (Book Three)
The Pict Wars: The Complete Series

Battle Eagle by Jayne Castel

ISBN: 978-0-473-54890-2 (paperback)

Published by Winter Mist Press
Cover designed by Winter Mist Press
Edited by Tim Burton
Cover design by Winter Mist Press

Cover photography courtesy of www.shutterstock.com and www.pixabay.com
Eagle image courtesy of www.pixabay.com

Map of 'The Winged Isle' by Jayne Castel

The Washer Woman song that appears in Chapter Five is adapted from a poem by Harry Boslem: www.ibuzzle.com/articles/the-washer-woman-bean-nighe-poem.html

The song that appears in Chapter Twenty is adapted from a Scottish Folk song, The Mist Covered Mountains: www.omniglot.com/songs/gaelic/chimi.php

Visit Jayne's website: www.jaynecastel.com

***

*To my readers—who make it possible for me to do what
I love!*

***

Maps of Scotland and The Winged Isle

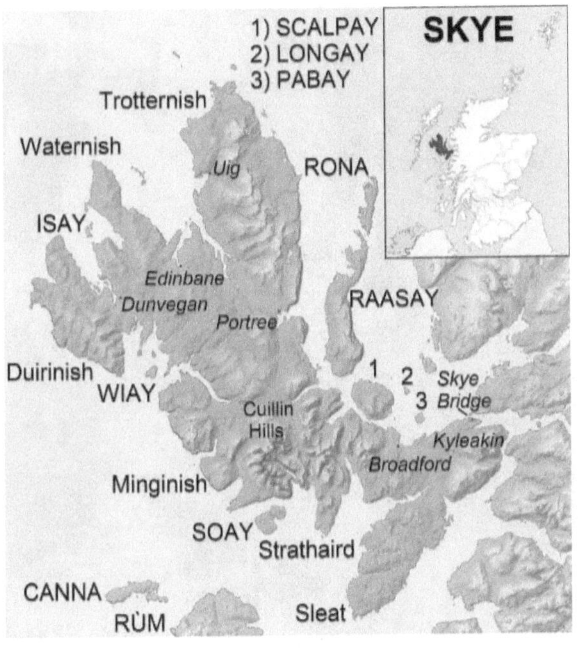

DUN
SKUDIBURGH
DUN
GRIANAN
THE
STAG
DUN
VEGAN
THE WOLF
DUN
ARDTRECK
THE
BLACK CUILLINS
LOCHANS OF
THE FAIR FOLK
MAINLAND
THE EAGLE
THE
RED HILL
DUN RINGILL
KYLEAKIN
THE BOAR
AN TEANGA
THE
WINGED
ISLE
(4TH CENTURY AD)

Three things there are that will never come back:
The arrow shot forth on its destined track;
The appointed hour that could not wait;
And the helpful word that was spoken too late.
—From the Persian, paraphrased by Louis Untermeyer

Prologue

Bitter Cold

Winter, 368 AD—The Winged Isle

The fort of Dun Ringill

DONNEL WENT TO his wife's cairn at dawn. He walked alone, leaving the outer walls of Dun Ringill and climbing up to the hillock east of the fort. Mist drifted in from the loch, giving the wintry landscape an otherworldly feel.

It was an eerie morning—it felt almost as if the Fair Folk were looking on.

Mid-winter was approaching, and the earth lay dormant. The caw of a raven was the only sound in the still, silent dawn as Donnel climbed the slope toward a row of stacked-stone burial mounds.

He stopped at the brow of the hill, before the cairns. There were a few new ones of late—too many. There was his father's, who had been slain in a skirmish with The Wolf just two years earlier. There was Alpia's, who had fallen in battle last spring.

And there was Luana's.

A year ago to the day.

Donnel exhaled slowly and lowered himself to his knees before the cairn. The stack of stone rose before him, its entrance guarded by a slab of rock. Inside lay his wife's body.

It hardly seemed a full turn of the seasons since the gods had cruelly taken her. Much had happened during the past year. He had gone south for a time, joining warriors from An t-Eilean Sgitheanach—The Winged Isle—and other mainland tribes. They had marched on the Great Wall. There, they had beaten the Caesars and returned home victorious. During that campaign, Donnel had proved himself as a warrior of no equal. He had slain many centurions during the siege, and the other warriors had hailed his bravery.

But none of it mattered. Without Luana his world was cast in shadow.

It was bitterly cold this morning, and the chill drilled into his bones. But Donnel did not care. It matched the ice in his heart.

He reached out and placed a hand on the door to his wife's tomb. "Luana," he whispered, his voice low and broken. "My love, my life."

His eyes burned, but he did not weep. He had wept upon her death but had not shed a tear since. Instead, the grief had burned inward, had grown into a seething rage.

Memories of Luana assailed him, and he closed his eyes. Her laughing blue eyes and her lovely face. Her long raven hair and gentle touch. She had been a kind soul; the best woman he had ever known.

He hated The Reaper for taking her from him.

Donnel dropped his hand from the tomb, his fingers curling into fists. She had borne him a son, Talor. He knew it was wrong to hate the lad—yet every time he looked upon him, he was reminded of her. Folk said Talor had his father's coloring and bone structure. But those eyes, the bright blue of a summer sky, were Luana's.

Donnel kept away from the lad. Talor was still too young to know or care who his father was. In the meantime his son was in the care of Luana's sister, Mael, and her husband, Maphan. They were bringing Talor up with their daughter, Ailene, as their own. He was grateful to them. Donnel could not raise a child. He was too angry—too bitter. He would just poison the lad, and his son would grow to hate him.

Another raven's caw, close by now, jerked Donnel back to the present. His knees were beginning to ache, pressed against the hard stone. He pushed himself upright, drawing his fur mantle close to ward off the bone-numbing chill.

"I failed you, my love," he whispered. He had told Luana he would protect her with his life. But on the day she had given birth to Talor, the day the birthing sickness had taken her, he had been helpless. He had done nothing as his lovely young wife died in his arms. He had hated himself since—every moment of the day— for his failure to save her.

And yet at Dun Ringill life went on. That angered him too—for he had wanted the world to stop after Luana died.

Donnel turned from the cairn, casting his gaze back to the fort, to where a large squat tower rose into the mist. He could see smoke drifting from its roof. There would be folk awake now, rousing the embers of the great hearth. His eldest brother, Galan, was likely to be among the first up, especially since he and Tea shared their alcove with a wailing infant.

Galan had recently become a father. At Gateway, Tea—his brother's fiery wife—had given birth to a son. They had named the boy Muin—after Galan, Tarl, and Donnel's father. Muin would grow up alongside Talor; they would both be warriors one day.

Meanwhile Donnel's other brother, Tarl, had found love. Last summer he had wed Lucrezia, a Roman woman he brought back from the Great Wall. Tarl and Lucrezia had not begun their story well—for Tarl had initially taken her as his slave. But after Galan had given

Lucrezia her freedom, Tarl had set out to win her love—
and he had succeeded in the end.

Donnel did not wish either of his brothers ill. Next to
Luana they were the two people he loved most in the
world. Yet their happiness only served to highlight his
own misery. He was hollow inside. Despite the biting
cold, which made his breathing steam before him—and
had already numbed his fingers and toes, Donnel was in
no hurry to rejoin his kin in the broch. He and Galan
argued often these days; indeed, there was little they
agreed upon.

Turning back to the row of mounds, Donnel's gaze
rested upon the most recent: Alpia's. The warrior had
fallen during a skirmish. A Boar warrior had thrust a
pike into her belly, and she had died shortly after.

Alpia had been young and brave. Like Luana she had
been taken before her time. Donnel clenched his jaw at
the memory. He wanted vengeance against the people of
The Boar, but Galan would not hear of it—the topic was
one of the main sources of discord between them.
Galan's quest for peace, once something he had
respected in his brother, now galled Donnel.

Anger, an old familiar friend by now, warmed his
belly, obliterating the ache of loss he felt whenever he
thought about Luana.

Enough. He turned from the cairns and strode back
down the hill toward the fort. *This won't bring her back.
Nothing will.*

He would grieve no more over his dead wife. But he
would make the world pay.

Chapter One

Fire

Six months later ...

"FIRE!"

EITHNI GLANCED up from where she had been harvesting chamomile. Ruith's garden was a riot of herbs. The seer did not use half of what she grew so Eithni, as the fort's healer, was allowed to gather what she needed for her remedies.

Straightening up, Eithni raised her gaze—and saw a column of black, oily smoke staining the pale morning sky.

"Fire!"

The call came again, but Eithni was already off, running. The smoke was rising from the far side of Dun Ringill, on the eastern edge of the scattering of houses that lay between the fort and the outer perimeter.

Eithni sprinted up the stone path, her bare feet flying. She passed low-slung round huts made of stacked-stone, with conical roofs. The smell of roasting meat wafted out of doorways, a reminder that the noon meal approached.

As she ran, Eithni caught sight of flames licking into the sky. Shouts and cries echoed over the village inside the walls. When she crested the hill, her gaze seized upon the dwelling that burned before her.

Her heart leaped into her throat. She knew this roundhouse well. This was the home of Mael and Maphan, and their daughter, Ailene. Talor, their nephew, also dwelt here.

Eithni choked back a sob and pushed her way through the amassing crowd. The fire roared like a stag. The roof looked like it was about to cave in.

"Gods ... no!" Eithni rushed forward, toward the open doorway. She had to see if anyone was trapped inside.

"Eithni—stop." A strong hand grasped her by the shoulder and pulled her back. She glanced back to see Lutrin, one of the chieftain's warriors, standing behind her. "It's too dangerous," he said, his ruggedly handsome face stern. "Tarl and Donnel have already gone in there."

Eithni swiveled round, her gaze returning to the narrow entrance. "But where's Mael ... and Maphan?" she gasped.

An instant later two figures burst out of the roundhouse's entrance.

Donnel, tall and dark, carried a child under each arm. He was swiftly followed by Tarl, his brown-haired elder brother, who dragged an unconscious man out behind him.

Maphan.

The two children Donnel held—Talor, who was now one and a half, and Ailene, who was approaching her third winter—were coughing and wheezing. Tears streaked their stricken faces, and their eyes were huge.

Donnel carried the boy and girl clear of the burning house, with Tarl at his heels.

The roof exploded behind them. Plumes of flame leaped high, sending showers of sparks into the heavens. The gathering crowd staggered back, but Eithni rushed up to where Tarl was laying Maphan on the ground. Behind him the two children were wailing in Donnel's arms. It was a good sign as it meant that the smoke had not gotten into their lungs. Eithni would check on them later, but for the moment it was their father who needed her attention.

She dropped to her knees beside the unconscious warrior. Maphan, a well-built man with long dark hair and sharp features, lay there as if asleep.

"Maphan ..." She shook him gently. "Can you hear me?"

"I found him face down by the fire pit," Tarl rasped, his face smudged with soot, his grey eyes streaming from smoke. "He'd been frying something in lard—but it fell onto the floor when he collapsed. I think that's what started the fire. The bairns were trying to rouse him when we entered."

Eithni frowned. Leaning over, she felt for a pulse. There was none. Then she lowered her ear to his chest, but there was no rise and fall of his rib cage, no rhythmic thud of his heart.

Eithni straightened up, her gaze meeting Tarl's once more. "He's dead," she whispered.

"Maphan!" A woman's cry split the air. Eithni looked up to see Mael, her skirts billowing and her dark hair streaming out behind her, as she sprinted up the path toward them. She carried a basket under one arm. Reaching them, Mael threw her basket to one side, the sorrel and parsley she had collected scattering over the ground. Then she dropped to her knees at her husband's side. "What's wrong with him?" Mael glanced up. "Eithni?"

Eithni inhaled deeply. She loved being a healer—preserving life, and bringing new life into the world—but she hated this part of it. Looking into someone's eyes and telling them their loved one was dead or dying tore her insides to pieces.

"I'm sorry, Mael," she whispered. "He's gone."

Silence settled over them. Mael stared at her as if she had taken leave of her senses. For a few moments the woman simply refused to believe it.

The gathered crowd hushed as they all realized that Maphan was dead. It was a shock; Maphan had been a healthy warrior of twenty-seven winters who should have lived for many more.

A wail went up, shattering the quiet. Mael slumped forward and threw herself over her husband's body. The two children howled as well, both of them struggling under Donnel's grip.

Shaking, Eithni rose to her feet, her gaze meeting Donnel's for the first time since he had carried the children to safety. Both of them wriggled against him, but he held them in a grip of iron. Talor's face had gone bright red. The wee lad wept, struggling under Donnel's arm. He was frightened and wanted Mael to comfort him.

But Mael was struggling to accept her beloved Maphan was dead.

Donnel's face was hewn from stone as his gaze held Eithni's. "What killed him?"

"I don't know," Eithni replied.

His mouth thinned. She could feel his disdain for her, could almost taste it. She had cured Donnel of a soured wound many months earlier. She had brought him back from the brink of death—and he had never forgiven her for it. She knew he resented her—that he thought her interfering—but she did not care. She would not stand by and let someone die.

The Battle Eagle. He had earned that name while fighting to the south. It suited him, Eithni thought, for these days Donnel was at war with the world.

It was hard to like Donnel of late, and yet there was something about him that fascinated Eithni. She often felt an odd restlessness well within her when he was near—a sensation she did not understand or welcome.

Under Donnel's left arm little Ailene was weeping piteously. "Da," she wailed. "Wake up, Da!"

Eithni stepped forward. "Give the girl to me, Donnel," she instructed gently.

He released Ailene without a word, and Eithni gathered the sobbing child in her arms. Ailene's thin body trembled with fear; like Talor she was too young to understand what death meant. "What's wrong with Da?"

There were no words of solace Eithni could offer. She could only hold the child.

Behind them the dwelling continued to burn. It had been a substantial roundhouse—one of the largest and most comfortable in the village. Maphan had built it just before he and Mael had wed three summers earlier. This house had been one of Eithni's favorite spots. She had spent many an afternoon here gossiping with Mael as the children played at their feet.

But now it was burning to ashes before them, along with Mael's life.

Still cradling Ailene, Eithni turned away from Donnel and closed her eyes. Tears escaped, burning down her cheeks.

"I'm so sorry, Mael."

Tea pulled the sobbing woman into her arms and hugged her tightly. Eithni stood behind them, still holding a sniffling Ailene in her arms, while Eithni's elder sister, Tea, did her best to comfort Mael. Tea and her husband, Galan—chieftain of The Eagle tribe—had rushed from their broch the moment news of the fire reached them. Tarl's wife had also joined them; Lucrezia stood next to her husband, her face drawn as she gazed upon the smoldering ruins of the roundhouse.

Galan's expression was grim. He hunkered down before Maphan and regarded the warrior silently.

"Maphan seemed well when I went eeling with him yesterday," Tarl spoke up from behind Galan. "What could have taken him?"

Galan looked up and grief flashed across his hawkish features. "Remember what killed our mother? Sometimes there are silent things at work within us that strike without warning."

Behind them Donnel snorted. He still gripped Talor under one arm, and although the lad had stopped crying, he wore a miserable expression as he hung there. Watching them, Eithni realized that Talor most likely considered Donnel a stranger. In the one and a half years of his life, this man had not come near him once. Talor wanted the comfort of someone he knew and trusted. Likewise, Eithni saw the tension in Donnel's broad shoulders as he held the lad. It was only the severity of this situation that kept him from casting the boy aside.

"Don't try to make sense of it," Donnel growled, his voice harsh. "It's just life, brother. The Reaper comes for us all."

Galan frowned. A tense silence settled over the gathered crowd.

Eithni held her breath, waiting for Galan to respond harshly to Donnel. The two of them had done nothing but argue of late.

When he did not, Donnel's lip curled. He thrust Talor at Lutrin, who was standing to his left. "Here ... take him."

Lutrin had just gathered the lad in his arms when Donnel turned and stalked away without another word.

Eithni watched him go, outrage flowering in her breast.

She was not like Tea; she had never been brave or forthright. Yet Donnel's attitude riled her. How dare he? His behavior was unacceptable—especially when Maphan's body, not yet cold, lay just a few yards away.

Wordlessly, Eithni passed Ailene to Tea and hurried off after Donnel.

She caught up with him just as he entered the stone arch that led toward the broch.

"Donnel!"

He ignored her, and so she reached out and grabbed his arm, pulling him up short. "Donnel—wait!"

He turned, his dark eyebrows rising in surprise. Not for the first time, Eithni was struck by just how handsome he was. The plaid breeches and leather vest he wore showed off his tall, muscular body. His chiseled features, beautifully molded mouth, straight nose, and long eyelashes were breathtaking. All three of the brothers—Galan, Tarl, and Donnel—were attractive but, to Eithni, Donnel was the most striking. Yet bitterness had cast a harshness over his features.

She had set eyes on Donnel mac Muin for the first time nearly two years earlier, at Tea and Galan's wedding. He had been married then, his lovely wife Luana heavily pregnant. Even so, Eithni had been captivated by The Eagle warrior. How she had wished to find a man so handsome for herself.

But that was before she had returned home to Dun Ardtreck—before Forcus.

"You can't keep doing this," she gasped, out of breath from running after him. "It won't bring her back."

His gaze narrowed. "What?"

"You have to let your anger go. Talor needs you."

His expression turned thunderous. "We've had this conversation before, Eithni. I don't need to hear this again."

She put her hands on her hips. "Clearly, you do. Talor has just lost his uncle—a man he sees as a father."

Had she imagined it, or did Donnel flinch at that?

Headless she pressed on. "Mael is on her own now. She needs your help."

A dangerous light ignited in those slate-grey eyes then. All three of the brothers had those eyes, the color of a stormy sky.

Donnel stepped forward, leaned down, and pushed his face close to hers. "I never thought you to be simple-minded," he growled, "but today I swear you have the brains of a goose. Heed me, woman. I do not wish to see the lad. Stop meddling and leave me alone."

He turned then and strode off, crossing toward the steps leading up to the broch.

Eithni did not follow him.

She dropped her hands from her hips, the fight going out of her. She suddenly felt shaky and close to tears. Confrontations were never easy for her at the best of times, but Donnel's grief had given his temper a vicious edge. He had left her badly shaken.

Eithni inhaled sharply and dashed away a tear that rolled down her cheek.

Enough. Don't let the man get to you—don't waste tears on him.

She should not have followed him—she realized that now. She had to accept that there were some things she could not heal. It tore at her heart to think of Talor growing up without a father. One day he would learn that the man who had sired him could not bear to look upon him. Donnel did not seem to realize this, or to care.

Yet Eithni now understood she could not make him see sense.

Chapter Two

After Sunset

ON THE EVE of Maphan's death there was a spectacular sunset. Eithni had been helping Mael prepare the warrior's body for burial. She emerged from the hut to be greeted by the sight of pink and gold ribbons decorating the western sky. She paused on the threshold, and her gaze swept over the heavens.

It seemed out of place that something so beautiful should appear on such a sad day. She pulled the door closed behind her, muffling the gentle sound of Mael's sobbing. She wanted to leave her friend alone for a while; Mael needed to say goodbye to her man.

Eithni walked away from the hut. Her steps were heavy this evening, as her feet felt leaden, her spirits low. Around her the air smelled of warm earth and grass, and of cooking. It had been a bright summer's day, and the colorful sunset promised another warm day to come.

The mood was subdued inside the fort, although the folk of Dun Ringill were making the most of the last of the light. Women brought in washing from the lines outside their homes, and children played in the dirt. Men washed their hands in water beside the stone well in the center of the village after spending the afternoon gutting and hanging the venison and boar they had brought home from their last hunting trip. It was an everyday scene, and a reminder that death only drew these hardworking people from their chores for a short while.

Life went on all the same.

Eithni liked Dun Ringill—she was happy here. She had once been happy at Dun Ardtreck too, where most of her kin still lived. Life had been good there—until her mother had died. After that her father turned vengeful, her sister bitter, and her brother withdrawn. Her brother, Loc, had become chief when their father died, and tried to forge peace. He had succeeded, until Forcus ruined it all.

Forcus. How easily he crept into her thoughts, even though she had done her best to cast him out. Nearly two years on the thought of him still made Eithni break out in a cold sweat. Her heart began to race.

Clutching her basket of herbs close, Eithni hurried down the last slope toward the south-eastern perimeter of the fort. She had to get home, to her sanctuary, where thoughts of Forcus could not reach her.

Eithni's hut sat just a few yards from the bandruí of Dun Ringill's ramshackle dwelling. Ruith, the fort's seer, had a wild but bountiful garden surrounding her hut, full of herbs and vegetables. There was also a messy enclosure which housed fowl. As it was dusk, the birds had gone indoors to roost; the soft sounds of their clucking drifted out into the soft evening air.

Eithni's garden was very different to Ruith's. She made her way to the front door, past neat beds of primroses, daisies, and foxglove. Honeysuckle grew up the stone wall of her hut. Eithni inhaled its sweet scent; the smell gave her solace.

This was not a day she wished to relive. Her home was a welcoming sight. It was an ordered, clean, and manageable world. Here, death, grief, and anger did not exist.

Opening her front door, Eithni stepped down into a small space. The pink-hued light of the sunset filtered in through the open door, illuminating a neatly-kept home, with a pile of furs in one corner, a long wooden bench along one wall, and a stone hearth in the center. The air smelled of heather, for she had sprinkled flowers amongst the fresh rushes on the floor.

Eithni went inside and sat down heavily upon a stool by her unlit hearth. A lump of peat lay in the fire pit. However, she would not light it until tomorrow morning, for she needed a fire then to cook her morning oatcakes.

Just twenty winters, and I feel as weary as a crone.

These days she sometimes felt as if she carried the weight of the world upon her shoulders. She had once laughed easily and often, but of late she felt it difficult to rouse a smile.

Today had not helped though—today had reminded her just how fragile, how short, life was. She would be glad to crawl into her furs later and leave it all behind.

Eithni sighed, rubbing her hands over her tired face. Supper was approaching; soon she would go to the broch and join the others. She was not in the mood tonight and would have preferred to eat at home. Yet she had no supper prepared, and her belly ached, reminding her that she had not eaten since dawn.

The interior of the broch rumbled with voices and bustled with activity as Eithni entered. Outside, the glorious sunset was starting to fade. It was late, for this time of year the setting sun and the rising moon almost overlapped. They had long passed Bealtunn—the spring equinox—and were now heading toward Mid-Summer Fire.

Eithni padded across the rushes, past the people who were taking their seats at the long tables that formed a square around the great hearth. She saw few smiles on the faces around her though; everyone had been saddened by Maphan's death. Dun Ringill was a tight-knit community. They would all feel the warrior's loss keenly.

Inside the hall the air was heavy with peat smoke and the rich aroma of venison stew. It took some getting used to after being outdoors in the fresh air, and Eithni was pleased she lived out of the broch. The chieftain and his kin resided in the alcoves that lined this wide circular space while many of his warriors and their families simply slept on the floor each night. When Eithni had come to live here, Galan had offered her an alcove; but she had chosen to have a hut of her own, like Ruith.

She spotted the seer now. Ruith, a small, wiry woman with greying dark hair braided into long plaits, was sitting at one of the long tables. She raised a hand to greet Eithni although her usual spry energy was missing this evening.

Maphan had been her nephew.

Eithni favored her friend with a sad smile and continued on her way across the floor. Stepping up onto the platform at the far end of the hall, Eithni edged around the chieftain's table. This was where the chief of The Eagle, his kin, and favored warriors ate their meals. As Tea's sister, Eithni was expected to join them.

Galan and Tea were already seated. Their son Muin—oblivious to the pall of grief around him—perched, gurgling upon his mother's knee. Already Eithni could see the lad would grow up to be the image of his father. He had the same striking features. Galan and Tea's heads bent close as they talked, their faces solemn. Watching them, Eithni felt warmth suffuse her.

She was so glad her sister had found a man like Galan to love.

He was a warrior—and could be brutal when needed—but he had a noble, kind heart. Tea had hated him initially, for theirs had been a forced marriage to forge peace between their tribes. The people of The Wolf and The Eagle had been long-standing enemies, but this union had ended the blood feud.

To Galan's right sat his younger brother Tarl and his wife Lucrezia. They also spoke quietly together. Tarl was usually in good spirits, laughing or teasing at mealtimes, but he wore no smile this evening. As they talked, Tarl reached out and stroked his wife's cheek. Lucrezia held his gaze, her hand fastening over his arm.

Eithni suppressed a sigh. Watching them reminded her that love existed. She would never know such happiness, but she was glad Tea and Lucrezia had found it.

She took her seat at the table, next to Donnel, who sat to Lucrezia's right. Eithni's seat was the one that Luana would have once taken—but Eithni had been given this place at the table. She would have preferred to sit elsewhere. There had been times over the past year when she had made excuses to shift seats. However, her behavior had just drawn attention to the fact that she and Donnel did not get on. So she had continued to sit here, swallowing her discomfort.

There was nowhere else to sit anyway for Cal, Namet, Ru, and Lutrin—Galan's four most trusted warriors—had joined them for supper this evening.

Donnel did not acknowledge her as she sat down, and likewise she ignored him. It was a habit for them both by now; one she had grown used to. Eithni reached for the basket of bread that was being passed down the table. She had long-since given up trying to draw the man into conversation.

Taking a bite of bread, Eithni caught the end of a discussion between Lutrin and Namet farther down the table.

"At least The Gathering will take everyone's mind off losing Maphan," Lutrin said.

Namet nodded, his brow furrowing. "Aye ... it'll be good to get away for a bit."

Eithni tensed. With everything that had happened today, she had forgotten that they were preparing to travel north, into the territory of The Stag. Their departure was only two days away. Every five summers The Winged Isle held a Gathering where all four tribes of the island—The Wolf, The Eagle, The Stag, and The Boar—met for days of revelry, games, and feasting.

"Do you remember Maphan at the last one?" Namet continued, his expression softening. "He left many Boar warriors with bloodied noses after that game of Camanachd."

Lutrin snorted. "Aye, but he won us the contest."

"And drank so much ale that night he ended up in Urcal mac Wrad's tent, challenging him to an arm-wrestling match."

This comment caused a ripple of laughter to go down the table, lightening the previously somber mood.

A melancholy smile tugged at Eithni's mouth as she listened. Maphan had indeed been a character, always in the thick of things at every festival. However, Eithni wasn't sure folk would be in the mood to celebrate so soon after his death. She glanced back up the table at where Galan was eating, his expression introspective.

"Galan," she called to him, raising her voice to be heard over the rumble of conversation around her. "With Maphan's passing ... are we still going to The Gathering?"

The question made conversation settle. All gazes swiveled to their chief.

Galan frowned as he considered the question. Watching him, Eithni reflected that it was a heavy mantle the chieftain of The Eagles wore. He bore the role stoically yet, in the past two years, there had been a number of difficult decisions for Galan to make. She supposed this one was easy compared to some.

"We'll go," he said finally. "This Gathering is an important one for us." He glanced over at Tea, his expression softening. "It is the first in many summers that both The Eagle and The Wolf will attend. The peace between our tribes is crucial ... we should be there this year."

The snort beside Eithni made her start. She glanced left at where Donnel was glaring down at his bowl of stew. "The Boar will be there also," he growled. "And I have unfinished business with them."

"There will be no bloodshed at The Gathering," Galan replied. "It is a time of peace. You would bring the wrath of all the tribes down upon us if you broke it."

A hush settled over the table. Next to Galan, Tarl was frowning. "Just leave this, Donnel," he warned, his voice low. "The argument between us and The Boar has ended.

I killed Wurgest in a fair fight, and now we must move on."

"It wasn't a fair fight," Donnel snarled. "Wurgest sent his men to ambush and kill the rest of us ... or have you forgotten?"

"And those warriors are dead now too," Tarl countered, his gaze narrowing. "Would you have vengeance upon dead men?"

Donnel shoved his bowl of stew aside, spilling it onto the wooden table. However, he paid his supper no mind. He was glaring openly now at both his brothers. "Have you both lost your balls now you've taken wives?"

Tarl stared back at him a moment before he grinned. "Now you're using my old insults," he replied. "Find some new ones of your own instead of stealing mine."

Next to Donnel, Eithni tensed. Her gaze flicked from brother to brother. Tarl was the only one smiling. Sometimes she thought he took very little in life seriously. Unlike Galan he rarely challenged Donnel on his behavior, but this evening was different.

"Maybe *your* balls are causing you trouble," Tarl continued. "Find yourself a woman to plow, and you might wipe that scowl off your face."

That sent a ripple of mirth down the table. Cal, Namet, Ru, and Lutrin roared with laughter. Lutrin, who had been swallowing a piece of bread started to choke, and Namet had to slap him on the back to dislodge it. Someone handed Lutrin a cup of wine to sip, and the warrior stopped coughing.

Donnel ignored them all. He had gone dangerously still, his handsome face hawkish. He gave Tarl such a glare that his brother's smile faltered for a moment. "Speak to me like that again, and I'll knock your teeth down your throat."

Chapter Three

Blood for Blood

EITHNI STRETCHED, AWAKING slowly.

Her eyes flickered open, and she noticed the bright beams of light filtering through the cracks in the doorway. She sat up, rubbing sleep out of her eyes.

I've overslept.

It had been a rough night; she had slept fitfully and dreamed of Forcus again.

Such dark dreams always drained her.

Clambering out of her furs, Eithni dressed swiftly, pulling on a long, sleeveless woolen tunic, which she belted at the waist. Usually, she would prepare herself some oatcakes and take her time over her first meal of the day. However, there was no time for that this morning. They were due to depart for The Gathering the following day, and there was still much preparation to get done.

Eithni left her hut, stepping out into the brightness of a warm, breezy morning. The sun was well up in the sky by now. She had indeed overslept. Everyone else was busy with their chores while she languished in her furs.

"Morning, lass."

Eithni turned to see Ruith working in the garden next to hers. The seer was on her knees, pulling up weeds.

"Good morn, Ruith," Eithni replied, stifling a yawn. She still felt half-asleep.

"Late up?" The bandruí smiled, a web of wrinkles forming around her eyes as she did so.

"Aye—I slept badly."

Ruith's penetrating gaze did not shift from her. "Bad dreams again?"

Eithni nodded. Ruith knew about the demons that plagued her sometimes although she wisely did not press Eithni about them.

"I know a charm that might help," the bandruí said after a moment. "Come by later, and I shall teach it to you."

Eithni smiled. "Thank you, Ruith." Her gaze shifted to the huge pile of weeds to the seer's left. "What's prompted this?" she asked, her smile widening.

"We're going to be away for a wee while," Ruith replied. "I don't want to come back to find the weeds have grown over my front door."

Eithni left Ruith to her weeding, making her way across the village to where a semi-circle of cone-roofed store huts sat. She could see Lucrezia and Deri there, hauling out wheels of cheese and haunches of cured meat for the journey.

"There you are," Lucrezia greeted her. The woman's high cheekbones were flushed from exertion. She was dressed in a skimpy leather vest that showed off the ample curves of her breasts and a short plaid skirt that left her legs bare. She looked as if she had just come from warrior training. "I was about to go looking for you."

"No need," Eithni said brightly. "Sorry I'm late."

Lucrezia shrugged. "No need to apologize ... I was worried, that's all." Once a Roman centurion's wife at the Great Wall to the south, Lucrezia had run a large home and even had servants. Yet here upon this isle, Lucrezia had embraced *their* way of life. She certainly was not afraid to get her hands dirty. Not only was she an excellent cook and gifted gardener, but she had learned to fight as well.

Eithni was a little in awe of her—as she would have been of Tea if she had not been her sister. Back in Dun Ardtreck, Eithni had been taught how to wield a sword and a fighting dagger, yet she had hated every moment. She loathed violence, now even more than when she was younger. She was not meant to be a warrior. Instead, she had chosen the path of healer, which suited her much more. Her sister was tall and strong, while Lucrezia, although the same height as Eithni, had a lithely muscled frame. Eithni felt like a weakling next to her.

"How are things with you these days?" Lucrezia asked with a smile. "I feel we never get to chat."

It was true—ever since Lucrezia had wed Tarl the two women hardly spent any time together. When Lucrezia had first arrived in Dun Ringill, she had shared Eithni's hut for a time. Eithni had enjoyed the company, and Lucrezia was easy to live with. When her friend had moved into the broch to share Tarl's alcove, Eithni had felt lonely for a time, although she had now gotten used to her solitary life once more.

"I am well," Eithni replied. It was the response she gave all who asked after her. No one wanted to hear that a shadow of hopelessness dogged her steps most days. There was nothing they could do about it anyway.

"You're just in time for a break," Deri chimed in, her eyes twinkling as she produced a jug of goat's milk and some clay cups. "Let's sit down for a moment."

The three women sat down on the ground while Deri poured them some milk. Eithni took a large gulp; the milk was so fresh it was still warm. Opposite her Deri stretched out her legs before her and pulled back her skirts so the sun could bathe her skin. Curvy, with a thick mane of brown hair, Deri was wedded to Cal, one of Galan's warriors.

"I hope this sun lasts for The Gathering," Deri sighed, turning her face up to the sky.

"Aye—after that bitter winter," Lucrezia replied.

Deri snorted. "Last winter wasn't that bad. We've had colder."

Lucrezia shuddered, reminding her companions that she hailed from a much warmer land far to the south of The Winged Isle.

Eithni watched Lucrezia with interest; her friend's homeland fascinated her. Lucrezia had spoken of long hot summers and a sweet fruit that they made wine from. She described a deep blue sea that you could swim in without shivering, for many moons of the year.

"Are you looking forward to The Gathering?" Deri asked them. "This is the first time The Stag have hosted one in nearly twenty summers."

"It sounds a bit like the festivals I grew up with," Lucrezia said after a pause. "I used to go into Roma every summer to watch them."

Eithni leaned forward, fascinated. "Roma," she said, rolling the 'r' the way Lucrezia did. Her friend had already described the great city to her: a grand place filled with great monuments of gleaming white marble. "The Eternal City?"

Lucrezia smiled back, her expression wistful. "That's right—you've a keen memory."

"You never told me why it's called that."

Lucrezia's smile widened. "There's a saying in my tongue: *Quando cadet Roma, cadet et mundus*—'When Roma falls, so falls the world'. The people of my homeland believe that the city will stand forever."

Silence fell as Lucrezia's companions digested this.

"Do you celebrate Mid-Summer Fire there?" Deri asked, her tone mildly curious. Unlike Eithni she did not hold a fascination for Lucrezia's homeland.

Lucrezia nodded. "A festival celebrating Summanus, the god of thunder at night."

"Really," Eithni leaned closer still. "You have a god for that?"

Lucrezia laughed. "Aye, we have too many to count." She leaned back, crossing her bronzed legs at the ankle. "These days, the god we call 'The Father of Christ' grows steadily ever more important. Those who follow him wish for all the other gods to be cast out—yet the old ways still endure."

"What happens on Summanus then?" Deri asked. Despite herself, she was starting to look intrigued.

"Folk gather at a great arena called the Circus Maximus in Roma. They offer cakes to Summanus, and then gladiators fight to the death, providing the blood sacrifice needed for the day."

Eithni listened, a shiver running through her. Although the people of this tribe and her own did not sacrifice folk to honor the gods, she had heard tales of those who did. The thought chilled her. It cast a shadow over the sunny morning.

The three women finished their milk and rose to their feet. They then resumed the task of carrying out food from the stores and loading it onto the carts that would be traveling north with them.

By the end of the morning, they had piled three carts full of provisions, all of which they had been stockpiling for many moons for The Gathering. The chore completed, the women covered the carts with oiled tarpaulins to keep the rain off and hitched ponies. Then they led the ponies into the yard outside the broch.

Leading her pony, its feathered hooves clip-clopping hollowly on the hard sun-baked earth, Eithni caught sight of Galan and Donnel standing at the foot of the steps leading up to the broch. They were deep in discussion.

Her gaze rested on the two warriors in silent admiration.

Despite that she had not let a man come near her since Forcus, she could still appreciate a handsome, virile warrior. Galan and Donnel were of a similar height, and shared the same grey eyes and jet-black hair, although the similarities ended there. Galan was of a heavier build than his youngest brother. He was also less classically handsome than Donnel—his features sharper. He wore his dark hair long, flowing over his broad shoulders, whereas Donnel had clipped his short. Both men wore tight-fitting plaid breeches and leather vests, clothing which emphasized their muscular bodies.

Eithni's gaze trailed down Donnel's torso, admiring the hardness of his abdomen.

"Stop staring," Lucrezia whispered in Eithni's ear. "Donnel will catch you."

Eithni jumped guiltily. She had not realized she had stopped short and was gawping at Donnel. "I wasn't," she snapped. However, Lucrezia was not fooled. She merely gave Eithni a knowing look and returned to her cart.

Eithni led the pony under the shadow of the wall and began to unshackle its harness. This was the coolest spot in the fort, and the supplies would remain here until the following morning. As she worked, Eithni's cheeks burned from being caught blatantly staring at Donnel.

What's wrong with me today?

It seemed she had been out of sorts since rising late.

The aroma of roasting meat wafted out of the broch above her, causing Eithni's belly to growl, and reminding her that she had missed her oatcakes earlier. She was definitely ready for her noon meal.

While Lucrezia and Deri finished unshackling their ponies, Eithni led hers across to the stables. On the way she passed Galan and Donnel. They were still talking and did not even notice her presence. As she neared them, she saw the look on their faces and tensed.

Galan looked angry, while Donnel wore a surly, mutinous expression.

"I want you to stay here," Galan growled, folding his arms across his broad chest, "to rule the fort while I'm away."

Donnel shook his head. "Namet and Ru are staying behind. They can look after Dun Ringill in your absence. You don't need me to remain here."

Galan scowled. "I'd prefer one of my kin stayed behind."

"Your warriors have ruled while you're away before." Donnel folded his arms across his chest, mirroring his brother's gesture. "Admit it—that's not why you want me back here."

Galan's gaze narrowed. "Peace is fragile upon this isle," he replied coldly. "I won't have you ruining everything I've worked for."

"What makes you think I will?"

Galan huffed a breath. "Every time you open your mouth you speak of vengeance against The Boar. Blood for blood. You talk of little else these days."

Donnel's mouth thinned. "So you don't trust me?"

"No, I don't." Galan stepped back from Donnel, signaling their conversation was over. "I'm sorry, Donnel—but you're staying behind."

Eithni walked on. As she entered the stables, she heard the low timbre of Donnel's voice, answering Galan. He was not about to let the matter drop.

Blood for blood. Eithni shivered. She saw Galan's point; Donnel was not himself these days.

She thought of Lucrezia's words earlier that day. She remembered her description of the blood-thirsty games of her homeland: the men and women who fought, died, and bled into the earth to please the gods. Was Donnel's quest for revenge that different?

Chapter Four

Departure

DONNEL READIED HIS pony in the dimly lit stall, slipping the bridle over the grey's head before swinging the saddle onto its broad back. Around him he could hear the rise and fall of warriors' voices as they prepared their own mounts to ride out.

The day of departure for The Gathering had come.

The pony—a gift from Donnel's father five summers earlier—shifted impatiently and stomped a heavy feathered foot, narrowly avoiding Donnel's booted one.

"Easy, lad," Donnel murmured. "We'll be on our way soon enough." He reached out and ran his palm along the stallion's neck. During the winter the pony grew a shaggy coat, but this time of year he was sleek. Donnel had named the pony Reothadh—Frost—and had broken him in himself. He remembered Reothadh as a colt; he had been a dappled grey then although now the years had faded his coat to match his name.

The pony whickered in response, and Donnel smiled. Since Luana's death, Reothadh had been the only company he could tolerate. The pony asked nothing of him. It did not judge or demand he mend his mood. The stallion accepted him, no matter how dark his humor.

"Donnel."

Galan's voice hailed him. Donnel tensed and cast a glance over his shoulder at where his brother had entered the stall, his tall, broad form blocking out the sunlight behind him.

"I thought I told you to stay behind."

Donnel heaved in a deep breath. He had been waiting for this moment. He turned, and their gazes met across the stall.

"Will you not heed me?" Galan asked.

Donnel's first instinct was to argue, but he had already tried that. Galan was as stubborn as he himself was; if Donnel wanted to join the others on this trip, he would need to take a different approach. Although it galled him to do so, he would attempt to be humble.

Donnel dropped his gaze. "I wish to travel with you, brother," he replied, softening his voice. "The last months have been hard. Everywhere I look there are memories of her. Time spent away from here would do me good."

It was a ruse. Donnel knew Galan had a soft heart. He would think he was doing Donnel a favor by letting him attend The Gathering. As Donnel had hoped, his brother's hawkish features gentled. "You're not planning to cause trouble at The Gathering then?"

Donnel's mouth curved. "You're taking Tarl with you. He's more likely to cause a scrap than me."

Galan snorted. "Not since he wedded. That Roman lass has tamed our brother it seems."

Donnel resisted the urge to roll his eyes. Tamed indeed. Tarl was still a bit of a rogue, but these days he was content with his life.

Galan watched him for a moment longer. "I need you to give me your word," he said quietly. "I need you to promise that you will shed no blood at The Gathering. It's too important for our people."

Donnel swallowed the irritation rising within him. He wanted to bite his brother's head off for that, but it would only result in Galan forcing him to remain at the fort. Donnel had to go north—he had to face those Boar bastards. However, he could not let Galan see what festered in his heart.

"Aye," he replied, forcing himself to hold Galan's eye. It was hard to lie to him. His brother was a good man, a fair man. "I give you my word."

Craven. Anger rose up within Donnel, biting at his throat. After their skirmish with The Boar a year earlier, Donnel had wanted vengeance, but Galan would not hear of it. Galan saw his decision as right, for he would keep the peace at any cost, yet to Donnel it was cowardice.

We've become strangers to each other.

Galan watched him a moment longer, considering his words. Then he gave a swift nod. "Finish saddling your pony. We ride out shortly."

Alone in the stall once more, Donnel tightened Reothadh's girth and slapped the pony on the rump. "Ready, lad? Off on another journey together."

The grey snorted, making it clear he was done waiting. Donnel led him from the stall and out into the bright sunlight. Mid-Summer Fire was close now. They would reach The Gathering Place to the north just in time to celebrate it with the other tribes. It was a glorious morning, and the atmosphere of excitement within the fort was infectious. A chatter of animated voices surrounded Donnel, yet he was immune to their mirth.

Around him the people of Dun Ringill readied themselves for departure. Children clambered excitedly up onto the backs of wagons, fighting for the most comfortable spot, while their parents finished loading up rolls of hide and packs of supplies. Shaggy ponies were everywhere. Their long tails were swishing and their feathered hooves stamping as warriors mounted up.

Donnel swung up onto his stallion's back, paying none of the bustling crowd around him any mind. He followed a line of warriors on horseback out of the yard and through the stone arch into the village beyond. There, more folk joined the throng.

Besides the group of warriors Galan would leave behind to protect the fort in his absence, a few others would stay on in Dun Ringill. Mael was among those; after losing her husband, she was in no mood for celebration.

As he approached the southern perimeter, Donnel's gaze shifted to the two huts to the right of the gate. He spied Ruith emerging from her hovel. The bandruí was dressed for travel in a long plaid tunic, belted at the waist. She wore a pack on her back and carried a wooden walking staff. At sixty winters the woman was still a force to be reckoned with, yet she lacked the stamina of the younger members of the party.

Eithni waited for the seer at the end of the path. Dressed in a long sleeveless tunic, a woolen wrap around her slender shoulders, the healer wore a pensive expression this morning. Her fine walnut-brown hair had grown long of late, and she wore it braided down her back. The young woman was gazing out over the procession of riders, her heart-shaped face composed, her hazel eyes shuttered.

Eithni annoyed Donnel, and yet he found his gaze drawn toward her. You would not think such a slight, fey-looking girl could be so irritating—but she was like a dog with a bone, constantly nagging him about his responsibilities as a father.

Donnel had taken vicious pleasure in defying her. And it was odd, for he noted that each fiery encounter between them cost her. Yet she persisted. He had heard rumors that she had been ill-treated at Dun Ardtreck before coming here. He believed it too, for he had seen fear in her eyes two days earlier when he had pushed his face close to hers and told her to leave him be.

There was another reason he resented Eithni though, not just for her interfering ways.

She had saved his life.

He had awoken after that deathly fever on his return home from the campaign to the south, only to find himself in the alcove where his wife had perished three moons earlier. Then, he had met Eithni's gaze and

resentment had consumed him. He had wanted to die—
why would she not let him?

Donnel tore his gaze from the healer, who now
hurried alongside Ruith to join the column, and urged
Reothadh forward. He rode up alongside Lutrin, who
journeyed upon a heavyset chestnut mare.

"Fine morning, Donnel," Lutrin greeted him. Donnel
merely grunted a response.

He and Lutrin were the same age, born just two days
apart during the same harsh winter. The warrior was
loyal to Galan, but it was Donnel with whom Lutrin had
grown up and sparred. The two of them had once been as
close as brothers, but these days they had little to say to
each other. Lutrin was unwed and seemed happy to
remain so. He did not understand what Donnel had
suffered.

"So, Galan let you come after all," Lutrin observed
with a wry grin. "He says you won't cause any trouble."

Donnel scowled. "I gave my word."

Lutrin gave him a speculative look. It reminded
Donnel that the warrior had a sharp mind; he was not
easy to fool. "And what weight does your word carry
these days?" he asked.

Donnel snorted, looking away. "We shall soon see,"
he replied.

Eithni was one of the last to leave Dun Ringill. She
walked up the slope, leaving the stone perimeter behind,
and paused. Twisting, she looked back over her shoulder
at where the fort spread out behind her.

Dun Ringill was glorious this morning. Perched on
the edge of the glittering waters of Loch Slapin, the fort
sat upon the western shores of The Winged Isle, looking
over a vast lake that led out to sea. To the north she
could see the dark craggy outline of the Black Cuillins.
The silhouette of those mountains would always remind
her of Tea and Galan's wedding, for they had been
handfasted in the shadow of those mighty peaks. To the
south a long headland thrust out into the water, and

beyond it rose layers of mountains that faded to grey blue against the clear sky.

Eithni sighed. She loved this land. The broch of Dun Ringill stood proud and solid against the sky, the conical roofs of the roundhouses spreading out around it gilded in the sun.

"You gaze as if this will be the last time you look upon the fort." A woman's voice, edged with amusement, reached her, drawing Eithni out of her reverie. She turned to see Ruith watching her. The seer had a penetrating stare, like she was trying to see into your very soul.

Eithni smiled in an attempt to mask her discomfort. "It's just that I miss my home already. I hope it doesn't get overrun with mice while we're away."

Ruith made a clucking sound. "Not this time of year, there's too much food for them elsewhere." She gave Eithni an assessing look. "Worry not, lass. Your hut will still be standing when we return. Sometimes it's good to have a break from our surroundings. You'll appreciate it all the more on our return."

The seer linked her arm through Eithni's, and the two women continued up the slope. They were roughly the same height although Ruith's body was hard and sinewy, while Eithni's was slender and soft.

Ruith cast Eithni a grin then. "The Gathering is always great fun. I attended my last one ten summers ago. There was a warrior of The Stag there who gave me many nights of pleasure. I wonder if he's still alive ... or if he'd find me too old and withered these days. I wouldn't mind some more nights in the furs with him."

Eithni's cheeks warmed at this. Ruith could be so frank about her relations with men. Too frank for Eithni's liking. She had never spoken of her past to the seer, but she sensed that Ruith knew. In a fort this size few of them had any secrets.

Perhaps the silence alerted Ruith to her discomfort, for the bandruí gave her arm a gentle squeeze, her grin transforming into a warm smile. "Come, lass. Wipe that worried look off your face. It's not good to remain in isolation—it breeds bad blood between the tribes. The Gathering is a time of joy, a time for us to mingle with the other folk of this isle. You will see."

Chapter Five

Songs by the Fireside

THE EAGLES OF Dun Ringill inched north, toward where the outline of a great red mountain thrust into the pastel sky. With such a large group traveling, many of them on foot, the company could not move swiftly. The warriors on ponies at the front of the column had to slow their pace to allow those trailing behind, especially the elderly and children, to keep up.

The journey did not dampen the travelers' excitement; if anything the chatter of their voices increased as the day wore on, echoing high up into the empty sky.

Eithni dawdled at the back of the group, listening to the rise and fall of conversation, the creak of leather, the thump of hooves, and the rumble of heavy wooden wheels from the carts.

After a while she realized that the seer had been right. It had been hard to drag herself away from her hut, from her daily routines. But now that she had left it behind, a lightness settled over her. Not only that, but it was a beautiful day to be traveling, and to be alive. A warm wind breathed in from the south-east, bringing with it the scent of heather and rich earth. Above, birds of prey circled in the cloudless sky, observing the travelers.

At the head of the column, some of the warriors—Galan and Tarl included—carried hawks aloft upon their wrists. The chief's hawk was named Lann—Blade—and the bird's sharp beak certainly lived up to its name. The birds would hunt for them on the way, and one of the contests at The Gathering also involved hunting with hawks.

Even though they had slowed their pace to accommodate those behind, the warriors on horseback drew farther and farther ahead as the day stretched on. Eventually, they became little more than specks on the horizon.

Eithni did not mind; she was content to make her way north at her own pace. Even Ruith had drawn ahead; she was chatting with a girl who had recently given birth to her first child. The young woman carried the infant slung across her front.

The day stretched out and Bienn na Caillich—the Red Hill—rose above them, before they skirted around its pebbly base. Eithni looked up at the mountain, the profusion of red grasses that grew upon its rocky sides giving it its name.

Folk also called this mountain 'The Hill of the Hag', and Eithni imagined that the goddess herself—who ruled sleep, dreams, winter, and death—perched up there looking down at their passage.

By the time they stopped for the day, The Red Hill lay to the south, a dark bulk against the sky. The company made camp in a pebbly vale next to a burn where clear water trickled over grey stones.

During the trek north their numbers had swollen, as folk from outlying villages joined them. The chorus of voices was almost deafening as the travelers erected a camp of hide tents under the shadow of The Red Hill.

Tea and Lucrezia, who had ridden with their husbands during the day, rejoined the other women as they prepared supper for the hungry travelers. The men were lighting fires—four large fire pits dominated the camp—and were dragging lumps of peat over for fuel. Few trees grew in this area of The Winged Isle, so peat provided the main source of heat.

The hunting hawks had brought down a number of birds—rooks and grouse—on the journey north-east, and Eithni sat next to Lucrezia, plucking them.

Lucrezia worked deftly, her slim fingers flying as she ripped feathers from the still warm carcass. They worked in silence for a while, before Eithni realized that Lucrezia's gaze kept straying to her.

Eithni glanced up and noted her friend's tense expression. "Luci ... what's wrong?"

Lucrezia's dark gaze shifted across the fire pit to where Tea was nursing little Muin. The babe's pudgy hands kneaded his mother's full breast as he suckled. "It's a year now since Tarl and I wed," she murmured, "and my womb has not yet quickened."

Compassion tugged at Eithni. She had wondered when this would start to bother Lucrezia. She was surprised her friend had not yet gotten with child. Although Eithni did not reside within the broch, she had heard the talk of how loud Lucrezia and Tarl were at night. It seemed that most eves they kept the other inhabitants of the roundtower awake with their groans and cries. They did not seem to know how to couple quietly, nor did they want to. Lucrezia was a healthy young woman; there was no reason why her womb should not quicken.

"Sometimes you must just give things time," Eithni replied after a moment. She met Lucrezia's eye then. "However, I can give you herbs and mix a special tincture which should improve your chances—if you're worried?"

Hope lit in Lucrezia's eyes, and Eithni realized that this had been preying on her mind more than Eithni had realized. She nodded, her full lips stretching into a smile. "I'd like that ... thank you."

Night fell and the aroma of roasting grouse and rook filled the air. It was a mild night, and as it was the warm season there was no need to sit huddled by the fireside wrapped in furs. Instead, there was singing and laughter.

After supper Eithni produced her harp and started to play. Tea, who had a lovely voice, sang beside her.

Tea started off by singing two songs the sisters had grown up with at Dun Ardtreck in the north: tales of the people of The Wolf. These were the songs of their people, of the building of the great broch perched on the wild cliffs where seabirds wheeled and puffins nested on the rocks.

After that she sang an eerie song of the Bean-Nighe— the washer woman. This fairy—a ghastly old woman who could be found by streams and pools—was an omen of death. She washed the clothes of those who were about to die.

Tell me, haggard washer woman,
Whose clothes are washed this day?
I see the cloak of a chieftain
Within your basket, lay.
And is this wife to lose her man,
My heart to be forfeit?
And shall the banshee sing tonight,
To wail his lament?

The sky weeps with blackened clouds,
And spills its rain of tears,
The wind howls through the glen,
To warn The Reaper is near,
The old broch looks forlorn,
As darkness drapes its veil,
I wash my husband's finest clothes,
That he may die well.

Tell me, haggard washer woman,
Whose clothes are washed this day?
I see a skirt that once was mine,
Within your basket, lay.

Folk always enjoyed the grim songs the best. Eithni loved them too, for she was used to feeling melancholy and could let the mood flow out of her into the music. She felt her freest when she played the harp. Her fingers flew over the strings, and she let the song carry her away. The music pulsed through her veins, and for a few moments she felt lifted out of her mortal body. Next to her Tea's voice grew more strident, the clear sweet notes lifting high into the night.

It was then that Eithni became aware of someone staring at her.

It was a strange sensation, like a physical weight pressing down upon her. It was making it hard to breathe. The fine hair on the back of her neck prickled, and her body grew warm.

Eithni's eyes flickered open. She looked over the amassed crowd, and across the fire she met Donnel's penetrating gaze.

Donnel had been glad of the music and singing. Unlike banter, boasting, and storytelling around the fireside—which just irritated him—the music soothed the darkness in him.

He sat on the edge of the firelight, as far as possible from the merriment, a cup of ale clasped in his hands. As the music continued, he found himself watching the sisters who sat next to each other at the fireside. They were so different. Tea was tall, dark, and proud—Galan's equal in so many ways. Next to her Eithni appeared delicate and fey.

His gaze remained on Eithni.

There was something entrancing about her this eve. The firelight played across her skin, highlighting the fineness of her features and her pretty face. Her eyes were closed, and she wore a peaceful expression. She had pulled up her hair this evening, exposing the slender length of her neck.

Donnel watched her, captivated.

It had been a while since a woman had caught his attention. He had only ever had eyes for one. He had only ever wanted Luana.

And yet tonight he felt a pull toward the young woman who played the harp as if it was an extension of her. He felt her sadness, the beauty of her being, and the aching emptiness of her soul.

Had they been camped by one of the mounds of the Fair Folk, he would have thought himself ensnared by magic—for the Aos Sí liked to play games with mortals. Yet there were no such places near here. It was Eithni herself who was bewitching him.

Eithni's eyes opened then, and across the fire their gazes met.

Donnel's breathing stilled. He saw her fingers falter, before she caught herself. She played on, but the enchantment had gone. Tea, still singing, glanced across at her sister, a quizzical look upon her face.

Eithni's slim fingers moved over the strings of the harp, but this time her attention was downcast. Her face had gone taut, and pink stained her cheekbones.

She had not welcomed his attention.

Donnel looked away, fixing his gaze upon the glowing embers of the fire pit. What was wrong with him? A woman he could barely tolerate—a woman who had spent the last year and a half nagging him—had just caught him staring at her like a mooncalf.

Turning away from the fire, as the strains of the harp lifted high into the night, Donnel took a deep draft of ale. He did not know what was wrong with him—but he did not like it one bit.

Chapter Six

Bodach an Stòrr

"ARE YOU SURE you don't want to ride up with us?" Tea adjusted her son in the sling across her front and glanced over at where Eithni was shouldering her pack. "I'm sure one of the warriors would let you travel with them."

Eithni smiled back. "I prefer to walk."

Tea snorted. "I can't understand why?"

"I like the feel of the earth beneath my feet."

Her sister gave Eithni an exasperated look. "I swear, I'll never understand you."

Eithni's smile faded.

Tea sighed, stepping close to her sister. Eithni saw concern in her midnight blue eyes and tensed. She had a feeling she knew what was coming next. "I worry about you sometimes, Eithni."

"You don't need to."

"Don't I?" A look of sadness flitted across her sister's proud face. "You've grown distant of late. Sometimes I look at you, and it's as if you're not even there ... like you've traveled far inside yourself."

Eithni held her gaze. She wasn't going to deny it. "There's nothing wrong," she murmured. "It's just how I deal with life. It makes things easier to distance myself ... sometimes."

"You'd tell me if something was worrying you?"

Eithni reached out and stroked the fine mat of dark hair upon Muin's head. "Of course I would."

She turned away from her sister then and joined the throng of folk heading north. She felt Tea's gaze upon her as she walked away but did not look back. Tea knew her better than anyone, but even she did not know all that had befallen Eithni during her time alone at Dun Ardtreck with Forcus. Tea had asked, and Eithni had evaded the question, telling her that she would confide in her sister when she felt ready. Many moons had passed since that conversation, and Tea had never asked again— likewise Eithni had never brought the subject up.

She never intended to again.

Eithni followed the others up a gentle slope, away from the shadow of Beinn na Caillich, continuing their path north. Unlike the bright sunshine of the day before, the sky was overcast today and the breeze chill. Eithni had wrapped a woolen shawl about her shoulders although she knew she would warm up soon enough.

Hearing the thunder of hoof beats behind her, she glanced right and saw warriors on horseback approach, Galan and Tea out front. The group cantered up the hill, the long manes and tails of their ponies flying out like banners behind them as they rode toward the front of the column.

Among them Eithni spied Donnel.

The warrior stared straight ahead, his handsome face impassive, and rode past without acknowledging her. Eithni did not expect him to, and yet when she had caught him staring the night before she was sure she had seen naked longing in his eyes.

It had reminded her of Forcus, although *his* eyes had been filled with a kind of crazed lust.

Eithni shuddered at the memory. Longing, lust—they were both just facets of the same thing. She wanted nothing to do with it.

And yet the look on Donnel's face had entranced her. The power of his stare had held her captive for an instant. For a heartbeat their surroundings had faded and there had only been the two of them watching each other across the dying embers of the fire.

Enough.

Eithni shook her head, banishing the memory. It was foolish to relive the moment. Donnel was a devastatingly attractive man; only a woman made of stone would not respond to him. Still, the warrior had made his dislike for her clear, had been rude to her on many occasions now. And yet she had caught him watching her as if she were the loveliest thing he had ever seen.

She did not understand it.

It took them two more days to reach The Gathering Place.

It was a journey over wild land, through wide valleys under the shadow of great mountains. Huge sweeping peaks, tawny brown and gold, reared overhead, dwarfing the travelers. The peaks' sheer majesty made Eithni feel very small in comparison—the band of travelers trekking through the vale was as tiny as a column of marching ants compared to these sleeping giants.

On the last afternoon before arriving at their destination, they drew near to a deep blue loch that stretched east. The terrain was barren and open here, the grass seared brown and studded with heather. To the north the land rose steeply, and at its crown a table of dark rock and the jagged outline of rocky pinnacles reared overhead. One in particular stood out, looming against the pale sky like an upraised thumb.

Eithni, who had never traveled to this part of the isle before, craned her neck up at the escarpment above her, before she glanced over at Ruith. "Is that where we're going?"

"Aye, that's Bodach an Stòrr," Ruith replied with a smile. "The Old Man of Storr."

"Isn't it supposed to be a giant's thumb buried in the earth?" Eithni asked, her gaze returning to the distinctly shaped column of rock perched high above them.

Ruith's smile widened to a grin. "There are plenty of stories about this place. But most believe the name comes from the tale of two giants—a man and his wife—who, while fleeing from enemies, made the mistake of looking over their shoulders as they ran. They were turned to stone."

The two women joined the others as they climbed the hill. It was hard going as the way grew steadily steeper. Eventually, the warriors who led the column were forced to dismount from their ponies and lead them the rest of the way.

Out of breath, Eithni crested the top of the hill, her face glowing with exertion, and turned back to admire the view. A vista of velvety green hills, an arm of headland, and glittering water greeted her. The day was drawing to a close and streaks of gold and purple decorated the sky.

A smile curved her lips. *What a magnificent spot for The Gathering.*

She had only ever been to one Gathering of the Tribes before, and that had been many summers earlier. She had been around six, Tea eight. They had traveled to the south coast, to the territory of The Boar. She remembered stuffing herself with rich cakes and playing knucklebones with the other children.

Turning, Eithni followed the others to the top of the hill, and there at last she saw The Gathering Place. Just below those soaring pinnacles of dark rock stretched a vast encampment of tents. Smoke rose into the sky from the cook fires, and she inhaled the aroma of roasting venison. A moment later the tinkle of laughter reached her.

There were many tents pitched here already, even though Mid-Summer Fire was not until the following night. Eithni's skin prickled with excitement as her gaze swept over the sea of weathered hide. It had been a long while since she had seen so many people gathered in one place; she wondered which of the tribes had arrived before them.

Had the people of The Wolf arrived? Eithni quickened her pace, her smile widening. She had missed her tribe more than she had realized.

She spied a heavyset warrior with flowing dark hair then, striding down the hill to greet them.

It was her cousin Wid—chieftain of The Wolf.

Tea, who was traveling up ahead, rushed forward to embrace him. They were laughing together, Wid admiring wee Muin, when Eithni rushed up.

"Wid!" She was gasping for breath now. That last sprint had finished her off.

"Bonny Eithni." Wid clasped her in a bear hug and swung her round. "Have you not yet found yourself a husband?"

Eithni laughed off the comment. "Have *you* not yet found yourself a wife to sing for you in the evenings?"

Wid's expression turned glum, and he shook his head. "There are few women my age in the fort, and raids and feuding have stripped our villages bare of all but bairns and crones."

Eithni grinned. "Just as well you've come to The Gathering then. There will be plenty of young women here eager to meet you." She stepped back, assessing him. "Your shoulders have grown as broad as an ox. What have you been eating?"

Other members of The Wolf tribe gathered around them then, and Eithni found her vision blurring with tears as she hugged them all. She loved her life at Dun Ringill. It had been a fresh start, and the fort had been in desperate need of a healer; but back among her own folk, who bore the mark of The Wolf proudly upon their right biceps, she felt a sense of belonging.

Still, she saw the curiosity on many of their faces as they greeted her. They all knew what had happened to her in the months after Tea's handfasting to Galan. They would all be wondering how she was bearing up.

That was one thing she had not missed. At Dun Ringill, most folk let her be—let the past remain in the past.

Wid slung a heavy arm over Eithni's shoulder, and they walked up the slope together. "The broch's felt empty ever since you left," he said. "No one else plays the harp as well as you."

Chapter Seven

Are We Friends?

EITHNI MASHED THE herbs to a thick green paste with her pestle and mortar. The potion was for Lucrezia: nettle and milk-thistle were known to help a woman's womb quicken.

Alone in her tiny tent, seated upon a fur where she would sleep later, Eithni continued to work the herbs together while listening to the sounds of the other Eagles finishing setting up camp. She was fortunate, as most unwed women merely shared a tent with kin. Yet she, as Tea's sister, had a privileged position in the tribe and so received her own tent.

Around her Eithni could hear the chatter of women's voices punctuated by the excited cries of children and the rumble of men's voices. The aromas of cooking were stronger now, wafting in through the crack in the leather flap covering the opening to her tent. The strains of music and laughter also reached her.

The sounds of celebration.

Eithni smiled as she worked. Seeing her kin again had buoyed her mood. She had missed Wid more than she had realized.

It was getting late in the day. Outside the tent the sun was setting, and the camp was preparing for the first of five long days of feasting, drinking, and games. Eithni would join them shortly; she just had to finish this potion for Lucrezia.

She stopped mashing the herbs and poured some water into the mortar. She then mixed the contents well before pouring them into a clay bottle, which she stoppered. Humming to herself, Eithni put away her pestle and mortar. She placed it next to the basket that she took everywhere with her—it was her healer's basket and contained a collection of herbs, powders, and ointments.

Her work complete, Eithni rose to her feet, slipped out of the tent, and walked toward the center of The Gathering Place. The trampled grass was prickly underfoot, and the ground was still warm from a sunny day.

The stone pinnacles, bathed in gold from the last rays of sun to the west, cast long shadows over the land. The ground beneath the rocky escarpment sloped gently for a spell, and this was where the tribes had pitched their tents. Farther on though, the ground fell away, the track winding its way down to the hills below.

Eithni continued to hum to herself, enjoying the sound of the bone whistle that now accompanied the lute. She had left her harp in the tent this evening for, although she would undoubtedly play during The Gathering, she wished to remain an observer tonight. She just wanted to relax and enjoy listening to the other musicians.

Four enormous fire pits had been dug into the clearing at the center of The Gathering Place, and a number of venison carcasses were now spit-roasting over glowing embers. Eithni's belly growled; she was ravenous after a day's hard journeying.

Spying Tea and Galan taking a seat at one of the fire pits, she crossed to them and sat down between her sister and Lucrezia. Wordlessly, she passed Lucrezia the small clay bottle. "Mix it with water every morning," she murmured.

Her friend nodded, her dark gaze gleaming, before she tucked the bottle away. "Thank you, Eithni."

Next to Lucrezia, Tarl was oblivious to the women's hushed words. He was deep in rowdy conversation with Lutrin. Between them it looked as if they had already finished a jug of ale and had started their second.

Eithni settled in front of the fire, tucking her legs under her. Her gaze traveled over the circular space where men, women, and children jostled for a seat. Their voices mingled with the crackle of roasting haunches of venison. It was a warm evening too, which had put everyone in high spirits.

A wide smile stretched Eithni's face as she soaked in the joy that thrummed around her. Life had become so serious of late, but here she could shed it all like a heavy winter mantle.

Eithni reached forward and poured herself a cup of ale. Taking a sip, she resumed her observation of her surroundings. Unlike inside the broch of Dun Ringill, where they all had designated seats at the chieftain's table, she could sit where she liked tonight. As such, it was a relief to see that Donnel was not next to her, but instead seated next to Galan a few feet away. The brothers were talking quietly, their voices muffled by the roar of the conversation surrounding them.

Next to Eithni, Tea cast her sister a smile. "Isn't it good to be here?"

Muin sat gurgling in his mother's arms. His fingers reached up and tangled in Tea's long unbound hair. Tea winced and unsnarled her dark tresses from his chubby hands.

Eithni nodded. "Aye—I'd forgotten what fun The Gathering is."

Tea was about to respond when excited shouts broke out across the clearing. Eithni glanced up to see a group of dark figures stride into the camp, approaching through a gap in the tents.

"The Boar have arrived!" A man shouted.

Roars of welcome went up as a huge warrior swaggered into their midst. Broad, both in shoulder and girth, Urcal mac Wrad was a sight to behold. The chieftain of The Boar had wild dark hair, threaded with grey, and a beard to match. His dark blue eyes swept the crowd with cunning. He was barechested, with swirls and circles painted in blue woad over his hairy chest. Urcal of The Boar was built like the beast after which his tribe was named.

Eithni tensed. After the events of last summer, relations between The Boar and The Eagle had been strained. She hoped this Gathering would smooth things. Without meaning to, she glanced over at Donnel. The warrior had gone still, his chiseled features hewn of stone, his gaze narrowed. Next to Donnel, Galan's expression was inscrutable. It was impossible to know what the arrival of The Boar meant to him, even if Donnel's hostility was clear. Misgiving feathered down Eithni's back. She hoped Galan would keep an eye on Donnel while they were here.

She shifted her attention back to where The Boar tribe filed into the clearing. Urcal walked beside a barrel-chested bald man with a scowling face, no doubt a relative or warrior of high-standing, while a small, dark-haired woman followed the two men. This would be Urcal's wife, Modwen. The chieftain's wife was a faded beauty, her features tired, her expression resigned. She carried a boy of around three winters on her hip. A plump girl of around thirteen walked a step behind Modwen. Both children had their father's wild dark hair.

However, when Eithni's gaze shifted behind them, her breathing hitched.

Her gaze alighted upon a man of around her own age, a warrior who strutted into the clearing as if it belonged to him. Unkempt dark hair and dark blue eyes marked him as Urcal's kin. The man could have been named handsome if it wasn't for the unpleasant smirk he wore.

Loxa mac Wrad.

Eithni remembered him from last summer. Urcal's youngest brother had traveled to Dun Ringill to deliver

Wurgest's challenge to Tarl. She would never forget the way he had stridden into the broch with the same arrogance he now walked into this camp with, or the challenge in his eyes as he had faced Galan and his brothers.

Loxa's gaze swept the crowd before settling upon Galan, and a wild smile split his face. Then he spotted Tarl, who had stopped laughing with Lutrin and was watching The Boar under hooded lids.

Lastly, Loxa's gaze alighted upon Eithni. And there it stayed.

His grin faded. He stared at her, stripping her naked with his eyes. He watched Eithni as if they were alone in this clearing and he was about to take her. The feral hunger she saw there made Eithni's heart begin to hammer against her ribs.

She knew that look; she had seen the same crazed expression in Forcus's eyes before he had defiled her for the first time. Eithni felt herself wilt beneath the raw heat of his gaze—and yet just like a year earlier, she did not look away.

She was not brave like Tea. She could not kill a man with a knife under the ribs or sword blade to the neck. Yet she had a stubbornness that was a type of courage, and it was that strength that made her hold his gaze. He was trying to dominate her, and she would not let him.

"Urcal!" A big man rose to his feet. Around his shoulders he wore the skin of a stag, the head and antlers perched upon his head. He had a handsome face although his looks were marred by a heavy scar that ran down his right cheek. Fortrenn, chieftain of The Stag, was an imposing sight as he stepped forward to welcome The Boar chieftain. "You're late!"

"Fortrenn!" Urcal boomed back. "You know I like to make an entrance."

The two men strode across the clearing and crushed each other in a bear-hug. A roar of cheers and shouts went up around them, and the newcomers took their seats at the fireside.

Loxa, who had kept staring at Eithni while his brother greeted The Stag chief, looked away for a moment while he took his place at Urcal's right hand. Eithni seized the chance and dropped her own gaze to her lap. Heart pounding, she stared down at her cup of ale. She would not look his way for the rest of the night. The man who had frightened her a year earlier terrified her now.

She could not believe she had forgotten about him and had not realized he would come to The Gathering. She had never met his elder brother Wurgest, but the man sounded like he had been a crazed, murderous brute. He had tried to rape Lucrezia and nearly killed Tarl. She hoped Wurgest's younger brother was not as dangerous.

"Galan!" Urcal raised a cup of ale toward The Eagle chieftain. "Good evening to you and your people."

Galan inclined his head and raised his own cup, smiling. "Welcome, Urcal."

Urcal favored him with a wolfish grin. "Making a name for yourself as a peace weaver, I hear?"

The Boar did not phrase that as a compliment. There was no mistaking the gleam of challenge in his dark-blue eyes.

Galan did not reply but merely inclined his head in acknowledgment.

"I remember you when you were still at your mother's tit," Urcal rumbled. "Your father was so proud. 'My firstborn son. He will make our people strong,' he said. What would he think of you now?"

"I hope I prove him right," Galan replied. His voice was quiet, but it carried across the space between the two men. "Making friends with our neighbors makes all of us strong. If we're not out killing each other, our tribes can grow and prosper."

"Well said," Wid called out from across the fire.

Urcal ignored The Wolf chieftain, his gaze remaining upon Galan. The two men watched each other for a moment longer before Urcal's mouth curved into a sneer. "And what about us, Galan mac Muin? Are we friends?"

Chapter Eight

The Games Begin

MID-SUMMER FIRE DAWNED with a pale blue sky promising fine weather for the day ahead. Eithni rose from her furs and padded barefoot out of her tent.

The air smelled of dew-wet grass, and the scent of peat and cooking smells from the night before still lingered. A babe's wail went up to her left—Muin was announcing his hunger to the world and ensuring his parents were awake to see to his needs.

Eithni smiled as she heard the rumble of Galan's voice, punctuated by Tea's feminine lilt. The pair were definitely awake. However, there were no sounds coming from the next tent—Tarl and Lucrezia had retired late and even two tents away Eithni had been able to clearly hear their cries and groans.

Eithni's smile faded. The others teased Tarl and Lucrezia over it, but the couple's blatant display of their passion for each other made Eithni uncomfortable. What they experienced was unthinkable for her; she could not understand it.

For Eithni coupling brought only humiliation, fear, and pain.

Leaving the tents behind, Eithni walked out to the nearest fire pit, where a group of women from all the tribes were preparing breads and cakes for the evening's festivities.

Eithni joined them and took charge of preparing The Warrior Cake, named after the god who governed over the warm months of the year. This was a moist cake made with oats, ground walnuts, butter, honey, and small tart plums. It was a rich sweet made only on special occasions and would be drizzled with warm honey before serving.

As she worked, Eithni gossiped with the chatty young woman next to her, who like Eithni was caught up in the atmosphere of festivity this morning.

"It feels like the morn of Mid-Winter Fire," the girl said with a giggle. "Only, without the cold and snow."

"And days of games to look forward to," Eithni added, grinning. "At Mid-Winter we do nothing but eat."

"Have you seen all the handsome warriors here?" the girl asked, her bright gaze roving over the surrounding crowd. "I hope to dance with at least six every night!"

Eithni laughed. "You'll be exhausted by the time The Gathering ends."

"Aye." The young woman gave her a sly look. "But I might have found myself a husband."

Soon the nutty aromas of baking drifted over the camp, and once the other women had prepared a huge batch of oatcakes on the griddle, Eithni broke her fast.

Excited chatter grew around The Gathering Place as the sun rose high into the sky and burned off the morning dew.

The first games of The Gathering were about to commence. Removing her Warrior Cakes from the stone oven the men had erected the day before, Eithni set the sweets out to cool and covered them with a cloth. Then she followed the tide of excited revelers out to the gentle slope beyond the ring of tents.

Eithni's gaze slid over the men amassing for the first of the strength contests: Clachneart—the Stone of Strength. This game called for the strongest men from each tribe. Lutrin, whose size and strength far outstripped any of the other Eagle men, even Galan, represented The Eagle. The two chiefs of The Stag and The Boar represented their tribes, and a young warrior built like an ox stepped up on behalf of The Wolf.

Roars went up as each contestant launched a heavy stone from the front of his shoulder using only one hand. The man who could throw it the farthest won—and that warrior was Urcal mac Wrad, chief of The Boar.

"Beast of a man," Lucrezia muttered from where she perched on the grass next to Eithni. "I bet he wins this contest at every Gathering."

Eithni agreed with her; there were few men here who could equal Urcal's size and girth.

The next game was The Warrior's Hammer. This contest challenged men to whirl a heavy iron hammer in circles before releasing it over their shoulders.

Urcal won this one too—and the shouts and cries of victory from The Boar supporters were deafening.

The last of the strength contests was the Clach cuid fir—The Manhood Stone. For this event the crowd gathered around the base of the rocky escarpment that towered over their Gathering. Here, there were a number of boulders and rocks scattered about, embedded in the soft earth—and the challenge was to see who could pick up the largest.

Fortrenn, chieftain of The Stag, won that contest, but only just. Fortrenn's son, a self-confident young warrior named Tadhg, took second place; while The Boar chieftain came in third. Urcal it seemed was a poor loser, for he glowered at Fortrenn, his heavy-featured face the color of liver after all his exertion. Not remotely cowed by The Boar's aggression, Fortrenn gave a great booming laugh and slapped Urcal on the back. "You can't win them all, old friend."

After an exciting morning the crowd filtered back into the encampment for the noon meal. The women served thick barley and mutton stew that had been simmering since dawn, fresh bread, and oatcakes. Mead and ale flowed, although many of the men held back, for there would be a game of Camanachd in the afternoon and the warriors wanted to be sharp for it.

The first tournament was to be between The Eagle and The Stag.

Once the noon meal had settled in their bellies, the crowds amassed on the slope once more. Eithni stood at one end, watching as twelve Eagle warriors—Galan, Tarl, and Donnel among them—strode out to meet their Stag opponents. Each man carried a curved stick.

Eithni watched, fascinated. She had seen men play Camanachd many times in Dun Ardtreck. It was a brutal if hugely entertaining game to watch; indeed, Eithni had seen matches that had gotten bloody.

She watched now as Galan barreled into Tadhg mac Fortrenn before slamming the smooth, round stone into their opponent's goal.

A roar went up around Eithni, the loudest shouts coming from Tea and Lucrezia. Her sister looked as if she wanted to be out there herself, and would have been, if she had not borne a babe on her hip. Tea's expression was fierce, her blue eyes alight.

The game quickly turned vicious. There were few rules—besides not being able to touch the stone with your hands or feet—and none of them prevented brawling. Yet the warriors seemed to love every moment of it. Tarl went down under a heap of Stag warriors who tackled him as he hit the stone to Lutrin.

Donnel lunged forward and beat the struggling men off Tarl with his stick before hauling his brother to his feet. Tarl's nose was bleeding, but he was grinning. Both men then set off after the stone again.

Eithni watched them with a shake of her head. She would never understand why men loved thrashing each other.

"Are you enjoying the game?" A man's voice drew Eithni's attention. She turned to find Loxa standing next to her. The thrill she had been enjoying, for The Eagles looked close to winning now, drained from her.

Eithni stared at him but did not answer.

"I am Loxa," he rumbled, staring down at her. He was a huge man although not the beast his elder brother was. "What is your name?"

Eithni swallowed. Her mouth had gone dry. "Eithni," she finally replied. Around them the roaring and cheering continued as the game reached its climax.

"Run, Galan—run!" Tea screamed.

"Smash it, Tarl!" Lucrezia bellowed.

The two women were oblivious to the fact that Loxa had drawn close and towered over Eithni.

Heart pounding Eithni glanced around her. She wanted to flee, but she knew she was safest here, in the midst of a crowd.

"I saw you last summer in Dun Ringill," Loxa continued, his gaze devouring. "Your beauty bewitched me then ... as it does now." He stepped closer still. "Are you promised to a man?"

Eithni shook her head. "I've no wish for a husband." Her voice came out in a croak.

He grinned. "What of a lover?"

A chill settled over Eithni, turning the warm summer's day to winter. Yet her reticence did not put Loxa off; if anything, his expression turned even more wolfish.

"I like a coy woman," he growled. "Makes my blood run hot."

Panic bubbled up within her. She stepped away from Loxa, hands clenched by her sides. And at that moment a roar went up on the slope below.

Eithni tore her gaze away from Loxa to see that Donnel had just scored the victory goal. For once his handsome face was creased in a grin. He laughed as his brothers lifted him high into the air. This game belonged to The Eagles.

Donnel let his brothers carry him up the slope, before they dumped him unceremoniously on the ground in front of the crowd of Eagle men, women, and children who had watched the game.

Lucrezia launched herself forward and pulled Tarl into a passionate kiss, not seeming to care that the warrior's face was covered in blood. Likewise, Tea's eyes were shining as she embraced Galan.

Donnel picked himself up off the ground and allowed himself to be slapped on the back from all angles.

He loved a good game of Camanachd. It was a bit like battle only without the risk of death. Joy had been rare of late, but the game had lightened his mood.

Stepping out of the crush of excited people, Donnel's gaze roamed over the rest of the crowd—and alighted upon Eithni. She was standing off to one side, pale and tense, her hazel eyes wide and frightened. A huge man with wild dark hair towered over her. He was whispering things to her, standing far too close. The girl looked as if she was either about to faint or flee.

Loxa mac Wrad ... what's he up to?

He remembered this warrior well, remembered the way he had strutted into their broch, and the arrogance with which he had addressed all of them.

Eithni did not welcome the man's attentions—that much was clear. She looked like a cornered fawn. Donnel was debating whether to intervene when Urcal roared Loxa's name from a few yards away. With one last quiet word in Eithni's ear, Loxa strode away.

Eithni stood there, staring down at the ground for a few moments as if she was trying to pull herself together. Then she looked up and straight at Donnel, catching him observing her.

Chapter Nine

Feasting and Words

A GREAT FIRE BURNED that evening next to The Gathering Place. Like many areas of The Winged Isle, the slopes below Bodach an Stòrr were treeless—so the men dug out a large fire pit and dragged in peat to burn for the night. While they prepared the fire, the others of the tribes readied the food for the feast.

Lads, their faces red from standing so close to the fire pits, turned haunches of venison and boar over the glowing coals. Mid-Summer Fire was a celebration of the bounty of the warm season, and so as well as Warrior Cake, the women had prepared a variety of breads. Some were studded with nuts and fruits, while others were enriched with milk, butter, and eggs.

Eithni worked alongside the other women, preparing vegetables to be boiled for the feast. She was glad to be away from the men, especially after her encounter with Loxa, but she was also angry.

With him—with herself.

Why can't I be like Tea? She would never let a man intimidate her.

When Loxa had started whispering filth in her ear, of all the things he would like to do to her, she should have slapped his face or at least walked way. Instead, she had remained there shaking like a reed in the wind.

Her meekness made her angriest of all.

"Eithni?" Ruith spoke up from next to her. "If your scowl gets any deeper it'll split your forehead—what ails you?"

Eithni glanced up. She had not even realized that Ruith was next to her; she had hardly seen the seer since their arrival here. It appeared Ruith had indeed found her old lover and had spent last night with him.

Eithni huffed a sigh. "I just wish I was braver."

Ruith's sharp, blue gaze narrowed. "Why's that?"

Eithni tensed. She had no wish to share what had happened earlier that day. It made her skin crawl to remember Loxa and the things he had said to her. "I'm just tired of being afraid, that's all," she replied. That was the truth too. Eithni's gaze flicked to where her sister was teasing Galan a few feet away. "Tea isn't afraid of anything."

Ruith snorted. "That's not true. Tea had to overcome her greatest fears in order to find happiness with Galan. We all have things that scare us ... even if we don't carry them for all the world to see."

Eithni raised an eyebrow. "Even you?"

The bandruí gave her a wry smile. "Aye ... even me. Why do you think I have remained alone all these years? I have no man ... no children. Being a seer didn't stop me from having them. It was me."

Eithni frowned. "What do you mean?"

Ruith held her gaze. "I had a difficult upbringing," she said quietly after a moment. She spoke plainly but with a different tone to the one she usually used. There was a brittleness Eithni had never heard before. "My parents were always at war. They fought like wolves, and when I was five my father killed my mother in a jealous rage after she danced with another man at Bealtunn." The seer halted there, her gaze suddenly far away. "He was exiled for his crime ... driven out of the tribe to die alone. I don't think I ever got over it, and I've never trusted a man since." Ruith glanced back at Eithni, her smile strained. "So you see, you're not the only one with fears."

At dusk the men and women of the tribes danced around the great bonfire, laughter and music lifting high into the night.

Eithni sat with two other musicians: one playing a lute, the other a bone whistle. She was glad to have a task—glad to be kept busy. Loxa would not bother her while she played her harp.

She had not seen him for the rest of the day. Yet she had the feeling the warrior was there, lurking on the fringes of the firelight. Watching her.

Eithni played energetically, her fingers flying as one song flowed after another. Mid-Summer Fire was a celebration of life, summer, and warmth, and the songs were joyous. Finally, when her fingers ached from playing, the dancing ceased for a spell, and the tribes gathered around fire pits at the heart of the camp for the Mid-Summer Fire Feast.

Eithni squeezed in between Tea and Lucrezia. She sipped a cup of wine and nibbled at a platter of roast meat and vegetables. However, she had little appetite this evening. Her encounter with Loxa had put her out of sorts; it reminded her of a past she had tried to bury. She could not regain the lightness of spirit she had arrived at The Gathering with. Even Ruith's words had not made her feel better. She appreciated her friend confiding in her. However, it was not the same—Ruith did not know what it was like to live each moment in fear.

The Boar and The Eagle sat close to each other this evening, sharing the same fire pit. Urcal sat across the fire, his gaze focused upon Galan.

Watching Urcal, trepidation curled in the pit of Eithni's belly—it was clear he had things to say to The Eagle chieftain.

As she suspected, a short while into the feast Urcal spoke. "When we found Wurgest's body ... crows had plucked out his eyes."

The words rang out across the fire, although The Boar chief's face was expressionless as he spoke. The brutality of the statement caused conversation to die, and all gazes swiveled to Galan to see how he would respond. There was no mistaking the challenge in Urcal's voice.

Galan swallowed a mouthful of roast meat, his tall, broad frame going still. There was little anyone could say to such a statement, and Galan was not a man to waste words. Wisely, he waited for Urcal to continue.

"We also found the bodies of Boar warriors slain on the hillside close to that valley." Urcal's voice was a low growl. "I take it The Eagles are responsible for their deaths as well?"

Galan frowned. "You speak as if you know nothing of that day. You know the reason Wurgest and Tarl met. Did you know Wurgest intended to betray Tarl's trust? Did you know he sent a group of warriors to ambush and kill the rest of us?"

"The rules of the fight dictated that the two warriors should meet alone," Urcal replied. "Yet you and your men rode out after Tarl."

Galan's scowl deepened. "Aye, we did—yet Tarl had no knowledge of it. Instead, Wurgest left your fort with a group of men. From the first he planned treachery. Did you know of this?"

The words hung in the air. Urcal glanced at the huge, bald warrior next to him, and the two men shared a look. "Treachery you call it?" Urcal finally replied. He spoke slowly, measuring each word. "I would say my brother was merely being careful."

Urcal had deliberately not answered Galan's question, making it clear he had known of Wurgest's plans.

"Your brother was mad." Tarl leaned forward, his face hard, his grey eyes narrowed. "He couldn't let the past lie, but when he challenged me, I honored his terms. He and I met and fought alone, and in the end I killed him. The matter should end there."

Seated a few feet away, Galan cast his younger brother a quelling look. Eithni knew why: Tarl could be a hothead at times, and even Lucrezia's influence could not erase a volatile temper. Galan would not want him starting a brawl—not here on a night like Mid-Summer Fire—not at The Gathering. Eithni remembered the night of Tea and Galan's handfasting; it seemed an age ago now. Tarl had drunk too much ale and had started a fight with one of The Wolf warriors. Galan had not been pleased.

Eithni's gaze shifted from Tarl to where Donnel sat next to him. His brother sat so still he looked to be scarcely breathing, only his burning eyes and the resentment in his expression gave him away. He glowered at The Boar chieftain with searing intensity.

Watching Donnel, Eithni remembered how he had witnessed her encounter with Loxa. After The Boar had swaggered away, she had looked up and found Donnel observing her. She wished he had not seen the incident, although at least Donnel would not question her. He did not care enough to do so.

Meanwhile Urcal had listened to Tarl, a sneer twisting his heavy features. Not acknowledging the warrior's words, The Boar chief shifted his attention back to Galan.

"Your father and I were friends. He wouldn't have been foolish enough to make an enemy of The Boar. Are you such a fool?"

"I don't wish to make an enemy of you either," Galan replied evenly. "What happened between Tarl and Wurgest was a personal matter that started far to the south and has been dealt with. This has nothing to do with the relations between our tribes. Would you let a dispute that got out of hand destroy the peace between us?"

Urcal's mouth twisted further. "Galan the Peacemaker." He spat out the words as if they were foul. "You're not the man Muin was."

Eithni's belly twisted at these words; they were deliberately inflammatory. Urcal sought to enrage Galan.

And yet The Eagle chieftain's expression did not change. Only the hardness in those storm-grey eyes hinted at any anger within.

"I'm not my father," he said finally. "I am my own man. You'd do well to remember that, Urcal mac Wrad."

The jaunty strains of a bone whistle drifted over the slope beneath the camp. Mead, wine, and ale had flowed over the feasting, and now the revelers returned to dance around the great fire once more.

Eithni watched the dancers, her harp tucked under her arm. This night represented a significant point in the wheel of the year. That roaring bonfire would give life to the sun and encourage mild weather to ensure a bountiful harvest.

The fire burned so bright that she could feel its heat caressing her face, even from many yards away. For a moment she closed her eyes, soaking in the warmth. When she opened them she realized Galan and Tea were standing next to her.

Neither of them had seen her. Instead, they were arguing together, their voices low. Galan was holding Muin, who wriggled in his arms, oblivious to the tension between his parents. Galan's expression turned hard as Tea snapped something at him. The cries and laughter from the surrounding crowd drowned out their voices, but Eithni knew what they were arguing about.

She tensed. The feast, which should have been the most joyous of the year, had been the most uncomfortable meal she had ever sat through. Galan had not lost his temper, something which awed Eithni, although both his brothers looked as if they would launch themselves across the fire pit at any moment and attack Urcal.

"He'll think you weak," Tea's voice, sharp with anger, reached Eithni through the roar of the surrounding crowd.

"He's dying for me to lash out," Galan countered. "You'd have me give him what he wants?"

Chapter Ten

Racing

DONNEL URGED HIS pony forward, letting the stallion have his head. Reothadh loved to race—for he hated to follow another pony. There were at least two dozen of them thundering along the wide valley. Far above rose wind-seared hills, with the dark outline of Bodach an Stòrr against a pale sky.

The race was on.

Donnel crouched low over the saddle, grinning as his grey gained on the leaders. Galan was up front on Faileas, fighting for first place with Loxa, who rode a heavy bay. Nostrils flaring, his powerful body surging beneath Donnel, Reothadh lengthened his stride.

Donnel drew level with the leaders—and glimpsed the exasperation on Galan's face and the fury on Loxa's—before surging ahead.

Reothadh's heavy feathered hooves flew. He reached the end of the valley, where a cheering crowd had gathered—and won by at least two lengths.

The stallion did not want to stop there, and it took Donnel quite a distance to pull him up. Once Reothadh's blood was up, he hated to stop running. He was strong too and fought the bit for a while. Donnel reined him in, in a wide arc, before circling back to the others.

The other riders had reached the finish now. Loxa had ridden off in disgust, while Galan waited for Donnel.

"What do you feed that pony?" he greeted Donnel with a grin. "He never used to be able to outdistance Faileas." That was true. The shaggy black stallion—Shadow—had always won races in the past.

Donnel shrugged, leaning forward and patting his pony's sweaty neck. "He seems to get feistier with age," he replied. "Reo's a leader, not a follower."

Ever since Donnel's return from the south, the grey had become harder to handle, his already fiery nature turning more aggressive. Donnel knew why—it was as if the pony sensed the change in its rider and had altered its nature to suit.

Now that the race was over, they began the ride back up the hill toward The Gathering Place. Half-way up, the going became so steep that the warriors were forced to dismount and lead their ponies.

Galan and Donnel made their way up, side-by-side. They walked in silence for a while, a breeze blowing in from the loch behind them, when Donnel eventually spoke.

"Has Tea ever said anything to you about what happened to her sister?"

Galan glanced at him, brow furrowing. "No ... why?"

Donnel shrugged. He was not sure why he was asking this—it was just that after seeing Eithni and Loxa the day before, he had been wondering about the healer. She had looked ashen, terrified—far more than the situation seemed to warrant.

"She just seems ... a bit strange at times."

Galan lifted an eyebrow. "You've always been harsh on Eithni—why?"

It was Donnel's turn to frown now. "She meddles where she isn't wanted."

"She healed you when you wished to die, you mean?"

Donnel compressed his lips. There were times Galan was far too astute for his liking.

Silence stretched between them once more, before Galan broke it. "I don't know exactly what happened to Eithni at Dun Ardtreck. I remember how she looked when I arrived there, just after Tea slew Forcus—like a ghost. I remember the terrified look in her eyes and that she had trouble walking. Tea's never said as much, but I think Forcus brutalized her."

Donnel's mood darkened at this news. That explained much—especially the fear in the girl whenever a man stood too close to her. A pang of self-recrimination assailed him then—a rare emotion these days. He had been harsh with her over the past few months; perhaps he should have been gentler.

Pushing the emotion aside, Donnel glanced back at Galan. Their gazes met. "What did you make of Urcal's words last night?" Donnel asked.

He saw his brother tense and knew he did not welcome the question. Donnel had seen Galan and Tea argue afterward. Tea chafed at The Boar's insolence, and Donnel was fully in agreement with her.

Urcal needed to be taught a lesson.

"I'll say to you what I've said repeatedly to Tea and Tarl," Galan replied wearily. "Urcal has the mind of a ferret. He came here with a plan: to bait me into losing my temper. He wants me to be the chief who brings shame on his tribe at The Gathering. He wants a fight, but he'll not be the one to throw the first punch." Galan's face went hard then. "I'll not give the bastard what he wants."

Donnel listened. Galan was right; Urcal did indeed have a plan. He did not miss an opportunity to hurl an insult in Galan's direction or to lay scorn at his feet. It made Donnel grind his teeth each time The Boar opened his mouth. The sneering faces of Loxa and that bald-headed lout who followed Urcal everywhere did not help either. Donnel wondered how much longer he would be able to keep a leash on his temper.

He was not sure how Galan was managing to suffer the abuse. Was he made of stone? The other two chieftains, Fortrenn and Wid, had noted the situation too, although they both refrained from involving themselves. This was a dispute that Urcal and Galan would need to work out between them.

When Donnel did not respond, Galan's gaze narrowed. "I know you disagree with me—but being chief isn't always about drawing your sword and cutting men down the moment they speak against you. It's more complicated than that."

Donnel held his gaze. "So what are you going to do about Urcal? He's not going to go away."

Galan huffed. "I'm aware of that. Once The Gathering is over, I'm going to seek him out so we can have a private word. Maybe a resolution can be reached."

Donnel stared at his brother. "You're going to negotiate with him?" Anger surged up, quick and hot, like a flame catching hold of fat. "Why would you do that? The Boar conspired against us last year. Seeing Urcal speak the last two nights, I'd wager he not only knew what Wurgest was planning—but even encouraged him."

Galan shook his head. "I still don't believe that."

"No, you *won't* believe it—there's a difference." Donnel saw irritation flare in Galan's eyes. *Finally.* Maybe if he pushed him hard enough, Galan would see sense. "The Boar don't want peace. Once The Gathering is done, Urcal will start raiding our villages. Folk will start dying—all because you wouldn't stand up to him here."

"Enough," Galan growled. "You sound like our father. All he cared about was defending our 'honor'. Where did it get him? Screaming while he tried to push his own guts back into his body." His brother gave him a hard look. "If things are to change they must start here."

And with that Galan strode forward, pulling Faileas after him, making it clear their conversation was at an end.

Eithni carried a basket of bread over to the fire pit and placed it down next to the platters of roast meat, boiled and braised vegetables, and rich stew. The aroma of the food made her mouth water. After a day traipsing over the hills, watching pony races, hawk hunting, and more games, she was both tired and famished.

Today had definitely been an improvement on the day before. She had successfully avoided Loxa, and this evening The Boar had taken a seat with The Stag at one of the other fire pits, leaving The Wolf to join The Eagle for supper.

Eithni sat down between Lucrezia and Tea and reached for a piece of bread. Her gaze traveled around the fire pit and rested upon Wid. Her cousin had done well with his hawk this afternoon. He had even beaten Galan and Lann, on one occasion. The young Wolf chief sat next to a girl Eithni had not seen before. She bore the mark of The Boar upon her right arm but had chosen not to sit with her people this eve.

Buxom and flirtatious with thick dark brown hair and moss-green eyes, the young woman did not take her gaze off Wid as he spoke to her. She wore a tight-fitting leather bodice, cut low to reveal a swelling cleavage. Eithni's mouth curved into a smile when she saw her cousin's gaze kept dropping to admire it.

Men.

She shifted her attention from Wid then, traveling farther around the fire pit to where Ruith sat with a grizzled-looking warrior. He was a formidable-looking man, with sinewy arms that were covered with tattoos and scars. His thinning dark hair had been cut short against his scalp, and he had sharp features—yet his eyes were soft and his expression tender as he spoke with Ruith.

Eithni watched them with interest. She had seen Ruith and her Stag dancing together the night before. The seer laughed now, casting the man a teasing look before cocking her head. She looked decades younger this evening, her eyes dancing in the firelight. Clearly, her friend's worries had been unfounded. Her old lover still remembered her—still wanted her.

Smiling, Eithni took a bite of bread and chewed slowly. She was glad Ruith was happy this evening.

She glanced to her left then, at where Galan and Donnel sat, and her smile faded.

Both men wore grim expressions, and despite that they sat shoulder to shoulder, they were not talking. Watching them, Eithni frowned. Had they argued?

Angry voices reached her, drawing her attention from Donnel and Galan.

Across the fire Wid and his companion had just been interrupted.

A tall man with long black hair and a scowling face had stepped between them. Wid was glaring at him, and the girl was no longer smiling. Instead, she looked petulant.

"Interesting," Tea murmured from beside Eithni. "Looks like the lass is already spoken for."

The Boar warrior took his woman by the arm and hauled her to her feet. Wid went to rise, protesting, but one of his men pulled him back down. Wid had already consumed a few cups of ale, and it had made him mouthy and reckless.

"Let the lass go," the warrior next to The Wolf chief advised him. "She's not worth the trouble."

They watched The Boar drag the protesting woman over to a fire pit on the far side of the clearing.

"Poor Wid," Eithni said with a sigh.

Beside her Tea huffed. "Not really—that one looked like trouble." Eithni's sister eyed her over a cup of ale. "Could you not see that?"

Eithni glanced back at where The Boar couple were now clearly arguing. The woman had gone red in the face and no longer looked pretty and flirtatious. "No, I didn't," she admitted. "I was pleased for him. He's been lonely of late."

Tea gave her a wry smile. "You see the good in all, don't you?"

Eithni thought of Loxa and shook her head. "No, not everyone."

Chapter Eleven

To Her Rescue

EITHNI WOVE HER way through the dancers—her harp in hand. The feasting was done. It was time to join the other musicians. She would lose herself in her harp for a while.

She made her way through the jostling, drunken crowd, heading toward where a young man played the bone whistle. However, she had gone just a few paces when a strong hand fastened around her arm and yanked her back.

"Where are you going, lass?"

Eithni swung round to see Loxa grinning down at her. He was not an ugly man, not like his frightening eldest brother. Yet the arrogance on his face, the lust in his eyes, made him terrifying to Eithni. She wilted under that stare.

"To play my harp," she replied, hating that her voice came out in a frightened bleat.

"Not before we've danced."

"No, I don't—"

But Loxa was not listening. His grip on her upper arm was so tight it hurt. He yanked her with him as he strode toward the heart of the dancers. Eithni's harp flew out of her hand. She dug her heels in and tried to retrieve it, but Loxa dragged her away.

Amongst the dancers he turned to her. They were close to the fire here, the flames dancing in Loxa's eyes. The heat was blistering against Eithni's skin.

Loxa yanked her against him, laughing as she struggled. "So you have some fire in you after all, timid Eithni?" He grinned down at her. "I can't wait to get you in the furs."

Donnel was not in the mood to join the revelry. Nonetheless, he found himself on the edge of the circle of dancers, a wooden cup of ale in hand. He did not wish to join the crowd, but he did wish to keep an eye on the warriors of The Boar, who were celebrating with raucous abandon.

Flexing his fingers against his cup, Donnel recalled his argument with Galan earlier and felt his anger rise once more. His jaw ached from clenching it.

Galan is wrong. The longer he ignores Urcal, the worse it will get.

Donnel's gaze flicked over at where his eldest brother stood on the edge of the crowd, arguing with his wife again. Tea had fire in her blood. Donnel continued to watch his brother. Over the past months he and Galan had argued frequently. He had accused his brother of cowardice on a few occasions, an insult that could get a man killed. Yet Galan had not lost his temper with him—not once.

Of course Donnel did not truly think Galan craven; those had been angry words spoken out of bitterness. Deep down he knew Galan to be the greatest warrior of them all. Donnel had earned the name 'Battle Eagle', but all the Caesars he had slain had been victims to his killing rage, his fury at the world.

Galan was more dangerous, for his anger was far slower to kindle. Donnel had rarely seen the beast unleashed, and he wondered what would happen here if

Galan's temper did eventually snap. Urcal was playing a dangerous game.

The music had increased in tempo, the bone whistle shrill in his ears. Shouts and cries from the dancers lifted high into the night sky. Laughter and cries of merriment drifted across the hillside, and at the heart of it all the great bonfire illuminated the night.

Donnel took a deep draft from his cup, his gaze sliding over the crowd of revelers. And there in the midst of them—surrounded by swirling dancers—his gaze alighted upon Loxa and Eithni.

The moment he saw her, Donnel knew the woman was not there out of choice. Her gaze was wild, her face the color of milk. She struggled against Loxa as he swung her around, his hand gripping her forearm.

Eithni wore a long green tunic this eve, belted around her slender waist. The garment was so long that it nearly brushed the ground. Her walnut-colored hair flew out behind her as Loxa swung her left and right. His face was alive as he watched her, grinning.

Even from this distance Donnel could see Eithni's eyes glittering with unshed tears. He could also see livid marks on her bicep, as Loxa released one arm before gripping the other.

The music stopped for a moment, and Loxa pulled Eithni into his arms and tried to kiss her. Eithni twisted her face away, pushing at the hard wall of his chest with her hands. The bone whistle and lute began once more, and the dancers resumed their frenzy. However, Loxa did not join them this time. Instead, he continued to try and kiss the reluctant Eithni.

Watching them Donnel clenched his jaw once more. He did not want to get involved, but Loxa had taken liberties with that lass ever since their arrival. Something had to be done. Not only that—this was an opportunity for Donnel to vent the aggression that had been growing within him since his arrival at The Gathering.

Donnel dropped his half-drunk cup of ale to the ground and shouldered his way through the crowd. Dancers shifted out of his way, although one or two warriors cast him dark looks as he jabbed them in the ribs with his elbows to get them to move aside.

Donnel paid none of them any mind. His attention was riveted upon Eithni. She was speaking to Loxa now; it looked as if she was pleading.

Reaching them, Donnel took hold of Eithni and pulled her out of Loxa's arms. "You promised me a dance, lass", he said, raising his voice over the music and laughter.

"Piss off," Loxa growled. He made a grab for Eithni, but she jumped back, cowering against Donnel. "The girl's mine tonight."

Donnel drew Eithni farther away from the warrior. "I think not, Boar. Look at the lass's face. Look into her eyes. Does that look like a woman who's keen for your company?"

"Dun Ringill dog." Loxa spat on the ground between them. "Leave the girl to me—she'll warm up soon enough."

"No, I won't," Eithni rasped from beside Donnel, speaking out at last.

Loxa's expression darkened at that, and his gaze narrowed. "What's this—the mouse speaks up for itself?"

To Donnel's surprise Eithni held Loxa's gaze. "Stay away from me, Loxa," she said, her voice shaking. "I've no wish to dance with you."

Donnel drew Eithni back farther toward the ring of dancers. "You heard her, Boar. Go and find a woman who is willing."

In truth, after Urcal's inflammatory words during yesterday's feast, Donnel was spoiling for a fight. He had never liked the look of Loxa and itched to pummel that sneering face. However, a fierce protective instinct overrode the urge to brawl. Eithni needed his help. His thirst for reckoning could wait.

Loxa's handsome face was twisted into a grimace of resentment. It was an expression Donnel knew well—one he had seen on Wurgest's face when he had challenged Tarl for Lucrezia. It was of a grievance that would not be forgotten.

Both Donnel and Eithni had wounded Loxa's pride. The warrior would remember. Donnel did not care—he hoped Loxa choked on his pride.

Instead, he drew Eithni close and stepped into the crowd of dancers. A moment later they were swallowed up by the revelry, and Loxa disappeared from view.

Eithni gasped, sagging against him.

Donnel looked down at her. "Are you hurt?"

She shook her head. "Just scared," she gasped. "He terrifies me."

Donnel's mouth twisted. "I'd wager most women feel that way about Loxa."

She glanced up at him then, and their gazes fused.

The world stilled. The sound of music and laughter faded and their surroundings drew back. Suddenly, there was just the two of them staring at each other, a breathless moment of silence.

Eithni's expression, the look in those huge hazel eyes, penetrated the shield Donnel had built around him. He had never seen such naked vulnerability, such fear. He could see the edge of panic that bubbled just beneath the surface. Even though he had rescued her, she was afraid of him. She was afraid of all men.

Looking into her eyes, he wondered once again what that man Forcus had done that she appeared so traumatized. It was like staring into the eyes of a wounded, frightened animal. Donnel's chest constricted. He did not want to leave her out here among the dancers; he did not want Loxa finding her again.

Without thinking he scooped Eithni up into his arms and carried her from the fire. On his way through the crowd, they passed Tarl and Lucrezia. Oblivious to their surroundings, the couple were kissing passionately, bodies entwined. Farther on, at the edge of the crowd of revelers, Donnel saw Galan and Tea.

They watched him approach, alarm on their faces. Tea stepped forward. "Is Eithni unwell?"

Donnel shook his head. "Loxa was bothering her," he said curtly. "I'm taking her to her tent."

Tea opened her mouth as if to intervene but shut it again when Galan placed a hand on her arm. They both remained silent as Donnel walked on.

Eithni said nothing either, curled against his chest. He could feel her exhaustion, her brittleness. Another wave of protectiveness crashed over him, unlike any he had known.

What's wrong with me?

Why did he feel this way over a woman who got on his nerves more often than most? Until now he had only ever thought of Eithni as a nuisance. He had been so immersed in his own bitterness that he had never really *seen* her before, he had never glimpsed the wounded soul beneath her role as healer.

They crossed the encampment, passed the smoking fire pits, and walked toward the line of Eagle tents. Donnel's tent sat next to Tarl and Lucrezia's, while Eithni's one was easy to spot. It was small and sat a few feet from Galan and Tea's.

Donnel ducked into the tent, pushing aside the leather flap covering the entrance. It was a cramped space illuminated by a tiny brazier that bathed the interior in a warm red-gold glow.

Stopping before the fur in the center, Donnel gently lowered Eithni to her feet. As he did so, he was acutely aware of her warm, lithe body sliding against his. He inhaled the scent of rosemary from her hair as the fine strands trailed across the bare skin of his arms.

A jolt of arousal went through him, and he felt his groin harden.

He had almost forgotten what lust felt like. He did not welcome the sensation though, for it brought back too many memories that he wished to keep buried. He could not understand why it had crept up on him now.

Eithni stepped back from him and pushed the curtain of hair out of her eyes.

"Thank you, Donnel," she said, her voice husky. "I appreciate your help."

"Will you be alright alone here?" he asked.

She nodded. "I'm sorry if I appeared feeble back there. Loxa seems to rob me of courage. I need to learn to be braver."

Donnel watched her a moment before shaking his head. "Don't apologize," he said gruffly, "and don't blame yourself. I know what men like Loxa are capable of. Tell me if he bothers you again."

Eithni stared back at him before she eventually nodded. "I will ... thank you, Donnel."

Filled with a strange emotion he did not understand, one that made his breathing constrict, Donnel nodded. He then turned his back on her and left the tent.

Out in the cool evening air, he heaved in a deep breath and walked away. However, there was a strange restlessness in him that would not give him peace.

Eithni sank down onto the fur, her limbs suddenly boneless.

The light from the brazier was dim, casting long shadows over the hide walls of the tent. Heaving in a long shuddering breath, Eithni brushed away the single tear that escaped and trickled down her cheek.

Enough, she chastised herself. *I must be strong*. She appreciated Donnel's words, although she could not bring herself to heed them. *I must learn to stand up for myself. One day the likes of Donnel might not be around to protect me—what then?*

Eithni had been so scared tonight. When Loxa had hauled her into the dancing, and then dragged her around like a doll, she had felt so frightened she thought she might faint. The way he had grinned down at her had dredged up terrible memories of the past.

Donnel had rescued her.

The feel of Donnel's arms around her had not frightened her. When he had picked her up and carried her out of the crowd, she had merely let go and huddled in his embrace. She had heard the steady beat of his heart as he had taken her to her tent.

Eithni lay down on her side. She was too tense to sleep, so she listened to the sounds of the revelry and laughter drifting up from the hillside below the camp. She wondered what had happened to her harp. She had dropped it when Loxa grabbed her. It had probably been trampled underfoot during the dancing; she would have to get another made.

Tears stung her eyelids, but Eithni blinked them back. She would not weep. Tomorrow she would talk to Tea; she would ask her for help. She needed to learn how to defend herself. She was tired of cowering. The likes of Tea and Lucrezia would not have needed rescuing tonight.

The night stretched out, and the revelry eventually died down. It took Eithni a while to fall asleep, and when she did it was more of a fitful doze halfway between sleep and wakefulness.

It was early morning, the time of night when the silence was always the deepest— the time when Eithni's weakest patients would often be taken by The Reaper, when a noise awoke her.

An odd ripping sound, like a sack being torn down the middle.

Eithni stirred and pushed herself up on her fur, blinking as the fog of sleep receded. The embers in her brazier had died, and the interior of her tent was pitch black. For a few moments she was completely disoriented.

Something was wrong. The whisper of cool air against her back alerted her—someone had sliced open the back of her tent. She was not alone.

Eithni's breathing hitched in her chest, and she scrambled toward the entrance, a cry rising in her throat.

A moment later a hand clamped over her mouth, smothering her scream.

Chapter Twelve

Taken

"EITHNI!" THE SHOUT jolted Donnel out of sleep.

He sat up, shaking his head to clear it.

That was Tea's voice, and there was an uncharacteristic note of panic and fear in it. In an instant Donnel was on his feet. He ducked outside into the misty early dawn, his gaze shifting to where a crowd gathered a few yards away—around the smallest of the tents.

Donnel's stomach clenched. *Eithni's tent.*

He strode over to the group—to where Lucrezia stood, her face stricken. "Eithni's gone," she told him.

Donnel moved past her to the back of the tent, where he saw a gaping hole. Someone had ripped it open with a knife. Tea stood there, her eyes wild with panic. Muin perched on one hip.

Tea's gaze met Donnel's. "Someone's taken her."

Donnel went cold.

Tea, who was watching him, stilled. "What is it? Do you know who took her?"

"Aye," Donnel replied. "Loxa mac Wrad."

Tea's blue eyes hardened.

"Where's Galan?" Donnel asked.

Her jaw clenched. "He and Tarl are searching the camp."

Donnel strode past her and pushed through the gathering crowd. He found Galan and Tarl up ahead. His brothers stood before the knot of Boar tents. They were speaking with Urcal.

Galan saw Donnel approach. His brother's sharp-featured face was thunderous.

"Loxa's taken Eithni," Galan informed Donnel.

"Were you part of this, Urcal?" Unbeknown to Donnel, Tea had followed him. She still carried her son on her hip, although her face was hard, her eyes murderous slits as she faced The Boar chieftain. "Did you know he planned to take her?"

Urcal shook his head. For once The Boar chief seemed unsettled, at a loss for words. One look at his rugged face, and Donnel knew that this had come as a surprise to Urcal as well.

"I never even knew he'd taken a liking to the lass," Urcal muttered. "I've just checked—his pony is gone."

Tea cursed before passing Muin to the woman standing behind her. "Then we'll ride out after him."

Eithni kept her eyes squeezed shut and gave herself up to the jolt of the pony's stride. Loxa had slung her across the front of his saddle like a sack of barley. Her mouth gagged, her wrists bound, Eithni had long since given up trying to get free. She could not run away; she could not fight. Her ribs were bruised. Each stride threw her up against the pony's sharp wither.

Her captor did not speak as they rode, although he kept one heavy hand clamped on her back, pressing it down between the shoulder blades just in case she tried to throw herself off the pony.

They journeyed for a long while, the pony racing over the uneven ground, before it eventually slowed to a bouncing trot. It was then that Eithni finally dared to open her eyes and look around her.

They rode through a landscape she did not recognize, possibly far to the north of The Gathering Place. She had been too scared, too blinded by the darkness, to take note of their direction of travel. The surrounding landscape was craggy, and they continued on up a hillside studded with huge blue-grey boulders. After a spell the ground grew steeper still, and Loxa slowed his pony to a walk.

Eventually they stopped, and Loxa swung down, his feet crunching on gravel. He pulled Eithni into his arms and turned her around to face him before untying her gag.

"Finally." His smile was oily. "Alone at last."

Eithni looked about her. He was right. They stood alone upon the rock-strewn hillside under an overcast sky. It was then that Eithni realized they were next to a large stone overhang. The ledge cast a long shadow over a damp and mossy space littered with stones and the remnants of an old fire pit.

Her knees wobbled, and her stomach clenched. It was suddenly difficult to breathe. "You won't get away with this," she gasped, her jaw aching from being gagged. "They'll track us here."

Loxa shrugged. "Eventually, aye. But not before I've had my fill of you. I've been wanting to plow you since I set eyes on you last summer." He paused here, contempt flashing across his features. "And this time the Battle Eagle isn't here to protect you."

He left her wrists bound while he hobbled his pony—a shaggy bay stallion with a white blaze. Eithni watched him, her body chilling. She wanted to run, but she knew he would only catch her and punish her for it.

Finishing the last knot of the hobbles, Loxa returned to Eithni, and he untied her wrists. Then he grabbed her by the arm and dragged her under the overhang.

Eithni's feet stumbled, her limbs struggling to obey. Like when Loxa had taken her from her tent and dragged her through the slumbering camp, fear threatened to paralyze her.

Loxa pushed her to the ground and stood over her. He then began to unlace his plaid breeches, leering down at her. "Lift your skirt. No use pretending to be coy now—we both know you want it."

Eithni stared up at him, aghast. She did not obey Loxa. Instead, she lay there frozen. *Do you really believe that?*

Loxa grinned. "You like to watch, eh?" He pulled down his breeches, revealing a dark thatch of hair and a huge swollen member that thrust arrogantly out at her. "Take a look at this, lass."

Eithni's gorge rose.

Loxa fell to his knees before her, hampered by the breeches, which he had pushed down to his ankles. He grabbed the hem of her tunic and shoved it up, revealing her legs.

"Lovely," he growled. "I've waited too long for this."

Loxa pushed her onto her back and lowered himself onto her, his breath hot on her cheek.

Eithni struck.

While Loxa had been distracted, she had picked up a blunt-edged rock from the ground behind her. With her right hand, and with every inch of her strength behind it, she smashed the rock into the side of Loxa's temple.

I won't let another man hurt me.

The warrior grunted and collapsed on top of her.

Eithni dropped the stone and wriggled out from under him, pulling down her skirt as she went. She did not stop to check on Loxa. He was knocked out but likely would not stay that way. She could not waste a moment, for Loxa would come after her as soon as he awoke.

Eithni ran onto the slope below the overhang. Loxa's pony stood cropping at dry tufts of grass. It was hobbled, so the beast had not gone far. Eithni hesitated. She wanted to steal the pony, and was just considering how long it would take to untie the knots on those hobbles, when she heard a low pain-filled groan behind her.

Gods, he's waking up already.

There was no time to untie the hobbles. She had to run—now. Eithni took off down the hillside, fleeing as if The Reaper himself had come for her.

They found Loxa's trail just north of Bodach an Stòrr—one set of hooves in the damp earth heading north-east, deep into the territory of The Stag.

Eight of them tracked Loxa: Galan, Tea, Tarl, Lucrezia, Donnel, Urcal, and two other Boar warriors. All of them, even Urcal and his men, wore grim expressions.

Donnel rode at the front of the column alongside Galan. Reothadh pulled at the bit. The stallion itched to outrun the beast galloping at his side. Galan's stallion, Faileas—as dark as Reothadh was pale—was his rival. The two stallions had to be kept apart at night or they fought.

Donnel urged his pony forward, letting him draw ahead of Galan. He tried not to think about what awaited them—he doubted they would find Eithni unharmed. He blamed himself; he should never have left her alone in the tent. Yet he had thought Loxa would respect The Gathering Place and leave her be.

He had underestimated the man's desire for the comely healer. Not only that, but both Eithni and Donnel had slighted Loxa the night before.

He was taking his revenge now.

Rage simmered within Donnel. He dug his heels into Reothadh's flanks, and the stallion responded, surging forward and leaving the others behind.

Loxa, I'm coming for you.

Eithni had never run so fast. Her feet flew over the rocky ground. Even barefoot, she barely noticed the sharp stones. Her heart pounded in her ears, her breathing now coming in ragged gasps.

She ran down a shallow valley in between huge boulders. There were few places to hide here, no dark spot where Loxa would not find her. Panic pushed any coherent thought from Eithni's mind; all she could think about was fleeing. Cold sweat bathed her skin.

Ahead she could see the land opened out into rolling green hills, but she would find even less cover there.

Don't stop running, or he'll find you.

Then she heard the tattoo of hooves behind her, audible even over the drumming of her heart. Eithni twisted her head back, her gaze alighting upon a figure many furlongs behind. Even at this distance, she could see Loxa's mane of dark hair and the white blaze on his pony's head.

Terror gave her feet wings. She had thought herself exhausted, that she had reached the limits of her endurance, yet she discovered another reservoir of strength. However, it did not matter how fast she sprinted, Loxa was gaining on her. She could hear his pony drawing closer with each heartbeat.

Despair rose in her breast. *He'll catch me.*

Eithni kept her gaze fixed ahead, her arms pumping by her sides, as she pushed herself on. She would not let him take her easily. She would fight him this time, fight till the end.

And then she saw them. Dark shapes approaching from the opposite end of the valley.

Eithni's heart soared. *Riders.*

Chapter Thirteen

Justice

EITHNI KEPT RUNNING. Loxa was drawing close. She could hear his curses and the snort of his pony's breathing.

Up ahead the riders were also approaching. She could make them out now. Donnel was out front, far ahead of the others, dust boiling up from behind his stallion's huge feathered hooves. Behind him Eithni spied Galan and Tea. Her sister's hair flew in the wind. Her son was not with her; instead, she was dressed for battle, a wooden shield slung over her left arm. Tarl and Lucrezia rode directly behind Tea, their faces grim.

Donnel thundered past Eithni, heading farther up the valley to meet Loxa. He did not even look her way; his gaze was focused upon the warrior who galloped toward her.

Tea and Lucrezia pulled up when they reached Eithni, forming a protective circle around her. Meanwhile the other warriors raced past, following Donnel toward Loxa.

Lucrezia bent double and gulped in deep breaths of air. When she had recovered enough to straighten up, she saw that Donnel had almost reached Loxa. The others were still far behind him.

As she watched, Donnel drew level with Loxa and threw himself from the saddle. He collided with The Boar warrior, knocking him off his pony, and the pair of them tumbled to the ground.

All three women watched, none of them speaking, as Donnel pounded into Loxa with his fists. The others had almost reached them now, Galan out front. He was yelling at Donnel, the boom of his voice echoing off the sides of the valley. However, Donnel was deaf to his brother. He was too far away for Eithni to see the expression on his face, yet she could see the savagery in his movements.

Donnel punched Loxa repeatedly in the face. The warrior tried to fight back, for he was a big strong man, but he was no match for Donnel's fury. Donnel smashed him in the face once again before drawing a knife. The blade glinted as it swiped downward, and Loxa's legs started to kick.

Donnel drew back, his face splattered with crimson, and watched while Loxa bled out on the ground beneath him.

Galan and the others arrived then. They swung down from their ponies, drew their weapons, and approached. However, they were too late.

The tension drained from Eithni's body, and her legs began to tremble. She was safe, and Loxa was dead. It was over—she could relax now. She watched as Galan left the circle of warriors and strode over to where Donnel staggered to his feet.

And then, to her shock, Galan lunged at his brother. His fist shot out and hit Donnel squarely on the jaw. Donnel, who had barely straightened up, reeled back and crashed to the ground—out cold.

"Donnel!" Eithni took off, pushing past where Lucrezia and Tea were dismounting from their ponies, their gazes riveted upon the scene that had just unfolded before them.

She sprinted toward Donnel and had almost reached him when Galan grabbed hold of her arm. He pulled her up short and swung her round to face him. "Stay back, Eithni."

Eithni gazed up at his handsome face, hard with rage, and saw a fierceness she had never witnessed before.

"Donnel's hurt," she gasped. "What have you done?"

"Get back." The words came out in a low growl. His voice had an edge to it that made her take heed, and she did as bid, stepping back from him. She found herself standing next to Tea, who had followed her up to the group of men. Lucrezia had also reached them, her dark gaze narrow as she surveyed the two men lying upon the ground.

Donnel stirred then. He groaned and shook his head before rolling onto his side. His eyes opened, and he fixed Galan with a baleful stare as he reached up and rubbed the side of his face. "You nearly broke my jaw."

"Get up," Galan replied. Eithni looked on, shocked. She did not recognize this enraged stranger. This was not Galan at all. Gone was the calm, fair-minded chieftain she adored and respected. It seemed that Donnel had finally pushed past the limits of Galan's endurance and patience. He would take no more.

"Brother." A few feet away Urcal lowered himself to his knees where Loxa lay, his throat slit open, his blue eyes glaring sightlessly up at the heavens. Then Urcal looked up, his own eyes glittering, and his heavy features twisting. "I'll make you pay, Battle Eagle."

Donnel, who had risen to his feet, spat out a gob of blood on the ground. "He had it coming."

"Murdering maggot!" One of The Boar warriors who had accompanied Urcal here, the heavy-set bald man, lunged at Donnel. However, Urcal struggled to his feet and hauled him back. The Boar chief stepped forward, his gaze locking with Donnel's.

"It's not for you to deal out justice," Urcal ground out. "You're not a chief. You rode ahead to reach Loxa first. You took matters into your own hands, but you had no right. My brother would have been punished ... I would have seen to it."

Donnel's mouth twisted, his gaze narrowing. "No punishment from you would have been sufficient."

"Enough, Donnel," Galan snapped. "You gave me your word that you wouldn't shed blood at The Gathering. You have dishonored me ... you have dishonored us all."

Donnel flinched at that. They were harsh words for a warrior who lived and died by his honor. "Loxa didn't care about honor," he replied, his voice harsh. "He abducted Eithni—he raped her."

"He did not," Eithni spoke up, the words bursting out of her. She knew she was not helping Donnel's cause, but she could not let the others think Loxa had defiled her.

All gazes swiveled around, pinning her to the spot. However, she stood firm, lifting her chin to meet Donnel's gaze across the yards that separated them. "He tried, but I hit him with a rock and managed to escape ... but he would have caught me if you hadn't arrived when you did."

Next to her, Tea put an arm around Eithni's shoulders, squeezing tight. "Well done," she whispered. "I knew you had it in you."

However, Galan was no longer looking at Eithni. His attention had returned to Donnel, his big body coiled with fury. "You've gone too far this time." Galan's voice sounded choked, as he forced out each word. "Urcal speaks true. Your act can't go unpunished."

"Let me split him open," the bald warrior growled.

"Kill him," Urcal agreed, coiling his huge body as he rose to his feet at Loxa's side. His face twisted into a sneer. "Cut the Battle Eagle down."

Galan turned slowly to Urcal, his expression savage. "I will not slay my own kin," he replied, his voice flat and cold. His attention returned to his brother then. "Donnel mac Muin ... you are exiled ... banished from our lands. Until you can mend the rage in your heart and the bitterness that has poisoned your soul." He broke off, his breathing ragged. "Until you can make amends for this, you are no longer welcome at Dun Ringill."

Donnel stared back at him, and under the light summer tan on his face the warrior paled. "You're casting me out?"

"Aye, that's right. You have shamed our tribe. You have—"

"Galan," Tarl cut in. Eithni had been so focused on Galan and Donnel she had forgotten that their brother stood a few feet away, observing the entire altercation. Tarl's face was stern, his eyes haunted. "Stop this. Don't say words you can never take back. Donnel's still our brother. He only did what he thought was right."

Eithni's gaze shifted, taking in the faces of Tea and Lucrezia. They both looked aghast.

Galan shook his head, vehement. "He knows the rules of our tribe, but he chose to ignore them." The torment on Galan's face pained Eithni; she could see every word cost him, yet he would not relent. "Donnel has become a danger to himself ... and to the rest of us. He must bear the consequences of his actions."

Galan looked back at Donnel, and the two brothers stared at each other. Time drew out, the tension in the air so heavy Eithni could taste it. Her heart pounded against her ribs like a battle drum. This was wrong. Galan could not cast Donnel out for killing a man like Loxa. The Boar warrior had deserved his end.

And yet Galan was.

Donnel's face turned to stone. Without another word he turned and strode away, toward the entrance of the valley Eithni had just fled from. He walked tall and proud, the only sign of turmoil visible in the tenseness of his shoulders.

The group watched him go, none of them uttering a word. A cool breeze sighed down the valley, feathering across Eithni's skin. Her chest ached as she watched Donnel go. Tea's arm tightened around her shoulders in an iron band, almost as if her sister knew Eithni wished to go after him.

When Donnel was little more than a speck in the distance, Urcal broke the long silence. "Do you think that will appease me, Eagle," he growled. "My brother lies dead at my feet."

The look in Galan's eyes was dangerous as he turned to face The Boar chieftain. "And I've just banished my own brother, stripped him of all honor."

"There is still a price to be paid," Urcal snarled. "Blood for blood."

Galan stepped forward, his face twisting. "Loxa abducted a woman ... and intended to rape her. I'm not sure I wouldn't have cut him down myself, if I had been the first to reach him. He broke the laws of our people, the peace of The Gathering. You have just lost a brother ... and so have I. We will leave it at that."

Donnel had been cast out from the tribe. It was a terrible fate. The Winged Isle could be a brutal place, with long, bitter winters. A man or woman alone rarely survived long, for if hunger did not kill you, the cold would.

A numbness settled over Eithni as she mounted. She could not bear the thought of Donnel being on his own, wrestling with his anger and bitterness without the support of his kin.

With Donnel gone, Galan had given Reothadh to Eithni. The pony jogged and tossed his head. The stallion was too strong for her, but Galan was too distracted to care. The Eagle chief's handsome face had turned fierce, his gaze hard.

It was a somber procession that turned south-east back in the direction of Bodach an Stòrr. Urcal led the way, with Loxa's body slung across the back of his pony. The two other Boar warriors followed close behind, and The Eagles brought up the rear. They all traveled at a sedate walk now.

Eithni rode at the very back of the group, alongside Lucrezia. Her friend had not spoken during or after Donnel's banishment, although her gaze was troubled, her full lips compressed. After they had ridden for a spell, Lucrezia glanced Eithni's way. "I'm so sorry." Her heavily accented voice was hushed, filled with sorrow. "After everything you've been through, I can't believe another man would try to hurt you." Lucrezia broke off there, warring emotions flickering across her face. "I'm glad Donnel killed that bastard."

Eithni gave a distracted nod, as if coming out of a trance. Her thoughts had turned inward. Her body was present, yet her mind had been far away. She glanced ahead at where Galan rode, Tea silent at his side. "Galan shouldn't have sent him away," she murmured.

"He did it to save Donnel's life," Lucrezia replied. "Urcal wanted blood. It was the only thing Galan could do to prevent it."

Eithni's mouth thinned. She knew that, yet she could not overcome the wrongness of deserting Donnel. He was angry at the world, but he was not a brute like Loxa. He had come to her rescue twice.

I can't abandon him.

She pulled up Reothadh, nipping him with her knees as he fought her. "I can't go with you," she gasped. "I have to go after him."

Lucrezia swung around to face Eithni, her features tightening. "That's not a wise idea. Donnel's proud and angry ... he won't welcome the company."

Eithni shook her head. "I don't care. I'm going."

She was aware then that the others had pulled up ahead and were turning in their saddles to look at her.

"What's wrong?" Tarl called back.

"She's going after Donnel," Lucrezia replied.

"No, she's not," Galan barked. "Eithni ... you're staying here with us."

Reothadh danced on the spot, his heavy feathered hooves beating out a tattoo on the dusty ground. He could feel Eithni's tension, her desire for flight.

"I am going, Galan," she called back, rebellion catching fire in her veins. "I'm a Wolf, not an Eagle. You can't command me. I choose exile. You have all given up on Donnel, but I will not."

With that she wheeled the stallion around and gave him his head. Reothadh leaped forward, kicking up his heels behind him. Together they tore off, back toward that lonely valley where Donnel had disappeared.

Chapter Fourteen

I'll Follow You

GALAN CURSED AND wheeled Faileas around.

He could not believe this—as if he was not wrestling hard enough with his conscience over Donnel, he now had Eithni to contend with. He could not let the healer go after his brother; he had to get her back.

But as he turned, Tea caught Faileas's reins, hauling him to a halt. "Leave her."

Galan met his wife's midnight blue stare. They had not spoken since his altercation with Donnel. During the whole ordeal she had neither contradicted nor applauded him, and he had been grateful to her for that. Sending Donnel away was like taking a knife to his own chest. He felt sick to his gut, the sensation worse with each furlong he rode.

"Tea," he growled. "Let me pass."

She shook her head, her expression pleading now. "Let her go. Eithni's the only one who understands Donnel, the only one who can help him. She's our only chance of saving him ... he won't be able to leave the darkness without help."

Galan stared back at her, the truth of her words filtering through the red haze of anger that had settled over him ever since he had seen Donnel kill Loxa. She was right. Grief twisted deep inside Galan's chest. Alone and isolated with his rage there was no telling what Donnel might do.

Galan ground his jaw. "I hope you're right, wife."

What are you doing?

The question repeated itself over and over in Eithni's mind, in time with each thud of Reothadh's heavy hooves. She cantered down the rocky valley in the direction Donnel had disappeared, the wind buffeting against her face as she rode.

She had acted on instinct. Her gut had demanded she follow Donnel, and she had answered its call. Only now that she had left the others behind did she question her decision. She slowed Reothadh to a trot, scanning the rocky sides of the valley to the north and the south of her.

The stallion was content to slow its gait for now, having been allowed to run for the first part of their journey. It was important they slowed down. She did not want to miss Donnel.

They continued down the valley, and Eithni spied the rock overhang where Loxa had taken her. Memories of those awful moments when she was sure Loxa would rape her resurfaced, and she shuddered.

Thanks to Donnel, Loxa was gone. *He won't threaten me anymore.*

Tearing her gaze away from the overhang, Eithni urged the stallion on. The valley grew narrower, its steep sides rearing up. Huge boulders the size of brochs studded the rough ground.

Eithni shivered in the wind that whistled down the corridor the valley created. Despite that it was mid-summer, the wind was cool, raising the fine hairs on the back of her bare arms. Ripped from her tent the night before, she carried no cloak to keep her warm.

Nervousness churned through her body. She was not used to traveling on her own. This landscape was so desolate, so lonely. The emptiness put her on edge, made her doubt her decision to follow Donnel.

What if I've made a huge mistake?

After a while the valley widened a little, and she and Reothadh splashed over a burn. It was here she spied footprints on the far bank. Even though she was no tracker, Eithni could see they were fresh.

Donnel has passed this way.

She continued with renewed hope and courage. He could not have journeyed much farther than this, for he was on foot.

The morning drew out, and Eithni saw that the sun was now directly overhead, a white disc burning through the bank of cloud that obscured the sky. She had been riding for a while, and she imagined the others had returned to The Gathering Place by now.

Her heart was racing, her stomach clenched in a hard ball; yet she was glad she had not gone with them. She could and would not abandon Donnel.

Her gaze swung ahead, and there, seated upon a flat stone, staring south-west, was a man.

Eithni's breathing quickened. *Donnel.*

She drew up Reothadh and watched the warrior for a few moments. He had not yet seen her, as his gaze was fixed upon the horizon. She could not help but notice that he was staring in the direction of Dun Ringill.

He cut a lonely figure there, as if carven from stone.

Eithni urged the stallion up the slope and rode toward him. Eventually, Donnel heard her approach. His gaze shifted from the horizon, swinging around to watch her.

His brow furrowed, and the look on his face was anything but friendly.

Misgiving stirred within Eithni, yet she continued up the hill toward him. She would not lose her courage now.

She had faced Galan, and she would face Donnel too. At the bottom of the stone, she swung down from Reothadh, tied the stallion up and climbed to join Donnel.

"Why are you here?" His voice was wintry. "I have no need of a healer. Be gone, woman."

That was a lie, for she could see he was bleeding. He had sustained a cut to his bicep during the struggle with Loxa, and although it was not deep, it needed tending to.

"I haven't come as a healer," she replied, lowering herself to sit next to him. She stretched out her legs before her and arranged her skirts. On a hot day the stone would be warm, but it was chill on this cool afternoon. "I'm here as a friend."

Donnel snorted. "We're not friends."

Eithni ignored his rudeness. "I don't know what we are," she admitted softly. "All I know is that twice you've saved me. I owe you a great debt ... I couldn't let you go into exile alone."

She glanced back at him and saw that his gaze had returned to the horizon. His face was grimmer than she had ever seen it. "Did Galan send you?" he growled.

"No, he didn't want me to come." She paused here before allowing herself a rueful smile. "However, I reminded him that I am not a woman of The Eagle, but The Wolf. He can't stop me from going after you."

Donnel looked back at her. "I didn't think you had it in you," he admitted, his tone softer than before. "But then I didn't think you had it in you to fight Loxa off."

Eithni was silent for a few moments, considering her words before she replied. "It was you, Donnel. After you brought me back to my tent I lay awake for a long while afterward. I made the decision that if I was ever cornered again I would fight."

His mouth twisted. "Only, the chance came quicker than you'd thought."

"Aye, he took me by surprise. But the moment I could ... I fought back."

Donnel watched her steadily. She could see the desolation in his eyes, the war within him that had carved deep lines either side of his mouth, making him appear much older than he really was. The rage and bitterness of the past year and a half was finally taking its toll. It would eventually kill him if he did not fight it.

"I don't want you with me," he said after a long pause. "I'm not fit company for anyone ... it's not fair on you."

She shook her head. "You're not getting rid of me Donnel mac Muin. I'll follow you like a dog ... wherever you go."

Donnel barked out a humorless laugh. "Gods, you're stubborn, woman. You've been a thorn in my arse ever since I got back from fighting the Caesars."

Eithni drew herself up, indignant. "Someone has to stand up to you." Her gaze narrowed as she stared him down. "You don't scare me, Battle Eagle."

He looked away. "Don't call me that."

Donnel strode down the valley, aware of the woman following close behind upon Reothadh. He had given her his pony to ride, for he noticed she was limping from cuts to her feet.

Donnel clenched his jaw. He did not want Eithni with him—she was a responsibility he did not need—and yet he could not dredge up the will to fight her. The scene with Galan had drained him. He felt empty, weary to the bone. He felt as if he could lie down and sleep for days. Before Eithni had arrived, shattering his solitude, it had felt as if the wind blew straight through him. He had felt as if he were the last man alive.

The unthinkable had happened—Galan had banished him. There was no worse punishment for a warrior. Death was preferable.

Battle Eagle. I'm not worthy of the name.

Galan's words still rang in his ears; he would never forget them. The look on his brother's face as he had banished him would stay with him forever. He would never be able to return to Dun Ringill—not unless he could humble himself to make amends for what he had done and erase the bitterness and rage from his heart.

Donnel was not sure he ever could.

Eithni's arrival had just made him feel worse. Not only had he been exiled, but he had involved her too. She was grateful to him, but the truth was he had acted selfishly. He had not killed Loxa for her but for himself. It was vengeance for the grudge he had carried against The Boar for a year now. He had enjoyed pummeling Loxa to the ground and taking a knife to the warrior's throat. He had liked that too much.

He had gone too far, crossed an invisible line. Galan had warned him, told him to rein himself in, yet he had not listened. The need for reckoning had turned him deaf to his brother.

Galan is right, he thought dully. *I'm a danger to myself, and to the tribe. I wouldn't trust me.*

Aye, for there was still a part of him that did not regret slaying Loxa, a part of him that would do it again if given the chance. Yet killing the warrior had not given him the sense of vindication he had expected. He was not victorious, just hollowed out, numb.

Ahead of the valley the land opened out, and he spied the dark line of a pine forest. It would not take them long to reach it, and they would make camp there for the night. After that Donnel was not sure where he would go. For the first time in his life he had no purpose.

The shadows were lengthening when they reached the forest of tall spruce at last. The resinous scent of sap lay heavy in the air, and there was a mattress of springy pine needles underfoot.

Donnel chose a small clearing to make camp and dug out a fire pit with a stone. Then Eithni went looking for firewood while he withdrew the flint and tinder he always carried in his saddle bag upon Reothadh and set to work lighting a fire. It was a slow, laborious process, but one he had learned to do as soon as he could walk. As the light started to fade, a fire roared in the pit. Eithni drew close, warming her hands over the flames, her pretty face drawn and pale.

Donnel straightened up. "We need food," he said roughly. Truthfully, he had no appetite at all; the day's events had sickened him, robbing him of hunger.

However, he could see that Eithni needed to eat. He had a bow, a slingshot, and a knife. He would go hunting. "I'll be back soon."

Eithni glanced up, those soulful eyes resting upon him. "You're not going to run off are you?"

He watched her, disarmed by the directness of her gaze. "No," he replied, too weary to care if she believed him or not. "I won't."

Chapter Fifteen

Tending Wounds

EITHNI TURNED THE grouse upon a spit, holding it over the hot coals. Fat dripped off the carcass, causing the fire to smoke. The aroma of roasting meat filled the glade, and her mouth watered. She hadn't eaten all day and was starting to feel light-headed. Neither she nor Donnel had rations with them. She was eagerly awaiting this meal, but the bird was taking forever to roast.

She glanced up then, her gaze settling upon the silent still figure sitting opposite her. Darkness had fallen now. Donnel was away for a while, and despite his assurance that he would come back, Eithni had been both relieved and pleased when he had appeared at the fireside once more. He had not had much luck out hunting, although he had managed to bring down a grouse with his slingshot.

Donnel's brooding was starting to become oppressive. He stared into the flames—his face a cold mask, his expression giving nothing away. His eyes looked almost black in the firelight.

"I shouldn't have let you come," he spoke up finally, breaking the heavy silence. "What if Urcal comes after us?"

"He won't," Eithni replied. "Galan will smooth things between the tribes."

Donnel's mouth twisted. "No, he won't. I killed Urcal's brother. He won't forget that in a hurry."

A long, awkward pause followed. Eithni did not know how to answer that, for he was right. She could only hope The Boar would return home after The Gathering and not hunt them.

"Supper is nearly ready," she said brightly, hoping the news would cheer him up slightly.

Donnel shrugged. "There's no hurry," he replied. "I've no appetite anyway."

Eithni huffed. "Well some of us are hungry—and you should eat something."

"Don't nag, woman," he growled. "It gets on my nerves."

Eithni frowned. His words hurt her. She had forgotten how sharp tongued Donnel could be. His words now reminded her that he tolerated her company, but that was about as far as it went. He had no wish for her to help him or talk to him.

"I'm not nagging," she said stiffly. "Don't speak to me like that."

Why is that it a man who speaks his mind is applauded, she thought bitterly, *but a woman who does the same is named a shrew or a nag?*

She removed the grouse from the embers and slid it off the skewer and onto a flat rock Donnel had brought back from the brook. Then, she set to work pulling the steaming meat off the bone. It burned her fingers, yet in her annoyance at Donnel she did not care. After all she had been through, she would not cower before a man.

When she had finished preparing the bird to eat, she glanced up to find Donnel watching her with a bemused look on his face.

"Well are you going to join me?" she asked.

He sighed and heaved himself off the ground. "Very well." He lowered himself down beside her and next to the steaming grouse. Eithni passed him a leg before helping herself to some meat. It was delicious, although the bird was small and they both could have done with another one each.

Once she finished, Eithni wiped her hands on some dock leaves before taking the skin of water Donnel passed her. She drank deeply. The water was cool and fresh, for he had refilled the skin at the stream when he caught the bird.

Eithni passed the skin back to him, her gaze shifting to the wound on his arm. "Can I take a look at that?" she asked.

He glanced down at his bicep, his gaze narrowing as if he had only just realized he was injured. "It doesn't bother me," he muttered.

"You know what happens to wounds that are left unattended," she reminded him. "It won't take me long. While you were hunting, I gathered some woundwort. It'll stop the wound from going bad."

Donnel inhaled sharply. "Gods, woman. Do you never give up?"

She held his gaze. "No."

He threw up his hands. "Go on then."

Eithni set to work preparing the herb. Without her pestle and mortar, she mashed the woundwort with a stone upon a flat rock, with a splash of water. She blended the flowers and leaves up into a pulp, and then once she had cleaned the dried blood off the cut to Donnel's bicep, she applied the paste.

Taking a closer look, she was glad he had allowed her to tend it. Wounds caused by battle weapons seemed to carry evil upon them, and soured easily. As Eithni applied the woundwort she murmured the words of a healing charm, one that Ruith had taught her. And as the seer had told her, she repeated the charm three times.

With my hands I heal
With these herbs

When she had finished, Eithni moved away from Donnel and resumed her place by the fire.

Donnel did not move from his spot. Instead, he stared at the dancing flames for a few moments. When he eventually spoke, his voice was weary. "I know I come across as harsh, Eithni—an ungrateful wretch. It's just that you shouldn't be here."

Eithni sighed. "I thought we'd already gone over this."

"Aye, but since then the reality of it has hit me. We're out here in the wild on our own. No food, no shelter—and no clothing or furs for the coming winter."

"It's still the warm season," Eithni replied. "We have plenty of time to organize all that. Together we're much stronger, for we have complementary skills." She smiled at him. "You need me."

He glanced across at her, his mouth quirking. "Is that right?"

"Yes."

"You seem to have an answer for everything this eve."

Eithni held his gaze. "I don't always, but tonight everything is clear to me. Back in Dun Ringill I felt so adrift at times, as if life no longer held any meaning."

"I thought you were happy at Dun Ringill?"

"I was." She paused here, looking away. "As happy as I could be anywhere, Donnel. I bear scars no one can see. Sometimes I don't think they'll ever heal properly." She glanced up, meeting his eye once more.

Donnel watched her. "I've heard a little of what you faced ... nothing stays secret for long in a place like Dun Ringill." He hesitated a moment before continuing. "I was sorry to hear it, Eithni. No one deserves such treatment. He deserved a far worse end than Tea gave him."

Eithni swallowed. Donnel was the first man that she had spoken of this with. It made her feel uneasy, exposed. "I thought that I'd escape my past when I left Dun Ardtreck," she replied quietly, "and it worked for a while. Dun Ringill was new to me, and I had much to learn ... your people were so welcoming. But after a time the memories started to come back. Some nights I dread going to sleep, for I dream of him and what he did to me."

Donnel continued to observe her, and for the first time since she had sat down by the fireside with him, his expression softened. Yet he said nothing, and she was grateful for that. Sometimes you did not need words; you just needed someone to listen. Donnel was good at that. She did not feel judged or pitied.

Donnel inclined his head slightly. "You were limping badly earlier," he said quietly. "Since you looked at my arm, shall I look at those feet?"

She waved him away. "They're fine."

"Who's being stubborn now?" he teased her. "Have you got any of that woundwort left?"

Eithni nodded, before motioning to the flat stone behind her where she had mashed up the herb. "Aye ... there's a little left."

"Let's have a look then."

Self-conscious now, Eithni stretched out her feet before him. They were filthy after a day's travel, and she felt embarrassed. However, Donnel did not seem to mind. He gently took hold of her left ankle and raised her foot so that he could examine her sole in the flickering firelight. She watched him narrow his gaze as he inspected the damage. "You made a mess of these," he murmured. "They definitely need tending."

Eithni nodded. She did not trust herself to speak. The feel of his hand on her ankle did strange things to her insides. His touch sent a frisson of pleasure down her leg to her groin as if he had just caressed her. His hand was warm and strong but his touch gentle.

Donnel began to wash her wounds, and pain lanced through Eithni's feet. She sucked in a breath, gritting her teeth. With all that had happened today, she had almost forgotten how she had sliced her feet open while running over the sharp stones in her bid to escape.

After he had cleaned the dirt and blood off her soles, Donnel administered the woundwort. Watching him and the crease that formed between his eyebrows as he worked, Eithni found herself devouring the handsome lines of his face. When he was concentrating like this, his focus outward rather than inward for once, his features softened, and the handsome man she had seen nearly two years earlier at Tea's handfasting resurfaced. There was a sensitivity there which had been absent all these long months. His eyelashes particularly fascinated her—they were long and dark, beautiful enough to make most women jealous.

Eithni relaxed under his light touch. Gentle yet strong and sure.

Eventually, Donnel set back on his heels, his gaze meeting hers. They stared at each other for a few long moments, and an awareness grew between them that had been absent earlier.

There was tension now, the same hunger that she had felt across the fire that evening on the way to The Gathering Place. He was not looking at her as an annoyance; he stared at her like she was a desirable woman.

Elation soared within Eithni. Excitement fluttered low in her belly, and a strange hunger clawed its way up her throat. She longed to reach for him then, to feel his stubbled jaw under her finger tips. She wondered what his lips felt like to kiss.

Discomfort followed swiftly on the heels of desire though.

Eithni stiffened. *I'll not be hurt again.*

Donnel blinked as if awaking and let go of her ankle. He moved away from her, and the moment shattered.

Despite the panic that now trembled through her, Eithni felt a sense of loss at him shifting to the opposite side of the hearth, as if a chill had settled over the clearing.

Stop it. She heaved in a steadying breath. *It's for the best.*

The fire needed more wood, so she turned, gathered a few of the branches she had collected earlier while Donnel had been out hunting, and added them to the flames. The fire roared to life, shooting golden sparks high into the darkness, devouring the dry wood.

Eithni stared into the flames. Her reaction to Donnel's touch had shaken her. Suddenly, she wished she had not followed him after all.

Chapter Sixteen

The Deer Hunter's Hut

THE RAIN FELL gently, pattering on the canopy of branches overhead and kissing the forest floor beneath.

Eithni walked a few yards behind Donnel. She enjoyed the feel of damp pine needles under her sore feet. Donnel led Reothadh this morning, for the pines pressed close in this part of the forest and the ground had grown uneven. Across his back Donnel carried his bow and a quiver of arrows so that he would be ready should prey of any kind cross their path. Fortunately, he had brought his bow with him yesterday when he left The Gathering Place, tied behind the saddle. It would prove very useful in the days ahead.

Eithni found her gaze following Donnel. She admired the breadth of his shoulders, his proud stance. He wore breeches made of a grey-blue plaid and a dark leather sleeveless vest that revealed his muscular arms. His tall body was tense with purpose this morning, his gaze sweeping left and right.

They had set off at daybreak as soon as the grey light of dawn filtered through the trees to the east. Shortly after that the rain had begun. It was not cold though, and the air carried the sweet, rich scent that only summer rain possessed.

Eithni's stomach growled as she followed Donnel west, reminding her that she had not yet eaten today. The full reality of the situation was starting to creep upon her—and for the first time she realized why Donnel worried about having her out here with him.

She was used to her morning oatcakes, warm off the griddle and dripping with butter and honey. But out here in the wild there were no oats—or any grains—for cakes or bread. There was no cream for butter, and no beehives for honey. Their diet would consist only of what they could hunt or forage. If they did not find berries or edible plants, or catch animals or fish—they would starve.

It was a sobering thought and apprehension knotted in Eithni's belly. It fully dawned upon her what Galan had done in banishing Donnel from the tribe. He had cast him out into a brutal world where even a warrior would struggle to survive.

They walked on, and the forest floor began to slope. Soon Eithni found herself picking her way down the steep, wooded side of a valley. Ahead she could see the land fell away into a deep cleft carpeted by dark bristling pines stretching out into the distance. Great bare carven peaks thrust up beyond the trees; rain clouds partially obscured the mountains this morning.

"Where are we?" Eithni called out to Donnel.

He paused and turned back to meet her eye for the first time since they had set off at dawn. "We're in the heart of the mountains that divide the territories of The Wolf and The Stag," he explained. "Uninhabited save for hunting parties."

"The Glen of the Stags," Eithni replied, smiling as she too realized where they stood. "That's what the folk of Dun Ardtreck call this place. You're right—the warriors hunt here." She glanced at the peaks rising into the clouds to the north. That is the Cruachan ..." She swept her gaze south to the lower, more rounded peaks. "And that must be Creagan Mora."

"Aye," Donnel replied with a tight smile. "Looks like you know this area better than me."

She shook her head. "I know *of* this place, for the warriors would return from hunting trips with stories of its beauty—but I've never been here."

They continued down the wooded slope, reaching the valley below where a clear creek bubbled over mossy rocks. There, they continued west until they spied a lonely hut.

The dwelling sat back from the creek under the shadow of the northern side of the valley, with a view south. Made of stacked river stones and mud, its sod roof caved in and full of holes, Eithni could see at a distance that no one lived there.

"A deer hunter's hut," Donnel called out, quickening his stride as he approached the dwelling, leading his pony after him. "I was hoping to find one."

Eithni heard the relief in his voice. Like her, Donnel had no doubt been mulling over the issue of how they would survive out here. Both of them were resourceful, but without shelter—a base of some kind—life would be hard.

As she approached, Eithni saw that there was still a stack of firewood piled up against the back of the hut. Donnel had already tied Reothadh up outside and disappeared into the entrance.

Eithni reached the hut and ducked through the low doorway into a damp, dark interior. Daylight filtered in through the huge gap in the roof, and rain pattered on the dirt floor. There was some moss growing on the walls, and a fern had taken root in one corner. However, Eithni could see at a glance that with a bit of work they could make the hut inhabitable.

Donnel, who had been taking a look at the dark recesses of the hut, turned back to her. "What do you think?"

"I think no one's going to mind if we repair it."

He watched her, his expression inscrutable. "It'll do then?"

She smiled back. "Aye, it will."

Donnel strode through the undergrowth and approached the deer he had just shot. It was a beautiful doe with a rich dark brown coat. He crouched before the beast and saw that his arrow's aim had been true. He had pierced her at the point where the back of the neck joined the skull. The doe had been dead when she hit the ground.

He reached out and ran his hand over the deer's sleek coat. Fortune had indeed shone upon him to bring this beautiful creature into his path. The doe would give him and Eithni enough food for days, and the hide would come in useful too.

He heaved the deer up, slinging it across his shoulders. Then he picked up his bow and made for home.

Home. A ruined hut in the midst of a forgotten valley. It was not the broch of Dun Ringill, but it was a roof over their heads. And after he had finished patching the roof, it would hopefully keep them warm and dry. When he had set out hunting, Eithni had been hard at work cleaning out the interior of the hut and making it livable. He had been gone a while, and he wondered how her afternoon had fared.

By the time he reached the deer hunter's hut, the light was starting to fade. The rain had stopped mid-afternoon, although a veil of damp still hung over the forest. A pink hue shaded the western sky promising good weather for the day to come.

As he approached the mud and stone dwelling, Donnel breathed in the scent of wood smoke—and the smell of cooking. His belly growled, and his mouth filled with saliva.

What has she found to cook?

Eithni emerged from inside. One look at her, and he could see she had spent the afternoon toiling. Dirt smudged her cheeks, and untidy wisps of brown hair had come loose from her braid, curling damply around her face. She carried a broom fashioned out of a pine branch. Her face lit up when she saw him.

Her reaction pleased him. An unexpected warmth spread out across his chest. He had almost forgotten the pleasure of returning home to find a woman awaiting him with a welcoming smile.

Then he remembered that Luana used to come out to meet him, and the warmth turned chill.

"A deer!" Eithni rushed forward. "On your first hunting trip too!"

Donnel forced a smile, trying to banish the lingering pain of memories he preferred to keep buried. "Aye, but what's that I smell? Fish?"

Her smile widened, and her eyes were warm. "Trout. I'm cooking it on a stone in the fire pit. Come inside. It's nearly ready."

Eithni picked the last piece of trout flesh off the bones and popped it into her mouth, sighing with pleasure. "That was delicious."

"I'll get to work on that deer carcass tomorrow morning," Donnel promised her. "You'll have a feast of roast venison tomorrow eve." He sat across the fire from her, the firelight caressing the handsome lines of his face.

Eithni watched him a moment. He had been quiet over supper, his gaze introspective. She did not question him over his mood; she was just relieved that they had found a place to live and that they had at least eaten once today.

She shifted her attention from Donnel then, her gaze taking in her surroundings. There were still gaps in the roof, which they would take a look at the following day, but she had done her best to clean out the interior of the hut. She had gathered ferns from the river bank and made two small beds for them. They would not make a particularly comfortable bed, but she would gather more ferns tomorrow and see if she could find something softer to place on top.

"You did well, today." Donnel broke the silence, his voice low. "This place looks unrecognizable."

Eithni huffed, covering up the rush of pleasure his comment brought. "I've still got plenty to do … but it is an improvement."

He gave her a speculative look. "You're tough, Eithni. I don't think I've ever met a woman so resourceful."

She smiled back, warming under the compliment. "All the women of my family are—we've had to be."

"And a healer too. Was your mother one?"

Eithni shook her head. "My grandmother was, on my father's side, but she died when I was wee. I barely remember her." Eithni paused here, her smile turning melancholy. "I look like my mother, although she was fiercer than me."

It was Donnel's turn to huff. "You're fierce enough, I'd say."

Eithni laughed, the sound lightening her soul. It had been a while since she had let mirth in. "With Tea as a sister, I have much to live up to."

He met her gaze. "You are different to Tea … but now that I've spent time with you I see you have the same iron will."

"That comes from my father," Eithni replied. "He could be as stubborn as a boar."

"Stubbornness runs in my family too. Galan, Tarl, and I are all bull-headed." Donnel's face grew grim as he spoke of his brothers.

"This isn't the end, you know," she said quietly. "Give Galan time to calm down, and he will welcome you back."

Donnel shook his head, his mouth thinning. "You don't know my brother as I do. He is slow to anger and endlessly patient with those he loves. However, when his temper snaps it takes a long while to mend. Some things he will never forgive."

Eithni watched him. "He was once angry with my sister, but that did not last. It will be the same with you."

Donnel's mouth twisted. "He was in love with Tea, and he realized he had misjudged her. This isn't the same … Galan's patience has slowly been stretching to its limit where I'm concerned. Before we set out to The

Gathering, he made me promise not to spill blood. I agreed, although that promise meant nothing to me—Loxa merely gave me the excuse I'd been looking for." Donnel looked away. "Galan knows that."

Empathy swept over Eithni. She longed to go to him, to put her arms around those strong shoulders and comfort him. However, she did no such thing. She was wary of touching him. Not only that, but Donnel would not welcome her sympathy. The man wore his grief, his anger, like a shield. No one would dare penetrate it.

Chapter Seventeen

In Search of Reeds

EITHNI STEPPED OUTSIDE and stretched, raising her face to the morning sun. The bed of ferns, although scratchy, had been more comfortable than she had expected. However, she was relieved dawn had broken.

She did not like the long dark of the night or the bad dreams that haunted her sometimes.

Forcus had visited her again. He had been hunting her through a stand of tall, dark trees. She had fled, terrified, but wherever she went he followed, his rough threats echoing through the forest. Finally, he had caught her—his heavy hands slamming down onto her shoulders—and she had awoken to find herself bathed in sweat, her heart galloping.

Outdoors, Eithni closed her eyes under dawn's kiss. Daylight always chased her fears away. The air was mild this morning; there was a little lingering dampness after the rain of the day before, but the sky above the trees was clear.

A noise to her right made Eithni open her eyes and turn. Donnel was already awake and was lighting a fire in a large hearth. It was more practical, and comfortable, to cook and spend time outside during the day, for their hut was dark and cramped.

The deer carcass hung from its hind legs behind them. They would both work on it this morning.

Once Donnel had gotten the fire lit, woodsmoke wreathing into the soft morning air, the pair of them perched on one of the larger rocks near the fire and shared the last morsels of fish Eithni had kept back from the night before.

Donnel was taciturn this morning. He had barely spoken a word to her, and his gaze had turned inward. Eithni understood his mood; dawn was often the worst time of day for bleak thoughts.

"Did you sleep well?" she asked finally, flashing him a warm smile.

Donnel grunted. "Well enough. And you?"

Eithni shrugged, her smile faltering. "A bit restless. I had a nightmare ... I get them sometimes."

Donnel glanced up from where he had been staring moodily into the fire. "I heard you tossing and turning," he replied. "Are they about *him*?"

She nodded. "Forcus has been dead over a year and a half, but his wraith still haunts my dreams." She shivered, as if the morning had suddenly turned chill. "I suppose the dreams will stop eventually with time."

He watched her a moment before nodding. "I don't dream at all," he replied.

Eithni raised an eyebrow before favoring him with a teasing smile. "Of course you do—everyone dreams."

He shrugged. "If I do, I never remember them." He rose to his feet then, shattering the quiet moment, his gaze shifting to the deer carcass behind them. "Come— let's get to work."

A warm summer's day settled over the Glen of the Stags. Above the dark bristling tree line, between the slopes of the encircling mountains, the sky was a deep unblemished blue. It was one of those days when Eithni could pretend that winter never existed, that the breeze was always warm, and the days forever long. But she knew that this warm weather would not last—it never did upon The Winged Isle. The bitter season was far longer than the warm one, and there would be many moons when the days were short.

Still, it made Eithni appreciate this fine day all the more.

She and Donnel worked side-by-side. They gutted the deer, saving choice parts of the organs—the kidneys and liver especially—for eating fresh. Then they skinned the doe, and Eithni left Donnel to finish preparing the carcass while she took the skin over to the creek and washed it. She then hung it over a wooden frame that Donnel had built for her, stretching the skin tight so that the sunlight could cure it.

They worked tirelessly before enjoying a rich noon meal of cooked liver and kidneys, flavored with wild garlic. Afterward Donnel went off to hunt while Eithni set to work once more on the hut.

When she had finished her chores inside the hut, Eithni went in search of reeds.

She wanted to make herself a basket, which would make foraging much easier. No reeds seemed to grow nearby, and so she headed along the bank of the clear waterway, traveling west. The creek bubbled over smooth, round rocks and down shallow ravines. Farther west it would lead out of the pine forest into the open stretches of the glen, yet for now it lay under the shadow of the mountains, shaded by tall trees.

Eithni enjoyed her journey. Above, a skylark trilled; it was the sound of summer. The sun was hot on her back, and the ground was soft under her feet. She felt oddly calm and at peace this afternoon, which surprised her, for the last few days had been difficult.

Reeds seemed hard to find. She walked quite a distance before finally spotting some. The creek rushed over the edge of a steep bank, causing a small waterfall and forming a pool at the bottom, before it continued its way west. There below, at the edge of the pool, she spotted a small reedbed.

Eithni made her way down the bank, her feet sliding on slippery moss. Once she reached the pool, she hiked up her tunic, knotting it around her waist, and waded into the water. Eithni unsheathed a small knife that Donnel had given her for boning fish and preparing food.

She cut the reeds deftly and ended up with a large bundle under one arm. Resheathing her knife, she then waded back to the edge of the pool. Despite that it was mid-summer, the water was chill, and her feet had gone numb.

Unknotting her skirt from around her hips, Eithni began to climb the bank—and she had nearly reached the top when a dark shape burst from the trees a few yards before her.

A boar—a massive hairy beast with yellow tusks—rushed out of the undergrowth, snorting.

Eithni gasped, stumbled back, and slipped.

A moment later she was falling, her rushes flying into the air.

Donnel returned to the hut in the early evening. Night fell late this time of year, so dusk was still a way off. He was in a dark mood. Unlike the day before, this hunting trip had yielded little—just two scrawny water fowl. None of his other arrows had found their mark.

He strode down the hill toward the small dwelling, his expression darkening further when he spied the smoking embers in the fire pit outside. Eithni had let the fire go out.

Dumping his bow, quiver of arrows, and catch upon a rock near the fire, Donnel glanced around. "Eithni?"

No feminine lilt answered him, and Donnel realized he had already started to get used to having a woman's company again.

Where is she?

Donnel's mouth thinned. He had told her not to stray far from the hut. Surely she had not wandered off and gotten herself lost?

"Eithni," he called once more, but his voice merely echoed back at him.

Donnel took a deep draft from his water skin. He was bone-weary and had been looking forward to stretching out next to the fire. However, he would not be able to rest, not knowing where Eithni was. If the fire had gone out it meant she had been away for a while.

He found her tracks just west of the hut, in the soft earth beside the banks of the creek, and followed them. It was a glorious evening; the sun still had warmth in it. Sunlight gilded the forest, releasing the scents of pine and moss.

Donnel followed the waterway, his concern deepening when he caught no sign of Eithni. There were still footprints on the banks, and so he pressed on.

Some time later the land fell away steeply, and he stood at the top of a small waterfall with a pool beneath.

There at the bottom, lying on her side upon a velvet-green bank, was a slender female with long brown hair.

Panic flared in Donnel at the sight of her lying so still. "Eithni!"

The sound of his voice roused her, and when he saw her move his fear subsided.

Donnel climbed down the steep bank to where Eithni was pushing herself up into a sitting position. Her face was pale and pinched with pain.

"What happened?" he greeted her.

"I was collecting reeds," she replied with a wince. For the first time Donnel noticed the reeds that lay around her. "I was climbing up the bank afterward when I fell." She looked embarrassed then. "I saw a boar and took fright."

Donnel tensed. Boar were dangerous creatures. She had been lucky it had not charged her. His gaze slid down over her body, checking for signs of injury. "What's wrong?"

"It's my right ankle. It twisted under me as I fell. I tried walking, but it hurt too much."

Donnel huffed out a breath. "You weren't supposed to stray far from the hut."

She gave him a penitent look. "I know, but I wanted to make a basket—I needed reeds."

"You could have broken your neck." He knew his voice was harsh, but he was tired, and this was the last thing he needed. Two days together and she was already becoming a burden.

"It's just a sprain," she replied, stubbornness catching light in her eyes. "I knew you'd come looking for me so I waited rather than risk worsening the injury."

Donnel sighed. He was not in the mood to argue. "Come on," he muttered. "Let's get you home."

He helped her to her feet. "Climb onto my back."

She frowned. "Are you sure?"

"Aye—hurry up."

His tone must have warned her not to dither further for she hastily did as bid. Eithni was slightly built, so he carried her easily. Donnel felt the warmth of her lithe body press against him, and the firmness of her breasts crush against his back.

His breathing caught. *Aye, this woman is trouble—in more ways than one.*

Eithni sat with her legs stretched out before the fire, a leather bandage wrapped tightly around her sprained ankle. Her belly was full of roast venison, and she was enjoying the soft evening air, coupled with the heat of the fire that burned a few feet away.

However, the sight of Donnel's scowling face on the other side of the fire pit took away her peace.

She knew he was angry with her.

She had focused on not being a burden but today had proved that indeed she was one. Donnel had said little during the journey back and hardly spoken a word while they roasted venison for supper. The silence was starting to wear on her, as was the thunderous look on his face.

"I have already said 'sorry'," she said, breaking the silence between them. "I don't know what else I can say? I didn't mean to fall. I told you what happened."

Donnel glanced up, his face hard. "If something happens to you, it's my responsibility," he replied.

Eithni shook her head. "No, it's not … that's ridiculous. You aren't responsible for me. I'm not your kin or your wife. I made the decision to come with you.

Across the fire she saw a nerve flicker in his cheek. Their gazes fused, and Eithni's breathing quickened. Even when he was angry, she was drawn to him. When Donnel had carried her back from the reed bed, she had not wanted the trip to end. The feel of his strong body against hers had filled Eithni with a conflicting blend of excitement and comfort. It reminded her that her feelings for this man were far from clear.

She would never tire of looking at him. Sometimes when his gaze was averted she found herself drinking him in—yet his moods and his bitterness made her wary. And when he touched her, as he had been forced to earlier, she was not sure what to think.

Watching Donnel now, she could see her words had angered him. And yet she would not take them back. "You're not sending me away," she said after a long silence. "So don't even try."

Donnel let out a curse. "All right, woman," he growled. "But let me make something clear. Before you wander off in future, tell me where you're going first. If you get lost in the forest, I may never find you."

"You found me today," she challenged, annoyed by his bossy tone. "Why wouldn't you do so again?"

His grey eyes hardened. "I'm not going to repeat myself. If you don't heed me, I'll carry you off—kicking and screaming if I have to—back to Dun Ardtreck. Then your cousin can deal with you."

Chapter Eighteen

Feast in the Forest

One month later ...

"WE'LL RUN OUT of food if I don't catch something soon."

Eithni looked up from where she was frying eggs upon a hot stone. She had stumbled upon the grouse eggs the day before. They were a special morning treat, for they had not eaten any eggs since arriving here. Eithni had been looking forward to them. However, Donnel's words had shattered her light mood.

Their gazes met across the fire pit, and she saw the tension on his face. Donnel had been withdrawn over the past few days. She had often caught him staring off into space as if he was not even there. Eithni had thought he had been brooding over his exile, but she now realized that survival preyed on his thoughts as well.

"You bring back enough to feed us," she said. The comment was more to reassure herself than him, and Eithni winced at how hollow it sounded. Like Donnel she spent most of her days obsessing over what they would eat in the cold months ahead.

Both of them had lost weight since arriving here. Already slender, Eithni's tunic now hung off her. Donnel's tall, muscular frame had become lean and hard.

"Hunters have cleaned out this valley," Donnel replied, holding her gaze. "I come home empty-handed most of the time."

"But we have enough food at the moment."

"Only just—and what about winter? We need to be filling our stores. If I'm having trouble finding game now, it'll be worse during the bitter season."

His words caused a chill to feather over Eithni's skin. Masking her worry, she bent over the eggs, flipping them with her knife onto two wooden plates that Donnel had whittled out of pine. "Here." She handed a plate with four eggs on it to Donnel and forced a smile. "Eat these before they get cold."

He nodded, his expression softening. "Aye ... thank you."

Eithni took her plate and perched upon a rock a few feet away. She sighed with pleasure as she took her first bite of egg.

"These are delicious," Donnel murmured. Eithni looked up to see that he had almost finished his meal.

"I'll see if I can find another nest today," she replied. Red grouse were plentiful in many places of The Winged Isle. The birds nested on the ground in hollows lined with grass near the riverbanks; she'd had to be quick, but had managed to grab one in her hands.

He nodded, his mouth curving into a rare smile. "Good, lass."

Holding his gaze, Eithni felt a surge of warmth flower under her rib cage.

The Maiden preserve me, he's irresistible when he smiles.

A month in this man's company had made her acutely aware of him. There had only been rare light-hearted moments between them since their arrival in this valley, for the chores associated with surviving from day-to-day weighed heavily upon Donnel especially.

This new existence had not been easy—she spent most of her days with an ever-present hunger gnawing at her belly—yet they had been the happiest days of Eithni's life.

It had not taken her long to realize that Donnel was the reason.

Sometimes he could be poor company; when his mood turned bleak he became taciturn and uncommunicative. On those dark days the shadows of the past dug their claws deep. Yet she still looked forward to waking every morning so that she could spend time with him, before they got to work for the day. Whenever he went hunting, she grew impatient for his return.

Eithni too had days when the ghost of Forcus haunted her—when she would awaken in the early morning, heart pounding, her body bathed in sweat. However, Donnel chased memories of Forcus away. Eithni's favorite moment of each day was after supper when they would sit before the crackling fire pit and talk. Eithni looked forward to these conversations so much that she would be impatient if the afternoon dragged too slowly.

He was quickly becoming the most important thing in her life—and she did not care.

It pleased her to see him smile now.

"So will you go hunting today?" she asked, looking away as she felt a blush creep up her neck.

"No, we need to build up our wood stores so I'll start chopping up that pine I felled three days ago."

Eithni glanced up to see the smile had gone and a look of grim determination had settled upon Donnel's face once more.

Watching him, she decided she would do something special for him today—something that would bring a smile to his face once more.

"Donnel," Eithni called. "Where are you?"

Basket under one arm, Eithni wandered through the dappled forest. A wind breathed through the spruce either side of her; the air was warm, with the scent of pine. She inhaled deeply, her gaze scanning her surroundings.

Where is he?

She was about to call his name again when she heard the 'thunk' of an iron blade hitting wood. It was faint, but Eithni immediately knew she had found Donnel. Smiling, she set off, her feet crunching over the forest floor. She wore foot wrappings made of deer-skin. Donnel had fashioned them for her from the doe he had killed on their first day out here.

She followed the thud of the axe and found Donnel halfway down a slope, chopping his way through the trunk of a pine. He was using a small hand-axe; it was woefully inadequate for the job but the only tool of its kind that he had brought with him.

Stripped to the waist, his naked back gleaming in the noon sun, Donnel was an arresting sight. Eithni halted and stared, losing herself in frank appraisal.

The Mother preserve her, she had never seen such a magnificent man. The muscles of his lean torso rippled with each stroke of the axe.

Feeling someone's gaze upon him, Donnel straightened up, his attention shifting up the slope to where Eithni stood.

Still captivated, her gaze roved over the carven plains of his naked chest and hard belly. A strange hunger swept over her—one that made her feel oddly light-headed and weak at the knees.

"Eithni," he greeted her with a smile. "What brings you here?"

Pulling herself together, her cheeks warming at being caught gawking at him, Eithni held up the basket. "I've prepared a feast for my brave strong warrior," she replied with a smile. "I thought you might be hungry."

The days had been long recently, and she was in a playful mood this morning.

To her surprise and delight, his mouth stretched into a mischevious grin. "Always, sweet kind lassie." Donnel embedded the axe into the trunk of the pine and motioned to the stump. "Let's eat there, upon the great feasting table."

Eithni laughed. It was good to see Donnel lighthearted for once. It also distracted her from the sight of him, half-naked and virile, before her.

She walked down to the stump and laid out the contents of her basket. Their 'feast' was nothing like what they would have enjoyed in Dun Ringill, although she was proud of what she had prepared. There were fillets of smoked trout and eel, strips of dried venison, and small wild onions. However, the item she was most excited about sharing with Donnel was the large earthen cup of scarlet berries that she placed in the center of the stump.

Donnel's gaze widened. "Raspberries! Where did you find them?"

"Downstream from the hut," she replied shyly. "There are a few bushes alongside the creek." She paused here. "Don't worry—I didn't venture far."

Donnel grinned at her as he reached for a piece of smoked eel. "What a woman you are, fair Eithni."

She found herself smiling back. "Fair, eh? I like the sound of that."

He huffed. "I'm sure you've heard it many times. You are as lovely as a fairy maid."

Eithni's blush deepened at that—cursing the heat that flamed across her cheeks. "I never took you for having a honeyed tongue, Donnel mac Muin," she chastised, feigning primness. She took a bite of dried venison and focused on chewing for a moment.

However, Donnel merely winked at her. "All the men of my family know how to charm when it suits them— even Tarl."

Eithni raised a disbelieving eyebrow. Donnel's elder brother was not known for his polished manners. Yet he had managed to win Lucrezia over all the same—in the end. It struck her then that Donnel was flirting with her.

She grew still, her belly fluttering before deciding that she liked it.

They ate in silence for a while, enjoying the meal, which they finished with the berries.

Donnel's eyes widened as he tasted the first one. "Gods, these are good."

Eithni smiled. "Better than oat and plum pudding dripping with butter and honey?"

He groaned. "Don't torture me. Of course they aren't."

Eithni watched him eat the raspberries, enjoying the look of pleasure on his face. After a moment Donnel glanced up. "Aren't you going to have any?"

"I'll pick more later ... you eat these."

He shook his head. "They taste better when shared ... here." He picked up a berry and held it up. "Open your mouth."

Eithni hesitated a moment before complying. He placed a plump berry upon her tongue, watching as she ate it. Then he fed her another. This time she felt his fingertips brush her lips as he pulled his hand away.

Eithni's breathing caught, and their gazes met and fused.

All playfulness between them had gone now. Donnel's grey eyes held an intensity that made her feel stripped bare.

"I should get back," she murmured, rising to her feet with a suddenness that sent her basket flying. "I—"

She never finished her sentence, for Donnel had gotten to his feet as swiftly as her, and he quickly stepped around the stump to face her. A heartbeat later he lowered his mouth to hers.

Eithni went still, losing herself to the pressure of his lips against her own. Then he groaned and drew her gently against him, deepening the kiss. When his tongue parted her lips, she did not resist him. She had gone weak, boneless, in the cage of his arms. She did not feel like herself at all. A storm of aching need gathered within her, and she gasped, her hands moving unbidden to his chest, sliding over the warm, smooth skin.

Donnel's kiss was exquisitely gentle—soft and sensual in a way that undid her completely. She let out a whimper and pressed herself against him. Who was this woman who tangled her hands through his hair, who pressed her breasts against the hard wall of his chest as he kissed her? Eithni's loins had turned molten. She felt as if she would simply melt in his arms.

Donnel ended the kiss suddenly. He ripped his mouth from hers and stepped back, his gaze limpid, his lips parted. He was breathless and his chest was heaving—but as Eithni watched him, she was aware of a barrier crashing down between them.

The cold distant warrior had returned.

She watched him take another step back, and he raked his hand through his short dark hair. His grey eyes had turned flinty and his handsome face grim.

"I'm sorry," he said after a long silence. His voice had a rasp that made her shiver with need. "That was a mistake."

If he had just thrown a bucket of icy water over her, Eithni could not have been more shocked. She stared at him, her throat constricting. The bitter irony of the situation was not lost on her.

It should have been her to end the kiss. After what Forcus had inflicted upon her, she had expected to dissolve into hysteria if another man ever came near her—to claw his eyes out in terror—but she had done the opposite.

Donnel's kiss had set her free. His touch had made all the terrible memories fade.

Only, one look at his face now told her he did not feel the same way. Eithni raised her fingers to her lips, which still tingled from his touch. Was she unpleasant to kiss? Had he just compared her to Luana and found her lacking?

A wretched sensation twisted her belly. "Don't look so fierce, Donnel," she whispered. "You didn't hurt me."

That was the wrong thing to say. His expression turned thunderous. "I shouldn't have touched you," he growled. "Not after everything you've been through."

"It doesn't matter. I—"

"I don't know what came over me."

Eithni stared at him, tears pricking her eyelids. With each word, he was making things worse. In his arms she had felt beautiful, desirable, protected, and wanted. She had felt safe to let out her passion, a desire for him that had been building for a long while now. With just a few words he had succeeded in wounding her deeply. If he had slapped her across the face, it would have hurt less.

Her vision blurred, but she blinked the tears back. She would not cry—not in front of him.

Eithni took a few rapid steps back, nearly tripping over in her haste. "I'll see you later," she mumbled.

Then she turned and fled up the slope, as if a pack of wolves were on her tail. By the time she reached the trees at the top, tears were streaming down her face.

Chapter Nineteen

Vows

DONNEL WATCHED EITHNI disappear over the brow of the hill and forced himself not to run after her.

The Reaper take me, what have I done?

He was not sure what had possessed him. They had been enjoying each other's company, eating and talking, and then he had made the mistake of feeding her berries. He had not been prepared for the animal need that had surged up within him when his fingers had brushed those rosebud lips.

He'd had to kiss her. Right then.

But to worsen matters, she had tasted better than he could have possibly imagined: her warm, slender body pressed against his, her hot mouth opening for him as he kissed her. She smelled of pine, sunlight, fresh air, and the sweet scent of a woman's skin. It had unraveled his self-control.

Trust was a fragile thing. He had just betrayed hers. Eithni had suffered terribly at a man's hands. She deserved better than to have him throw himself at her. Not only that but kissing her brought back memories he wished to keep buried.

Luana.

Had he betrayed her memory?

He had enjoyed kissing Eithni too much. After his wife had died, he had made her a silent promise he would never touch another woman. Luana would never have demanded that of him. She would have smiled in that gentle way of hers and told him to find another to love, and to share his life with. Only, he could not. It tore him up inside to think of lying with another woman. Luana would truly be gone then. Would he then completely forget her in time?

Donnel cursed, spun on his heel, and yanked the axe out of the soft pine trunk.

Donnel returned to the hut with reluctance that evening.

He had not stayed away out of anger toward Eithni but fury at himself. He hacked at the trunks until sweat poured off him—until the muscles in his back, shoulders, and upper arms screamed. He had worked in a frenzy—hoping to drive away his demons—yet as the light faded and the air cooled he realized he had only succeeded in exhausting himself.

The feel of Eithni's mouth under his and the hot pulsing need he had felt for her were still there.

And now he would have to face her.

Donnel breathed in the aroma of roasting venison as he approached the hut. He walked down the mossy bank of the creek, his gaze taking in the humble home he and Eithni had made for themselves over the past moon. It looked vastly different to the ruin they had found. Smoke drifted up from the neatly patched sod roof, and the area around the dwelling was no longer overgrown with weeds and foliage.

He skirted the edge of the hut, glancing inside. A low fire burned in the hearth, and his gaze slid over the sprays of heather that Eithni had scattered over the floor. She had also collected bunches of meadow flowers, which were hanging, drying, from the ceiling beams. It was a cozy, domestic sight, but it just made him feel worse over his treatment of her.

Donnel found Eithni on the western side. She was turning a haunch of venison upon a spit over a glowing fire. They would soon run out of fresh meat. Donnel would have to go hunting again the following day; he just hoped he would not come back empty-handed. Red deer roamed the Glen of the Stags, although not in the numbers he had hoped.

Eithni had her back to Donnel and did not see him approach. As such, he was able to observe her for a few moments as she worked.

The long sleeveless tunic she had worn the night of her abduction was growing faded and threadbare. It was also far looser than when she had arrived here. She would need warmer clothes for the coming winter. Harvest Fire was almost upon them, a celebration that heralded the last moon cycle of warm weather before the leaves began to turn. Back in Dun Ringill folk would be reaping barley from the lower fields and harvesting the last of the summer produce. They would also be putting food aside for the long, bitter months, but Eithni and Donnel had little food they could store apart from dried meats and smoked fish. This fact worried Donnel constantly.

Unbidden he found his gaze sliding up Eithni's girlish form. She wore her brown hair in a long braid; it had fallen to one side as she bent over the spit she was turning. The position drew her tunic tight over the pert roundness of her bottom.

She was a lovely sight.

Enough. Donnel shoved the lustful thoughts aside. *Get ahold of yourself, man.*

Had he not resolved to think nothing but sisterly thoughts toward Eithni from now on? His decision had lasted till the moment he had seen her again, before it fluttered away like leaves scattered in the wind.

Eithni turned then, having heard him approach. Her gaze was shuttered and her face composed. "That was well-timed," she greeted him. Her voice was neutral, giving nothing of her emotional state away.

He nodded, tried to smile, and failed.

"Shall we eat out here?" she asked, turning to retrieve a pine platter. "The evening is too fair to be indoors."

"Aye," he replied. "Shall I carve the meat then?"

She nodded and handed him the platter, before moving away from the fire. Her gaze avoided his. He did not blame her for being guarded around him; he had been rude earlier, and he owed her an apology.

"I'm sorry ... I upset you earlier, Eithni," he said softly. "That's wasn't my intention."

She shrugged and took a seat upon a wide rock near the fire. She watched him unsheathe a knife from his belt and slice the meat off the bone with it. Yet she still refused to meet his eye.

When he was done, Donnel carried the platter of meat over to the rock. There, they sat side by side and enjoyed the supper with some dandelion leaves and wild onions Eithni had foraged. It was a simple yet delicious meal.

The pair of them did not speak for a while as they ate, and despite the still, warm evening, with the last of the sun dappling through the pines and the creek tinkling beside them, a tension lay heavy upon the air.

"I will not break, you know. I'm not as fragile as you think." Eithni's words, spoken softly, yet with determination, caught Donnel by surprise. Her directness disarmed him.

He swallowed a mouthful of venison and swiveled to face her. "It's not that," he replied, holding her limpid gaze. The Hag protect him, he wished she would not look at him in that way; it made it difficult to concentrate. "I shouldn't have kissed you." He tore his gaze away from hers. "After Luana died ... I vowed I would never touch another woman."

He could feel Eithni's gaze upon him. "Why would you make such a vow?" she asked, incredulous. "You are still young. You could find another to love."

He shook his head, negating her words. "Watching my wife die broke something in me. I never want to care for someone like that again. My soul belonged to her, and she took part of me with her when she died."

He glanced back at Eithni to see she was listening to him, her elfin face solemn. "Then you've chosen a lonely life. Whether or not you believe it, we need others. Loss is a part of love for all of us ... none of us escape The Reaper's touch."

Donnel's mouth thinned. "Aye, and that's why I'll have no part of love ... or the pain it brings."

She looked at him squarely. "Is that why you avoid Talor? I thought you blamed him for Luana's death."

Once again, her directness disarmed him. He had met few folk who spoke as plainly as Eithni. Yet, unlike back in Dun Ringill, he was not angered by it.

"At first that was it," he replied, considering her words as he spoke, "but now I do it for his own good ... I can't give him the love he deserves."

"That makes no sense," Eithni countered, a crease forming between her finely drawn eyebrows. "You're lying to yourself, Donnel. Whether you'll admit it or not, you care for your son. You'd be devastated if anything befell him."

"Don't tell me how I feel," he growled in response. "You can't read my mind."

She stared back at him, not remotely cowed. "I understand more than you know," she replied calmly. "After Forcus I told myself I'd never let another man near me ... that I'd go to my cairn without ever taking a husband or bearing children. I felt tainted and believed I would poison any who came in contact with me." She paused here, and her gaze met his. "But knowing you has opened my eyes. It has changed me. You've taught me that I can trust others ... that I can welcome a man's touch, his kiss. Even though you don't want me—I should thank you for that."

Donnel stared back at her. She made him feel wretched, ashamed. She was far stronger than him, this wisp of a woman. He wished he could be like her, could face the things that scared him most, yet he could not.

Eithni made him feel things he did not want. He was relieved to know his kisses had not traumatized her, but what had blossomed between them had to be stopped.

For both our sakes.

Eithni crouched by the creek and washed the carcass of the water fowl she had just gutted. This would be tonight's supper. It was a cool afternoon, for a brisk wind blew in from the north-east. It had an edge to it. Harvest Fire had passed and autumn now approached.

She suppressed a shiver at the thought of the warm months' ending. The weather had been mild of late, and it was easy to forget that The Winged Isle endured long freezing winters.

Both she and Donnel were working hard to prepare for the winter, yet it was not nearly enough. She had prepared deerskins for the cold weather: a vest for them each, and a new pair of breeches for Donnel. However, they really needed furs—seal or wolfskin ideally. They also needed more food.

Eithni straightened up from the creek and carried the carcass over to the fire pit, where she skewered it. A few feet away sat their store hut, which they were slowly starting to fill with dried meat and fish, as well as edible roots. Eithni had found some crab apple trees a few days earlier and picked them clean—the fruit was sour, but the apples would store well over the winter.

Lost in thought, Eithni counted the moons she and Donnel would have till the cold arrived—until Gateway at least. She would need to work harder.

The heavy thud of hooves on damp ground ripped Eithni from her thoughts. Heart racing, she glanced up, and her hand reached for the boning knife she carried at her waist.

Warriors upon shaggy ponies were approaching from the west.

She looked around frantically. Donnel was away hunting and would not be back for a while yet. She was alone here, and it was too late to run, for the men had seen her.

What if Urcal has come to seek vengeance for his brother?

Eithni straightened her spine, her hand still clasped over the hilt of her knife, and watched them draw near. If The Boar had indeed found them, she would have to face them on her own.

A moment later her fear dissolved as she recognized the warrior leading the group: big and broad, with a swarthy complexion and a mane of jet-black curls.

"Wid!"

Her cousin's face creased into a wide grin, and he waved, urging his pony into a brisk trot. Eithni rushed across to him, her feet flying over the mossy ground. Wid reached her, swung down from his pony, and threw his arms around her, crushing Eithni in a bear-hug.

"I thought we might find you around here," he greeted her, still grinning as he pulled back. His gaze shifted behind her, sweeping left to right. "Where's Donnel?"

"He's out hunting."

Wid's gaze returned to Eithni. "How are you, cousin? You're too thin, but you look well enough. Your cheeks are rosy ... your eyes bright."

"I'm well." Eithni stepped back from him, uncomfortable under the close scrutiny. "It's just the fresh air and hard work." Her gaze shifted to The Wolf warriors who had pulled up behind Wid. A wide smile stretched across her face, for she recognized them all.

When she looked back to Wid, her eyes stung with tears. "You are all a very welcome sight. Out here, I'd begun to think the rest of the world had disappeared."

Wid huffed. "No, the rest of us are still here." He paused, his smile fading. "I went to Dun Ringill a few days ago. The mood there is grim—Galan is worrying himself sick although he will admit it to no one.”

Eithni nodded, sadness dulling her joy at seeing her cousin again. “It’s not right,” she murmured, “this bad blood between brothers.”

“Aye,” Wid replied with a grimace. “Let us hope they resolve it.”

“I don’t see how they will,” she answered. They continued on their way toward the hut. “Donnel is even more bull-headed than Galan. He’d starve out here in the wild rather than humble himself before his brother.”

Wid frowned. “Aye, and that’s what worries Galan.” His gaze settled upon the hut then and the seriousness faded from his face. He turned to Eithni grinning. “This place was falling to pieces—you’ve transformed it.”

Eithni shrugged, a smile tugging at her mouth. “It’s hardly a chieftain’s broch, but we’ve made it comfortable enough.”

He inclined his head, his gaze searching her face. “Donnel’s mood was bleak the last time I saw him. He doesn’t mistreat you, does he?”

Eithni held Wid’s gaze, a warmth suffusing her at her cousin’s concern. Wid was a good man. “No, quite the opposite,” she replied. “He has looked after me well and even tolerates my prattle.”

Wid snorted. “I don’t remember you ever being the sort to talk a man’s ear off?”

Eithni laughed before turning to the others who were all dismounting. “See to your ponies and take a seat by the fire. We don’t have much food for supper, but we can share it with you.”

“Put it away for yourselves; we’ve got plenty of food to share,” Wid replied. “Oatcakes, butter, eggs, and cheese.”

Eithni’s mouth filled with saliva at the mention of her favorite foods. “It will be a feast then.”

“We’ve got ale too,” one of The Wolf warriors called out.

Eithni grinned across at him. “Donnel had better get back soon then before you drink it all, Beli.”

Chapter Twenty

Visitors

THE FIRELIGHT CAST a golden veil over the faces of the men seated around the fire. The eve was warm, and so the warriors sat on their cloaks rather than wearing them around their shoulders. Their faces flushed from the fire—and with a good meal and ale inside them—Wid and his men relaxed around the hearth.

The crackle of flames accompanied Beli's voice as he sang them a ballad about the beauty of the mountains upon their isle.

> *I see the mist covered mountains*
> *High peaks with lonely slopes*
> *I see woods, I see thickets*
> *I see fair, fertile fields*
> *I see the deer on the ground of the corries*
> *Shrouded in a garment of mist.*

The atmosphere was very convivial. Even Eithni, who did not usually like strong drink, had downed her fair share of ale. She had washed down the slabs of bread, butter, and boiled eggs she had eaten with glee. Her stomach stuffed and limbs drowsy, she now leaned up against a rock a few feet from the fire.

Beli sang on, his voice rising as he described the bleak yet starkly beautiful mountains of their homeland. Eithni wished she had her harp, that it had not been crushed underfoot at The Gathering. She wanted to play it now, to lose herself in the music.

Eithni's gaze traveled around the fire to where her cousin sat next to Donnel. The latter looked as if he was about to fall asleep. Like Eithni, he was not used to eating so much and had not touched ale for some time.

Eithni's attention rested upon Donnel. It had been a while since their kiss and the words that had passed between them afterward. She had regretted her frankness at the time—for there had been an awkward tension between them for a spell—yet after a day or two they slipped back into their usual routine.

However, Donnel kept his distance from her now, and Eithni took care not to accidentally brush up against him in the hut or to do anything to put him on edge. She had not knowingly done so before, yet ever since that day in the forest, she was aware of the attraction between them.

It lay dormant now, but the ghost of it was always there, coloring every interaction.

Still, Donnel seemed determined to ignore it.

His behavior saddened her, as much for him as for herself. The kiss had been freeing for Eithni, unlocking a fear that had gnawed at her ever since she had left Dun Ardtreck.

The fear that she would go mad with terror if a man ever touched her again.

Beli finished his song, and the warriors around the fire pit applauded him.

"How long will you stay?" Donnel asked Wid when the cheering had died down. "It's good to have company again."

"A few days if we can," Wid replied. "We've come to the glen for some hunting. Yet there doesn't seem to be much prey about. Have you hunted it out?"

Donnel grimaced. "Hardly ... the deer seem to have moved on this year."

Wid gave a shrug. "We'll try our luck again tomorrow."

"Can I join you?" Donnel asked. "Stalking deer on my own gets tiresome."

Wid grinned back. "Of course ... I'd take offence if you didn't join us."

Eithni watched them, a smile curving her lips. She was glad Donnel had male company again—even if it was only for a few days. She and Donnel had fallen into a comfortable routine, but he was used to having other warriors around. She had suspected he missed his brothers, and his ease with Wid confirmed it.

Donnel liked to think he needed no one. He thought he could cut himself from everything that made life worthwhile, yet it was like trying to hold back the tide with your hands—impossible.

Having Wid here will do him good, she thought, leaning against the rock sleepily. *He spends too much time on his own during the day.*

The heat of the fire, a full belly, and a skin of ale all had a soporific effect upon Eithni. She worked hard during the day and usually crawled onto her ferns early. This eve though, she was having trouble keeping her eyes open. The rumble of men's voices lulled her, and before she knew it she drifted off to the sound of Beli beginning another song.

When she awoke again, Eithni found herself pressed against a man's chest.

She stirred, looking up to find herself in Donnel's arms. He was carrying her toward the hut.

"Donnel," she mumbled, still half-asleep. "The others ... I need to organize furs for them."

"They've brought their own and will sleep outside around the fire," he replied. "Don't worry about them."

He ducked inside the hut and carried her across to the mound of ferns covered with deerskins in the left corner of the space. "You're exhausted, lass," he murmured, his voice a low caress. "Get some rest."

Donnel lowered her onto the furs and released her. A sense of loss swept over Eithni as he stepped away; waking up to find herself in his arms had bathed her in warmth. Now that she was away from the fire and the heat and strength of his body, she shivered. The evening had been warm earlier, but now the air had cooled.

"Here." Donnel lay something heavy over her. "Your cousin brought us furs. You will be more comfortable now."

Eithni wanted to thank him, but sleep was pulling her under once more, and her eyelids felt incredibly heavy. Moments later she sank into a deep sleep.

Donnel stepped away from Eithni and watched her sleeping face. The glow of the moonlight through the open doorway illuminated the sweetness of her features, captivating him. For a long moment he stood there, observing her.

She's lovely.

Eithni made keeping his distance very hard. It was not her fault—ever since their kiss she had kept away from him—it was his. He found it hard to concentrate whenever she was near, found himself staring whenever she was not looking his way. He had awoken the sleeping beast with that kiss, and despite his adamant words to Eithni, it would not go easily back into its cage.

The Reaper take him, he wanted her.

She had fallen asleep by the fireside while the men sang, talked, and drank around her. Donnel had not wanted to wake her, so he had picked her up to carry her to her bed. It had been a mistake, for the moment he felt that warm supple body against his, the moment he inhaled her scent, his body betrayed him.

This was no good. He had put up a convincing front— and had even believed the argument he had put forward—yet his need for Eithni grew with each passing day. He did not want this, but his body had other ideas. It was betraying him. He needed to find a way to regain control, or one of these days he would throw Eithni down on the ground and take her—and there would be nothing tender about it.

Ignoring the ache in his loins, Donnel turned from Eithni and crossed to his pile of ferns, covered with the deerskins that Eithni had expertly cured. He lay down on his side, facing the door. Snores filtered in, as one of Wid's men fell asleep.

Donnel tried to relax his body; the bed of ferns and deerskin was surprisingly comfortable. He was tired, and he ached from days out hunting, yet sleep would not come.

He needed to do something before he gave in to the beast.

Eithni said she was not afraid of him, yet he had done nothing more than kiss her. There was a heartbreaking innocence about her at times; one he did not want to destroy. She trusted him and wished to see only the good in him.

Eithni thought she could heal him, but he knew better. She did not see the blackness that rotted his heart. She did not realize that he was beyond help.

Donnel clenched his jaw and shut his eyes. *I can't have Eithni live with me any longer. She has to go.*

The stag bounded through the trees, narrowly escaping the fletched arrow that thudded into a nearby trunk.

Wid let out a curse and pulled up his pony. He then swung down from the saddle and strode over to where the arrow still quivered in the tall pine. "I almost had him."

"You were yards out," one of Wid's men called. "Are you losing your eyesight, man?"

"Belt up, Canaul," Wid growled, yanking the arrow out of the soft wood. "When was the last time one of your arrows found its mark?"

That was a fine stag he just missed, Donnel thought bitterly. *It could have fed us for a moon.*

He rode at the back of the group, although Reothadh chafed at the bit.

Wid vaulted onto his pony's back and they were off again, moving through the trees. The Wolf party had stayed with Donnel and Eithni for three days now, and every day the warriors had ridden out on a hunt. Even though they had not had much luck, they had managed to bring down a boar the day before. Two of Wid's men had stayed with Eithni today, helping her to gut, skin, and hang the carcass.

Donnel had enjoyed the men's company. Wid's boyish exuberance reminded him of Tarl, although as chieftain of The Wolf, the young man could be serious at times, and at those moments he reminded Donnel of Galan. The reminders were painful. Until his banishment, Donnel had taken the bond with his brothers for granted. The three of them had always been close growing up, and though their father had tried to pit them against each other at times—to make men out of them he had said— he had never succeeded in creating bad blood between them.

It was Donnel who had done that. Wid brought back to him all the things he missed the most: the banter with Tarl, the easy companionship with Galan. Without them he felt strangely incomplete.

As they traveled deeper into the woods, Wid reined his pony back so that he and Donnel rode side-by-side. "No thirst for the hunt today?" The Wolf chieftain asked. "It's not like you to hang back?"

Donnel's mouth curved into a sardonic smile. "I've done nothing but hunt for the last moon and a half. Today I'd rather watch others do it."

Wid shrugged, smiling back. "I can see how you'd feel that way."

Donnel watched him a moment, studying the younger man before speaking once more. "Have you seen my brothers of late?" He tried to keep his voice neutral, but his chest constricted as he spoke. He had put off asking this but could no longer wait.

Wid nodded, his face turning solemn. "I was in Dun Ringill a few days ago. Your brothers are both well … but …" Wid paused here, as if uncertain he should continue.

"But what?" Donnel asked, his voice harsher than he had intended. If anything was amiss in Dun Ringill he would know of it.

Wid's moss-colored gaze met his. "The mood in the broch is somber," he replied quietly. "Tarl's humor is foul, and Galan speaks to no one. They all feel your absence."

"It was Galan who sent me away," Donnel ground out. "There's no use him feeling sore over it now."

Wid nodded, making it clear he was not going to argue with Donnel about the subject. "Aye, but words spoken in the heat of anger are usually the ones that torture us afterward."

Silence stretched between them. The other riders drew ahead, leaving Wid and Donnel alone.

"So he didn't send you to check up on me then?" Donnel said finally.

Wid laughed. "His pride wouldn't let him. He'd geld me if he knew I was here."

"But you came anyway?"

Wid huffed. "To see if Eithni was well … Tea begged me to. Galan has no idea."

Donnel went still. This was the moment he had been hoping for. He met Wid's eye once more. "Take her away, Wid. This is no place for Eithni, and her healing skills will be missed in Dun Ringill."

Wid's face grew serious. "I've already asked her to travel back with me, but she refuses."

Donnel tensed. "She did? When was this?"

"Last night."

"Take her back with you anyway … it's for her own good."

Wid shook his head. "I'll not take the lass anywhere if she doesn't agree to go."

A beat of silence stretched out between them before Donnel spoke again. "I don't want her here."

Wid shrugged. "Then you tell her that yourself."

Chapter Twenty-one

Pride

WID AND HIS men left at dawn the following day.

Donnel and Eithni were awake to see them off, both wrapped in the fur cloaks The Wolf warriors had brought them. The ponies stamped and jangled their bits in the early dawn, keen to be away.

Eithni drew her cloak close; there was a definite nip in the air this morning. She stepped forward to say goodbye to her cousin as he finished tying the last of the packs to his saddle.

"I'm so glad you visited us, Wid," she said softly. "When you see Tea again, tell her I am well ... tell her not to worry."

The Wolf chieftain turned to her, his green eyes shadowing. "You can tell her yourself," he replied. "Come with us."

She shook her head, not wanting to have the same argument with him as two days earlier. "I'm staying here. Tell Tea it's my choice."

He nodded, although she could see from the flexing of his jaw that he wanted to say more.

Wordlessly, Wid stepped close to Eithni and wrapped her in a fierce hug. "Go well, cousin," he murmured into her hair.

"And you." Eithni stepped back, her eyes misting.

Wid moved across to Donnel then, and the two men faced each other for a heartbeat before embracing like brothers. When Wid stepped back, his youthful face was more serious than Eithni had ever seen it.

"I shall say this only once, Donnel, for I know you don't want to hear it. Pride has killed many a man ... has turned the days of his life to dust and ruined any chance of happiness. I see that might happen to you. You have the chance to put things right ... only you'll have to humble yourself to do it."

Wid broke off here, yet Donnel did not answer. To Eithni his face looked carved from granite in the grey morning light. She was pleased her cousin had spoken, although she could see his advice had fallen upon deaf ears. She had already encountered Donnel's stubbornness.

"Your fate is in your hands," Wid said after a long pause. "Don't wait till it's too late."

After Wid and his men had departed, the last of the ponies' long tails disappearing into the trees, Donnel turned to Eithni. Feeling his gaze boring into her, Eithni tore her attention from the west and met his eye. She knew from the tenseness of his jaw and the hardness of his eyes that he was angry.

"Wid said you refused to go with him. Is that true?"

"Aye," Eithni replied, holding his gaze. "It was my choice to make ... wasn't it?"

She watched him clench his jaw. "Winter is coming. Despite the supplies that Wid has left us, despite that I spend every day out hunting and you spend every waking moment storing food, it won't be enough. You know that. You can't stay here with me."

Eithni folded her arms over her breasts, drawing herself up to face him squarely. "It has to be enough," she countered. "There are only two of us to feed. I'll not leave you here on your own."

His mouth twisted. "I'm not a bairn. I can take care of myself. It's you I'm concerned about."

Irritation flared within Eithni. "I'm tougher than I look, and I'll not abandon you. Wid respected my decision. Why can't you?"

He glared at her, clearly infuriated by her defiance. Yet Eithni held firm. She would not be sent away.

Donnel stepped back from her. "Very well," he replied, his voice hard and cold. "Be it on your head then."

Eithni watched him stalk off, his back stiff with anger, before her gaze shifted west to where her kin had ridden away. It had been difficult to say goodbye to Wid and the other Wolf warriors, but her place was here.

Donnel would just have to accept that.

Eithni knew the moment she opened the door to the store hut that something was wrong. The sweet smell of rotting meat wafted out, hitting her in the face.

Eithni drew back, her bile rising at the stench. "Gods ... no!"

"What is it?"

Donnel was crouched next to the fire pit, attempting to light the damp wood. It had rained overnight; the deluge had leaked through the turf roof of the hut in places. A heavy cloak of drizzle hung over the wooded valley this morning, bringing with it a damp cold that made Eithni's limbs ache.

Eithni turned, her body tensing as she met his gaze. "The meat has gone off."

"What?" He rose to his feet, his expression thunderous. "All of it?"

"I'm not sure."

Together they hauled out the haunches of venison and boar that hung inside the store house and inspected them in the watery morning light.

It was not good. Over half the meat they had stored was rotting; some of it crawling with maggots.

Eithni looked down at a haunch of venison that was writhing with the little white worms. She swallowed, forcing down a wave of nausea. "How has this happened?"

"Damp has gotten into the store," Donnel replied, his voice flat and bleak. "We mustn't have sealed it properly."

Eithni did not look his way as they carried away the ruined meat and rehung that which could be salvaged. She knew what he was going to say.

Ever since Wid's departure over ten days earlier, relations between her and Donnel had been awkward. They spent most days apart, and whereas in the past she had looked forward to their mornings and evenings together, there was a growing tension between them.

After disposing of the rotting meat, they sat down next to the fire. Neither of them had much appetite after their discovery, so they merely broke their fasts with some weak broth. Eithni perched on a damp rock, her fur mantle around her shoulders, her fingers curled around the earthen cup she had made.

For the first time since coming to this valley, despair welled up within her. She actually felt like weeping over the ruined food, yet she did not. The tears would be weapons Donnel could use against her. She had to remain strong, stoic.

"Eithni," he said finally, his voice gentle. "Look at me."

Reluctantly, she complied. He was watching her, those storm-grey eyes troubled. "You know what this means?"

Eithni clenched her jaw, stubbornness rising within her. "You're wrong. There's still enough for the winter if we're careful. It's still another moon till Gateway."

She watched him sigh and rake a hand through his hair—it was a gesture she had come to know well. It warned her his patience was thinning.

"Come winter, food will be very scarce," he replied. "The deer will move to lower ground, and there will be little for you to forage in the forest. We risk starvation. Wid won't be at hand with supplies of oatcakes and boiled eggs to fill our bellies. He risked much coming here ... if Galan ever found out it could jeopardize their relationship."

She stared at him, hating him for his logic. She wanted to argue with him, deny his words, yet she knew in her heart he was right.

"What will we do?" she asked finally. "We can't go back to Dun Ringill."

"I can't ... but you can."

She shook her head, stubbornness rising once more. "No. I won't leave you."

Donnel watched her steadily. "We're not traveling down this road again. This isn't about what either of us want ... it's about survival. I'll not keep us out here in the wild without food."

Eithni heaved in a deep breath. "I can see that ... but Dun Ringill isn't an option. Maybe we can go to Dun Ardtreck. Wid would happily take us in for the winter if we asked."

His features tensed and a muscle bunched in his jaw. "Doing that could easily sour relations between The Eagle and The Wolf," he pointed out. "I've already caused a rift with The Boar ... I'll not worsen the situation further."

"We don't have to make a decision right away," Eithni replied. "The cold won't settle in properly until after Gateway. Let's see if we can replenish our stores before then."

He gave her a rueful look. "You don't give up easily, do you?"

She shook her head. Their gazes held, and she smiled. "A healer never does."

Donnel walked through the dense stand of spruce, a bow slung over one shoulder and a quiver of arrows on his back. The sun warmed him, but the muscles in his shoulders and neck were tense.

He was in a bleak mood. After discovering half their meat store had gone off that morning, the day had not improved. He had been out hunting all afternoon, and the light was now starting to fade. He had not managed to catch anything; it was as if the forest creatures sensed his mood from afar and fled before he reached them.

Donnel paused, glancing around. *This is hopeless.*

Of course, it did not help that he was distracted. He kept thinking about their ruined food stores and the fact that he would soon need to make a decision about what to do over the winter.

Donnel exhaled loudly and glanced up at the darkening sky.

The way things were going, there was no way he and Eithni could remain in this valley over the winter. Snow often lay deep and heavy for many moons. He would not be able to hunt regularly, and Eithni would not be able to forage for food under a thick crust of snow. That was why their stores were so important.

Donnel turned on his heel and headed for home. His belly rumbled, and he wondered what Eithni was preparing for supper. It took him a while to reach their hut, for his hunting trips now took him far afield. As such, the light had almost faded when he caught the scent of woodsmoke and the aroma of roasting meat.

Donnel found himself smiling. *Roast grouse.*

Despite everything—despite the worries that would not let his mind rest—there was something about his life here in this forgotten valley with Eithni that he loved. It was easy to believe the rest of the world did not exist.

Things had not been easy, and Donnel was sure he had not been pleasant company at times. Yet he had come to enjoy the simplicity, the routine, of their days. He liked waking in the morning to the musical sound of Eithni's humming outdoors, as she roused the fire pit and went about her first chores of the day. He enjoyed sitting by the fire inside the hut in the evenings, watching her sew and mend clothing while he whittled utensils out of wood. Living with Eithni was like living with a warm summer's breeze. Her presence in his life brought sunlight into what would have otherwise have been very bleak days indeed.

He returned to the hut to find Eithni sitting on a rock near the fire, drying her hair. She had clearly just finished bathing in the stream. As he approached, Donnel found himself imagining her standing knee-deep in the clear water, the last of the evening's sun kissing her naked skin as she bathed. He imagined her nipples, pebble-hard in the cold air, and the nest of hair between her thighs. Would it be walnut brown like that on her head?

His body's response was swift and violent.

Gods ... what's wrong with me?

He unslung his quiver and held it in front of him so that Eithni would not see the sudden bulge in his breeches. He had to stop these thoughts. His body did not seem to know the difference between what was real and what was not. One of these days he was going to embarrass himself.

"Evening." Donnel sat down on a rock opposite, making sure to keep the quiver of arrows on his lap.

Eithni favored him with a warm smile and flicked her wet hair back off her shoulders. "Welcome home ... how was your afternoon?"

"Long. Nothing ... again."

Her smile faded. However, she did not reply, and Donnel was grateful. There was no point going over what they had already discussed at length this morning. They would have to make a decision about what to do over the coming winter—but it would not be tonight.

To warm the mood, he forced a smile, his gaze going to the small bird that roasted over the coals. "You caught a grouse ... well done."

Her smile returned, and pride lit in those warm hazel eyes. "Aye ... I finally learned how to use that sling-shot you made me."

Chapter Twenty-two

Night Demons

THE NIGHTMARE STARTED as they often did—with Forcus's voice.

Nearly two years on, the sound of his voice terrified Eithni still. She hated the commanding, brutal edge to it. Then came the hot blast of his breath in her ear as he took her—hurting her with each savage thrust—his hands rough and brutal. Then the pain that knifed through her and made her want to claw her way out of her own skin. It had hurt her terribly the first time, for she had been a maid, and he had not been gentle, but the pain was worse afterward. Far worse. He had taken pleasure from that too, his gaze devouring the agony that twisted her face.

Don't touch me! Leave me be!

"Eithni!"

The voice—a different voice—came from far away, seeming to reach her through a tunnel.

"Eithni!"

The voice was louder this time, puncturing the shroud of darkness and fear that held Eithni fast. She clawed her way out of sleep into wakefulness. A man's hands held her shoulders, and panic crashed over her in a great wave.

"No!" she shrieked. "Get off me!"

"Eithni ... it's me ... Donnel."

The darkness drew back. Suddenly, Eithni realized that the hands gripping her by the shoulders now were not rough; this man's fingernails did not dig into her flesh. Instead, his hands merely held her firm, protecting her.

Eithni's eyes flickered open, and her gaze met Donnel's.

The fire pit inside their hut had burned low and was on the verge of going out. However, the last coals still emitted a red glow, illuminating Donnel's worried face.

Eithni stared up at him, her heart galloping in her chest.

"M'eudail," he said softly. "Are you well?"

My darling.

Eithni swallowed, her gaze holding his. "It was a bad dream," she gasped. "The worst in a long while."

"You dreamed of him again?" Donnel asked, his brow furrowing.

Eithni nodded and inhaled deeply, her pulse steadying as the last remnants of the dream drew back. Having Donnel here, hearing his voice and feeling the firm reassurance of his touch, made her feel much better.

"Come here, lass." There was a tremor in Donnel's voice that she had never heard before, and an aching tenderness. Donnel pulled her gently into his embrace and wrapped his arms around her. Eithni felt him kiss the crown of her head, before he buried his face in her hair. "I will keep the night demons at bay, m'eudail."

Eithni relaxed against the warmth of his body and felt that heat soak into her own. She was suddenly aware that Donnel was naked to the waist. It was usual to sleep naked, although while Donnel and Eithni lived together, they had both taken to sleeping partially clothed. As such, Donnel wore plaid breeches.

Melting into him, Eithni breathed in the clean scent of his skin mixed with a male musk that made excitement curl in the pit of her belly. She loved that smell. Tentatively, she reached out and wrapped her arms around his muscular torso.

Donnel inhaled sharply in response. He breathed her name, and the tattoo of his heart against her cheek increased in tempo. He was no longer merely comforting her; something between them had subtly shifted.

Eithni drew back and looked up. Their faces were just inches apart, and in the dim light his grey eyes looked almost black. She drank him in; he was so beautiful it hurt her to breathe. She raised a trembling hand, her fingertips tracing the lines of his finely drawn mouth. All the while he watched her, his breathing growing shallow and his body becoming still.

"Eithni," he groaned her name. "Do you have any idea what you do to me?"

She shook her head. It was the truth. When it came to Donnel, she had no idea how he really felt about her. He was shrouded by layers of armor. It was difficult at times to reach the man beneath.

She wanted to understand him. This was the closest she had ever come to doing so.

Their gazes held for long drawn-out heartbeats. Eithni did not speak, for she did not want to shatter this moment. However, she ceased breathing when he lowered his mouth to hers and kissed her.

The kiss started gently, heartbreakingly so. It was as if he was afraid she would shatter in his arms. Yet the feel of his lips on hers, the taste of his mouth, had the opposite effect. The last of the night demons fled, and with a gasp she moved her arms up to link around Donnel's neck and kissed him back.

A growl rose up in Donnel's chest. He pulled her hard against him, his hands sliding down the length of her back over the thin tunic she wore to sleep, to finally cup her bottom. A moment later he pulled her onto his lap. Her tunic rode up as she moved to sit astride him, but Eithni paid it no mind.

She was lost in this kiss. She did not understand why it felt so good, only that she never wanted it to end. Just a short while earlier she had been in the throes of a nightmare, suffering the touch of a man who had left deep scars upon her. Yet in the arms of this warrior, she felt unleashed. She was no longer the timid mouse Forcus had reduced her to. Instead, she was a goddess.

Donnel's hands tangled in her unbound hair as he deepened the kiss. His mouth was not gentle anymore: it was hungry and demanding. Eithni felt the hardness of his shaft pressing against her lower belly, and a sensation leapt within her—an odd blend of excitement and fear.

He wanted her.

Donnel broke away then, breathing hard. He stared down at her, his high cheekbones flushed, his lips bee-stung, and his eyes shining. "I shouldn't be doing this," he said, his voice rough. "I shouldn't be touching you now ... especially after that dream."

Eithni shook her head. She did not want him thinking that. She had to make him understand that his touch healed her. "I want you, Donnel," she whispered. "Please don't stop."

His eyes widened, and he stared down at her. Perhaps he had expected her to shrink back from him, fear and repulsion in her eyes. Yet it was taking all Eithni's self-control not to throw herself at him. Watching Donnel—her heart hammering against her ribs—she waited for his desire to cool, for his shields to go up as they had the day when she had brought him that feast in the forest. She would not blame him for it, although she was not sure she could suffer the agony of disappointment. The agony of not having his hands on her body.

"There is nothing wrong with this," she whispered finally, her chest aching from need. "Whatever the wounds of the past. I'm a woman, you're a man ... and we want each other. There's nothing more natural—"

Donnel's mouth came down hard on hers, cutting off the things Eithni had been about to say. She had only just begun to open her heart to him; she had been ready to get down on her knees and beg him to touch her.

However, it seemed that Donnel mac Muin was not made of stone after all.

His kisses were wild now, and Eithni matched him. It did not even feel as if her body, her will, belonged to her any more. She was not sure who this woman was who raked her fingers down his back, who tangled her tongue with his. She liked this woman though—for this was how Eithni had dreamed of being.

Once, when she had shared her hut with Lucrezia, she had confided to her friend about her past. There had been great sadness in her that day, for she had seen the burgeoning passion between Tarl and Lucrezia and had believed she would never experience the same herself.

Breathing hard, she pulled back from Donnel and yanked her tunic over her head, exposing herself to him. His gaze was hot as it raked over her. He then lifted her to her knees and pulled her close so that he could touch her. Eithni sighed, closing her eyes and giving herself up to sensation. He ran his hands over the length of her body, before his mouth fastened upon her breasts.

She gasped and looked down to see he was suckling one. Her breasts were small and peaked. She had always lamented her lack of bust—comparing herself unfavorably to Tea. She had thought men would not find her attractive, yet now Donnel worshipped her breasts.

"Perfect," he mumbled, releasing one swollen nipple before he fastened on its twin.

Eithni groaned, closed her eyes, and gave herself up to sensation once more. Her knees were starting to wobble under her.

Donnel reared back and started to unlace his breeches. Watching him, Eithni stifled a gasp.

The Mother and the Maiden save me. Could there be a man alive more beautiful than this one?

Naked he was more breathtaking than she had imagined. Even his shaft—a part of the male body she had deliberately avoided thinking about—was magnificent. It was swollen and hard, straining against his belly.

"You can touch me … if you want, Eithni," Donnel said. The rasp in his voice excited her beyond measure. Her lower belly felt molten, and a strange ache pulsed between her thighs.

Nervously she reached out, her fingertips trailing up the hard length of him. "Your skin is so soft," she whispered. "But you're so hot … so hard."

Her words inflamed him. With a growl he pulled her into his arms and kissed her deeply. They fell back on the furs, Eithni beneath him, and she moaned at the velvet feel of his skin sliding over hers. Without even realizing she was doing so, she parted her thighs for him, wrapping her legs around his hips.

A heartbeat later she felt the tip of him pressing against her core.

And for a moment the shadows of the past intruded, dimming the passion that had made her fearless. Eithni's body went rigid under Donnel's.

He stilled, propping himself up on his elbows so he could look down at her. "I would never hurt you," he whispered. "If you wish it … I will stop."

"No, don't," she gasped. The memories faded, and she was with him again. "It was just a surprise that's all."

He smiled down at her before reaching out and stroking her face. "Let me make it a good surprise then."

Donnel entered her slowly. He was large, and she was still tense, so he took his time allowing her to get used to his size—to stretch around him.

Eithni forced herself to breathe, to relax her body, and to her surprise it did not hurt at all. Instead, she felt a wondrous aching fullness. When he was buried deep inside her, Donnel moved his hips in a circular motion, and a shaft of pleasure arrowed through Eithni's lower belly.

She gasped, and when he did it again, she gave a soft cry of pleasure.

"Is that good, mo leannan?" he murmured.

My lover. His words caressed her, like his hands that had returned to her breasts, like his shaft that was now buried to the root within her.

"Aye," she groaned. "Please ... don't stop."

He reared back, withdrawing from her slightly while he lifted her legs, placing them over his shoulders. Then he began to rock back and forth, sliding deeper into her with each movement.

Exquisite pleasure rippled out from her core.

Each movement of his hips lifted her higher and higher toward some nameless goal. Eithni let out a choked gasp and whispered his name. She opened her eyes, gazing up at him under heavy lids. Donnel towered above her, his naked skin gleaming with sweat in the dying light of the embers.

She noted the tension in his shoulders, the fierce expression on his face, and realized that he was reining himself in. He was going slowly and gently on her account. A feeling of safety settled over Eithni at the sight. This powerful, passionate man was afraid of hurting her. He was holding back for her pleasure.

"Please," Eithni breathed. "I need more, Donnel ... I need you."

His face twisted, a nerve flickering in his cheek. "I can't," he ground out. "I don't want to—"

"I want it," she cried as the pressure mounted within her.

With a curse he parted her legs wide and thrust deep between them.

Eithni cried out, shivering as excitement mounted within her and uncontrollable tremors began radiating out from her loins. She arched back against the deerskin and dug her fingers into his broad shoulders as he rode her.

He was her rock in a harsh cruel world.

Donnel's self-control snapped then, unraveling like a ball of yarn cast down a hill. He plunged deep, and Eithni felt him release inside her as she climaxed once again, her cries splitting the night.

Chapter Twenty-three

Making Things Right

EITHNI LAY UPON her back, breathing hard, and waited for the world to stop spinning. Her body felt weak and boneless, her loins still ached with pleasure. She felt completely undone—it was as if Donnel had slowly taken her to pieces and put her back together again. He had shown her what it should be like between a man and a woman. No fear, shame, or pain—just abandon.

Raising a trembling hand, she pushed her damp hair out of her eyes and glanced over at where Donnel lay sprawled on his back next to her. He too was breathing hard, his chest rising and falling fast. His eyes were closed now, with his lashes long and dark against his cheeks.

A wave of tenderness rose up within Eithni. She reached out and placed her palm upon his chest. Donnel's eyes flickered open, and he covered her hand with his. Then he turned his head to look at her.

His expression was still tender, but his gaze was haunted. Eithni had not one regret about what had just transpired between them. How could she regret the most magical experience of life? However, gazing into Donnel's eyes, she realized he did not feel the same way.

"I lost control," he said huskily. "Sorry about that."

He was so serious that she had to smile. "I'm glad you did," she replied, her cheeks warming under the intensity of his gaze. "This has been growing between us for a while ... I'm glad we gave into it. Tea once told me that desire isn't like other emotions. You can't wish it away, for it only gets worse if you do."

Donnel huffed a laugh. "I suppose she should know—she and Galan had a rocky start." His expression grew serious once more. "I've really made a mess of things ... haven't I?"

Eithni favored him with a soft smile. "No ... not of everything."

She slid over to him and propped herself up on one elbow, gazing down at him. He looked up at her, a half-smile tugging at his lips. "You're quite a woman. You surprised me."

"I feel safe with you," she replied, meaning it. "You make me feel ... as if I can be myself."

A shadow moved in his eyes, and she saw his jaw tense. Once again he was at war with himself; she could sense it.

"I can't give you my heart, Eithni," he said after a moment. "I don't have one left to give."

Eithni's chest constricted, and the blanket of wellbeing their lovemaking had wrapped her in slipped away, making a chill feather across her skin. She had wanted to think what had just happened between them had changed his world the way it had hers. However, he still carried his wife's ghost with him.

She did not blame him for it either, but the sting of disappointment this realization brought punctured her happiness. She had heard that Luana had been an incredible woman—beautiful, kind, and strong. Such a ghost would be hard to leave behind.

Perhaps sensing her change in mood, Donnel reached up, his fingertips tracing the lines of her face. "You're beautiful," he murmured. "Like a maid of the Fair Folk ... not of this world."

Eithni heaved in a breath. A few moments earlier she would have welcomed those words, would have basked in them. Now they just made her feel lonely. She had not lain with Donnel expecting him to profess his love for her, yet his words seemed empty after what they had just shared.

Foolish girl, you know nothing of the world, she chided herself, pulling back from him. *You play with fire and then are surprised when you burn your fingers.*

Without another word Eithni moved away from Donnel and reached for her tunic.

The grey dawn light filtered into the hut, drawing Donnel out of a deep sleep. Yawning, he stretched, awaking slowly. A sense of wellbeing filled him this morning; his limbs felt loose, his muscles relaxed, and his mind clear.

He opened his eyes to find himself lying naked upon the pile of ferns. There was an indentation on the deerskin where Eithni had lain during the night, yet there was no sign of her now.

Donnel sat up and stretched once more. Gods, he had not slept that well in a long while. Rising to his feet, he retrieved his clothing from the floor and quickly dressed. It was cold inside the hut, for the embers had died overnight. When he emerged outdoors, he saw a mantle of ominous grey cloud looming overhead. The air was damp and charged with the promise of rain.

He found Eithni before the fire outside, warming her hands over the low flames. She had not seen him emerge from the hut and had her back to him. At a glance he saw she was tense. There was a rigidity in her back, and her shoulders were slightly rounded.

Watching her, self-recrimination twisted Donnel's gut. What was wrong with him? Last night he had crooned endearments in her ear and made love to her as if she were the only woman alive—and then afterward he had informed her he could never love her.

What insensitive bastard does a thing like that?

Him, it seemed. The words had been out before he could stop them, but that was no excuse. He could not use Luana as a justification either—she was not to blame for anything. He had poisoned his own heart with his bitterness and anger; Eithni did not deserve that. She was worth so much more. She had a good heart, a kind soul, and a passion that had surprised and delighted him.

Yet as he watched her, he wondered at the wisdom of giving into his desire for her. They had done nothing wrong—what had happened between them was as natural as breathing—but it could not lead anywhere.

Not while he felt as he did about the world.

Eithni heard him approach and turned. His chest constricted when he saw her eyes were glistening and her cheeks were damp. She'd been crying.

"Lass ... I'm sorry."

She shook her head. "For what?" she replied, injecting a brightness to her voice that her eyes belied. "I'm fine. It's just the smoke from the fire."

Donnel crossed to Eithni, pulling her close. He folded his arms around her, noting how stiff she was in his embrace. So different to how she had been the night before. The lass was plucky and brave, yet she was also vulnerable and fragile. He should not have lain with her unless he had been prepared to give her his heart. But he could not take the words back now. Like an arrow loosed from a bow, he could only stand back and watch it find its mark.

"Forgive me, Eithni," he murmured against her hair. "I didn't mean to hurt you, but I can see I have."

She drew away, raising her tear-streaked face to meet his eye. "I'm just being a goose," she replied huskily. "I don't know ... what I expected. I'm a foolish woman."

Donnel shook his head, reached down, and brushed away a tear that trickled down her cheek. "You're neither of those things. You're a beautiful woman, and you deserve better than the likes of me."

He had messed up yet again. He knew it the moment the words were out. A shadow moved in those large hazel eyes, and she stepped back from him, out of his embrace.

The Reaper take him, he had never had such problems with women. It seemed that every time he spoke he dug a deeper hole for himself. He blundered about like a rampant boar in a flower bed, trampling everything.

They broke their fast together before the fire, while the clouds grew darker overhead. In the distance, thunder rumbled. It was a tense meal, and Donnel did not enjoy his smoked meat.

"Doesn't look like a day for hunting," Donnel observed, glancing up as the first fat drops of rain fell. "I'd better see to Reothadh. He's not fond of storms."

Eithni nodded. "I'll get a fire lit inside."

A short while later Eithni and Donnel sat at opposite sides of the glowing hearth while the rain hissed down on the sod roof and thunder boomed overhead.

Perched upon a wooden stump, Eithni sewed together pieces of deerskin to make clothing for the winter, while Donnel carved at a large lump of wood with a knife. He was fashioning a bowl so that Eithni could use it for cooking.

They worked in silence for a while, and as they did so, Donnel's thoughts turned inward. They did that too often these days. He had never been like that before Luana's death. Galan had always been the one who brooded. Donnel and Tarl were more light-hearted. Brooding did a man no good—it made problems loom to monstrous proportions.

Donnel's thoughts turned to the last words Wid had spoken to him before leaving them. He had been angry with The Wolf chieftain for speaking up—giving his opinion when it had not been asked for—but his words had haunted him ever since. The situation with their winter stores made him consider Wid's advice once more.

You have the chance to put things right ... only, you'll have to humble yourself to do it.

After a while Donnel's thoughts turned full circle and he looked up, his gaze fastening upon Eithni. She was bent over her sewing, her brow furrowed as she thrust a bone needle through the hide before inserting a thin leather lace to bind two sections together.

"Eithni," he said, raising his voice to be heard over the drumming rain on the roof. "Wid was right."

She glanced up, her eyes widening. "About what?"

"What he said about me needing to put things right. I've known the truth of it for a while but losing half our food stores has forced me to face it."

Eithni went still. "Will you return to Dun Ringill and speak to Galan?"

He shook his head. "No, that wouldn't be enough. He needs more than my word. I've broken it too many times. I need to give him proof that I've changed. Loxa deserved his end, but it wasn't for me to give it to him. Urcal and Galan were right about that ... it was their decision." Donnel paused here, considering his next words before he spoke them. "To make things right, I must go to Urcal and kneel before him."

Eithni gasped. "You want to go to An Teanga?"

He nodded.

"But Urcal will kill you."

"I don't believe he will. He's rough, but he's a different man to Wurgest and Loxa. He understands the importance of peace. He respects our tribe ... or did before The Gathering. He doesn't want a blood feud. It galls me to do so, but I must humble myself before him."

Eithni watched him, her heart-shaped face pale in the hearth light. "Then I will go with you," she murmured.

Donnel frowned. "That's not wise. It could be dangerous."

"But you said he would listen to you. Were you lying to me?"

He huffed out a breath. This woman never let him get away with anything. "No—but I'd rather not take the risk of you coming to harm. It would be best for you to return to Dun Ringill. If Urcal did turn on me, you'd be in danger too."

She put down her sewing and glared at him. "If you're going to An Teanga then I shall too."

"Eithni … I don't want to argue with you again."

"Then just accept it … or choose another path."

Donnel huffed. "There isn't any. I wish there was … but this is the only way."

"Then don't go." Her voice was almost pleading now.

Donnel's gaze met hers once more across the firelight. "Avoiding the truth isn't going to fix what's broken in me. Do you want to continue living with an angry bitter man?"

Her mouth thinned. "I'd prefer that to a dead one."

Donnel gave a humorless smile. "And I'd prefer not to lie awake at night worrying how to feed us, and wondering when Urcal will attack our people. I slighted him terribly, and he'll not forget it. The man deserves my apology."

Eithni stared at him. He could see the warring emotions on her face. He knew she could see his point, but she was also scared for him. She did not believe Urcal mac Wrad was to be trusted.

Truthfully, Donnel was not sure either. However, one thing he did know about the warrior was that pride and honor mattered greatly to him; he remembered his father speaking of it a number of times. *Never wound a Boar's pride,* he had warned his sons, *for he has a long memory and sharp tusks.*

Donnel's mouth twisted at the memory. His father had not been a fool. Neither Donnel, nor Tarl had heeded Muin's words—although they would have been wise to do so.

Chapter Twenty-four

The Shadow

EITHNI FASTENED THE last bag behind Reothadh's saddle and glanced back at the place she had called home for the past two moons.

The morning sun had just touched the top of the turf roof, casting its soft light over the glade. This lonely hut, encircled by pines, had been their haven, their shelter. It was a wrench to her gut to leave it.

Eithni looked over at where Donnel was saddling his stallion. "What about the rest of the food we've stored?" she asked. "It'll surely spoil."

He shook his head. "We're leaving it for the hunters who will pass this way soon. This place was a mess when we found it—the warriors of The Wolf will appreciate us repairing it and filling the stores."

Eithni sighed, her gaze returning to the store hut and the smoking embers of the fire she had just doused with water. "Spoken like a man," she replied, unable to keep the edge of bitterness out of her voice. "Women don't find it so easy to leave a home they have made."

Donnel ducked under the pony's neck and faced her. Two days had passed since he had made the decision to ride south to An Teanga, and in that time they had been so busy preparing for their departure that they had barely spoken of anything save practicalities.

His gaze was hooded this morning, his face hard to read. "I've been happy here too," he said, stepping so close she had to crane her neck to meet his eye. "But the weather has been fair, and we've barely managed to fill our bellies. You know things were about to get much harder for us."

Eithni sucked in a deep breath. "Aye ... so you say."

He stepped back from her. "Are you ready?"

"Almost. I just need to check inside once more."

"Go on then—we've got a long day's ride ahead of us."

Eithni stepped around him and went back into the hut. She had tidied it up this morning, leaving the two piles of ferns covered in deerskin for the next occupants. She had also laid the fire with sticks so that whoever came next would not have to search for kindling.

Sadness settled over her as her gaze swept the dim interior. It had been a humble abode, but she had been happy here. Her belly clenched when her thoughts shifted to what lay ahead. The future was suddenly uncertain. Donnel would face Urcal, and then what? If Urcal pardoned him, would they then return home to Dun Ringill, to their old lives? She the healer, he the warrior?

Circumstance had pushed them together, but would he want anything to do with her when they returned to Dun Ringill?

Goose. Eithni pushed this thought aside and pulled her fur mantle tight about her shoulders. *What a thing to worry over.* She had no control over the future. The situation between her and Donnel was tense enough without her working herself up over what might happen between them later. *Let's just get this visit to An Teanga over with.*

She turned, ducked under the low lintel, and emerged into the dawn. Donnel had mounted his pony and was waiting for her. Reothadh, an impatient beast at the best of times, pawed at the ground, his nostrils flaring.

Eithni crossed to Donnel, and he reached down, grasped her hand, and pulled her up onto the saddle in front of him. Eithni tried to get comfortable, adjusting her skirt to cover her legs. She was acutely aware of Donnel sitting behind her, the warm solid strength of his body seeping into her back.

Eithni pushed down the desire that fluttered like a caged moth under her ribcage. Donnel had not touched her—had not kissed her—since their one night together. They had been busy over the past two days, but she had not failed to note that he kept his distance physically from her. At night he retired to his side of the hearth.

Disappointment had flared in Eithni's breast both nights, yet she had fought it. She wanted to curl up on her deerskin and weep, for she knew that there would be no other man besides Donnel for her. However, instead she had rolled onto her side so that she faced the wall and squeezed her eyes shut, forcing back the sadness that rolled over her in waves.

Sitting pressed up against him now was a reminder of the effect this man had on her. Her breathing quickened, and heat flowered across her chest. She was grateful he could not see her face.

Without a word Donnel urged his stallion forward. They forded the creek and rode up the bank. Eithni forced herself not to look back at the deer hunter's hut. Instead, she kept her gaze forward—focused on the dark line of pines before her.

They rode west for a spell, following the valley in the cleft between the two mountains. After a while the vale opened out, the trees drew back, and they rode into the Glen of the Stags—wild open grassland under a pale blue sky.

At noon they stopped and ate some dried meat and crab apples upon a sun warmed stone at the rise of a hill. Eithni was surprised to find that she was hungry. The fresh air and early start had done much to restore her appetite.

Neither of them said much, for each had retreated into their own thoughts. Leaving the hut, and the simple life they had built there, had affected them both it seemed. Eithni felt cast adrift, and not even Donnel's presence could reassure her.

After a brief rest they continued on, turning south now over an open landscape bordered by soaring peaks. And as they rode, the dark outline of the Black Cuillins inched ever closer. By dusk they reached the foothills and made camp by a stream near the path leading up to the Lochans of the Fair Folk—the Fairy Pools where Tea and Galan had wed just under two years earlier.

Eithni sat on the grass near the small fire pit as Donnel coaxed a lump of peat into flame, and craned her neck to take in the majesty of those black crags. This close the mountains had a forbidding quality, for they appeared carved out of coal, all smoky hard edges against the blushing dusk sky.

The Lochans of the Fair Folk were nestled above them in the foothills of the mountains—a mystical place for their people. Gazing up at the last of the sun bathing the tips of the Cuillins, Eithni found herself remembering Tea and Galan's handfasting ceremony. It had taken place before a great storm. Her brow furrowed when she recalled the potion she had made for her sister; one that stripped her of her inhibitions and allowed Tea and Galan to consummate their marriage. Their brother, Loc, had put her up to it. He had been desperate for peace between The Eagle and The Wolf, even if it meant drugging Tea to do it.

I shouldn't have done that, she thought. It had nearly ruined her relationship with Tea forever.

Still, Tea had looked beautiful and fierce as she stood there at the edge of The Wishing Pool and made her vows. Galan—bare-chested, his naked skin painted in swirls and circles—had made Eithni's girlish heart flutter.

She had envied Tea. She had wanted a handsome, noble-hearted warrior like that for herself.

"It all began that day," Eithni murmured, voicing her thoughts aloud without even realizing it. "The story of our people uniting."

Donnel looked up from where he had just managed to light the peat. Pungent smoke drifted up into the still night air. His gaze narrowed as he too looked up at the Black Cuillins. Watching him, Eithni wondered if this place brought back memories.

"Luana insisted on coming to the handfasting," he said after a moment. "She was heavy with child and had not carried Talor easily. We argued before leaving Dun Ringill ... but in the end I relented." A shadow passed over his face. "I shouldn't have."

"It wouldn't have made any difference," Eithni replied gently. "If the birthing sickness took her, the trip here wouldn't have caused it." She paused, remembering the laughing dark-haired beauty she had seen with Donnel at the handfasting. She felt mousy in comparison. How could she possibly live up to the memory?

"What did you love the most about Luana?" The question surprised her. She did not want to cause him pain or remind herself of his lost love—yet at the same time she was curious about the woman he had loved so deeply.

She was worried the question might anger Donnel, but instead he smiled. "Her kindness," he replied without hesitation. "She was big-hearted and cared deeply for others." He paused here, his gaze shifting from the mountains to Eithni. "Not that different to you really."

Eithni warmed under the unexpected compliment.

He turned from the Black Cuillins and glanced back at the smoking peat. The tender gold flames were growing now. "You are different to her in many ways though. Luana was earthy, straight-forward, and practical, but you ..." He paused here, as if searching for the right words. "... you are elemental. Like the first blush of warmth in spring, the sparkle of frost on a winter's dawn, or the breeze that rushes in from the loch and steals your breath from you. Sometimes I wonder if you are really of this world."

Eithni stopped breathing. "That's beautiful, Donnel," she murmured. "I'm not sure I do your words justice."

His mouth quirked. "Aye, you do. Don't let the likes of me steal your light, Eithni." He paused here, pain shadowing his eyes. "These days I cast a shadow over all who come near me."

Eithni watched him a moment. She was starting to feel lightheaded, and then realized she had been holding her breath. Sucking in a lungful of air, she noted the atmosphere between them had changed. A tension had grown while they were talking, one that made her acutely aware of him.

They stared at each other, and the sensation grew. Eithni's pulse quickened as she saw his pupils dilate. He felt it as strongly as she did, she realized—this quickening, this desire—he was just bent on denying it.

"You won't steal my light, Donnel," she said after a long silence. "You lifted a shadow from my heart."

Chapter Twenty-five

All of You

DONNEL URGED HIS pony into a swift canter—
Reothadh's heavy feathered hooves eating up the
distance. This was the third morning of their journey.
They were passing through the heart of Eagle territory.
To the west was the peninsula where Dun Ringill sat, yet
Donnel did not turn in that direction. Instead, he
continued on, crossing a land he knew as well as the lines
of his own palms.

Eithni perched before him, her body jolting against
his with each stride. They both had layers of clothing
between them, for she wore a heavy fur mantle, but the
warmth and feel of her body against his had been
painfully distracting.

Her unbound hair tickled his face, and he inhaled the
scent of rosemary from her clothing. He was aware of her
long legs next to his. Her skirt had ridden up, exposing
milky skin. His fingers itched to caress it.

As he rode, he thought about the things he had said to
Eithni the night they camped under the shadow of the
Black Cuillins. There was something about this woman
that made him speak recklessly—and yet he could not

bring himself to regret those words. The fact of it was that she enchanted him.

It was early afternoon when they reached the boundary between The Eagle and The Boar territories: The Valley of the Tors.

Donnel slowed Reothadh to a walk as they rode down the steep, rock-studded slope. Great tors rose from the damp earth: dark sentries against the sky.

"Is this the place where Tarl fought Wurgest?" Eithni asked, speaking for the first time since they had rested at noon.

"Aye," Donnel replied. He remembered following Galan into the valley and seeing Tarl, bloodied but victorious, sitting on the ground with Lucrezia in his arms, Wurgest dead next to him. Black, brutal rage had fueled Donnel that day. He had helped cut down all The Boar warriors who had ambushed them, but it had not been enough. He had wanted to drown the whole world in blood.

With a jolt Donnel realized that he no longer felt that way.

The fury, the bitterness that had gnawed at his gut day and night, was gone. He no longer sought vengeance for a wrong that could never be put right. He no longer wished he was dead.

This woman sitting before him in the cradle of his arms was the reason.

"It was a dark day," he murmured, "for we lost Alpia. It was that anger I carried with me to The Gathering ... it was why Galan didn't want me there." His gaze swept across the empty valley. "And now it's as if it never happened. You expect the earth to carry the stains of battle forever, but as soon as the first rain comes they're washed away."

A cool, slender hand enclosed over his forearm. "If only it was the same with us," she replied softly. "If only the rain could wash the past away."

Silence stretched between them while Donnel struggled to master his feelings. A wave of tenderness hit him; it almost hurt to breathe. This woman had no idea what she did to him, how just the sound of her soft voice tore down the walls he had so painstakingly built.

"You were my rain," he replied, his voice coming out as a rasp. "The only reason I'm able to face Urcal is because of you. Being with you lanced the poison from me ... you truly are a healer."

Her hand squeezed his, and he heard her inhale deeply. They rode across the wide valley floor now, and Donnel reached out with his free hand, wrapped it around her, and drew her back against him so that their bodies pressed close. It was no good. He had been fighting this for days now; he could no longer deny it.

The wind had blown her hair to one side, and he leaned forward, kissing the soft skin of her nape. Eithni moaned, and his body reacted to the sound, his groin hardening against the curve of her bottom pressed up against it.

The Reaper take me—I must have her.

The more he resisted his need for her, the worse it got. He had to give in to it or go mad.

At the far side of the valley, he drew up his pony and swung down from the saddle. He helped Eithni down after him and pulled her into his arms. Their mouths collided, hot and hungry. She melted against him, linked her arms around his neck, and pushed her body along the length of his. Her firm, pert breasts thrust against him, and when her tongue timidly stroked his a hunger wilder than any he had known reared up within him.

His hands slid down Eithni's back and cupped her bottom. He picked her up, lifting her against him so that their hips were joined, and carried her over to where one of the tors rose above them, blocking out a mackerel sky. Donnel paid his surroundings no mind. Instead, he drank Eithni in, exploring that soft mouth, those beautiful pink lips.

He longed to rip the clothes off that supple body and kiss his way down it. But there was no time for that. His need to be inside her was driving him to distraction.

Eithni was unraveling him, robbing him of any coherent thought.

During their only night together, she had been passionate. Yet there had been a slight reserve—due to her fear of being physically hurt—that had held her back.

Today he sensed no such reserve. She devoured him, her hands roaming his chest before sliding down his belly to the bulge in his breeches beneath. Her small hand cupped his girth, her fingers caressing him through the plaid.

Donnel growled low in his throat and tore his mouth from hers. Reaching down, he unlaced his breeches and freed his shaft so she could touch it openly. He watched her gazing down at it, her slender fingers gripping him as she slid her hand up and down his length. Excitement gleamed in her eyes, and her lips parted as she stroked him.

He threw back his head and groaned.

Eithni gave a soft, throaty laugh. "You are beautiful, Donnel."

He could not stand any more of this. He had to have her.

Hitching up Eithni's skirt around her waist, he pinned her up against the sun-warmed stone, kneed her thighs apart, and thrust into her.

Eithni took him, all of him, to the hilt—her velvet heat closing around him, drawing him deeper still.

"Eithni," he gasped. She was so wet and tight it nearly pushed him over the edge. She made him want to lose control completely. Yet he did not want to do that—he did not want to frighten or hurt her.

She gave a deep moan and arched back, grinding herself against him. He stared down at her: the long sensual line of her neck, the way her lips parted as she gasped her pleasure.

Donnel responded in kind, rotating his hips and grinding himself deep inside her. She made a breathy mewing sound, and he felt her body start to tremble, the walls of her womb contracting against him. Her nails dug into his arms, and their gazes met.

The moment was so intense that Donnel nearly spilled within her there and then.

He could feel the shudders of her release rippling through her, yet she kept her gaze fixed upon his so that he could see what it did to her.

"Please," she panted. "I want you. All of you."

Her words were like dry tinder to a flame. He spread her thighs wider still and took her in slow hard thrusts, their gazes locked. Eithni cried out, the sound ringing across the valley, and Donnel felt a wet heat release deep within her.

Donnel went wild, his restraint finally snapping. He plunged into her, gripping her buttocks so he could penetrate deeply. Eithni met each thrust, her cries throaty now. Donnel leaned down, his mouth branding her neck as he took her.

He lost himself completely at that moment—for the first time ever during coupling. Life had left its scar upon the soul of Donnel mac Muin, but in doing so had given depth to him. His coupling with Luana had been passionate, yet he had always held himself back with her—just a little. When she died, she truly had taken the man he used to be with her. The man who took Eithni up against this tor was a warrior who had seen the darkest side of his being. He had tried to destroy himself and failed. He had nothing to hold back anymore.

For the first time in his life, Donnel was not afraid of surrendering himself. He lost himself in Eithni: the taste of her skin, her heat, her wild passion. White-hot pleasure crested within Donnel, setting every part of him alight. He bucked hard against Eithni as he came, threw his head back, and roared.

Eithni hung in the circle of Donnel's arms. She felt utterly spent, her limbs boneless and weak. Had he not been holding her up, she would have slid to the ground.

Her head rested against his chest, and she could hear his heart galloping in the aftermath of their frenzied coupling.

Eithni was having trouble gathering together her scattered wits. Her thoughts felt like clouds blown adrift upon a windy sky. Donnel had literally driven all rational thought from her. Days of tension between them, building steadily after that night together, had led to this.

Eithni's loins still pulsed and ached with pleasure. She longed to strip the clothes off him and do that all again on the mossy, damp ground. She did not care they were out in the open. This was a desolate valley with only the gods to witness their coupling.

Eventually, she raised her head and glanced up at him. Donnel looked down, his mouth curving into a sensual smile that made her catch her breath. He reached out, gently pushing a lock of hair out of her eyes. "I meant what I said earlier," he said. His voice held a husky edge, the look in his eyes so tender that Eithni's pulse fluttered. "You have healed me … you know?"

She smiled back, reaching up to caress his face with the back of her hand. "You make me sound much more powerful than I really am."

He shook his head, his smile fading. "I couldn't have let go of the anger and bitterness without you. I'm sorry I've been so ill-tempered. I promise to be a better man … the man you deserve."

Hope flowered in Eithni's breast at his words. After all that had happened of late, she had started to believe she and Donnel would never be together. However, this afternoon changed all that. She could see the sincerity in his eyes, the vulnerability he usually hid.

"You already are," she said softly.

His mouth thinned. "I will be after I face Urcal, and once I make peace with Galan."

He pulled back from her then, and a sense of loss flooded over Eithni. She was suddenly aware that the sky had clouded over and that the afternoon had turned cold. She and Donnel had been so taken up with each other, they had not even noticed.

"Come," Donnel said, adjusting his clothing and taking her hand. "We'd better get a move on if we want to reach An Teanga by nightfall."

Eithni nodded and stepped away from the tor. Her legs wobbled under her. She was exhausted, and she could have easily made a bed for herself and taken a long rest. However, she knew Donnel was right.

Her gaze shifted behind him, to where the stallion was sedately cropping grass a few yards away.

"Luckily the pony didn't run off," she observed with a smile. "Or we'd be in trouble."

Donnel grinned back. "Not Reothadh. I've had him since he was a colt—he'd never stray far from me."

Eithni held his gaze, her smile widening. *And neither will I.*

Chapter Twenty-six

Into The Boar's Lair

NIGHT HAD ALMOST fallen when they reached An Teanga at last.

Seated before Donnel, Eithni spied the broch rising against a sparkling sound. The fort sat upon the western side of a bay, upon a velvet-green spur of land that jutted out into the water.

Fertile farmland stretched around the fort: a patchwork of tilled fields and low stone huts with cone-shaped turf roofs. Smoke rose from the roofs, and Eithni inhaled the scent of peat and the aroma of stewing meat and frying oatcakes. Saliva filled her mouth.

How I miss oatcakes.

The closer they got to the outer walls of the fort, the tenser she felt Donnel become. She sat side saddle, curled up against the wall of his chest. The events of the day had drained her, and she had even dozed in his arms during the journey from The Valley of the Tors. However, despite her weariness, Eithni's senses sharpened as they approached An Teanga.

Urcal mac Wrad had been enraged and grieving the last time she had seen him. He would not give them a warm welcome.

As if reading her thoughts, Donnel shifted in the saddle. "We must tread carefully here, Eithni," he murmured in her ear. Up ahead the warriors keeping watch over the gate had spotted them. Tall dark silhouettes, spears in hand, moved to bar their way.

"Don't lose your temper then," she warned him.

"No chance of that," he whispered back. "Do you think I'd give Urcal further cause to gut me?"

A rough voice called out, as one of the warriors stepped forward brandishing his spear. "Halt. Who goes there?"

Donnel pulled up his stallion. "I am Donnel mac Muin."

A stunned silence followed before the sentry spoke up again, his voice aggressive. "What's your business here, Battle Eagle?"

Eithni felt Donnel grow tenser still, although his voice was steady in reply. "I'm here to see your chief."

The Boar warriors led them into a massive two-tiered broch that reminded Eithni of Dun Ardtreck. Built out on the edge of the spur, a row of twisting stone steps led up to the entrance. Peat braziers burned around the base of the broch, gilding the grey stone. The flames guttered in the cool wind that gusted in off the sound.

Donnel and Eithni walked into a vast circular space lined with curtained alcoves. Like the broch of Dun Ardtreck, a set of steps led to the upper level where the chieftain, his wife, and children would sleep.

A massive hearth dominated the space below, where chunks of peat glowed red. There were a number of people inside seated at tables that formed a square around the hearth, although Eithni's gaze did not linger upon their hard, unwelcoming faces. Instead, her attention shifted to the chieftain's table at the far end, where Urcal mac Wrad watched their approach.

His wife, Modwen, and his daughter, sat to Urcal's left. There was no sign of the young boy Eithni had seen with them at The Gathering—Urcal's son. However, Eithni did recognize the bald, barrel-chested warrior who sat to Urcal's right from The Gathering.

None of those seated at the chieftain's table watched Donnel and Eithni approach with friendly eyes.

Misgiving twisted in the pit of Eithni's belly. She had never been enthusiastic about Donnel's decision to come here—but now that they were standing in the broch of An Teanga, her instincts told her it had been a grave mistake.

"So the Battle Eagle has flown in, has he?" The bald man next to Urcal drawled. Eithni watched him, her gut clenching tighter. Urcal scared her—he was a huge bear of a man with arms like tree branches and a forbidding face—but this warrior had eyes that truly frightened her. They appeared almost black in the flickering light of the cressets burning behind him.

"Aye, Gurth—it appears so," Urcal murmured from next to him.

Eithni noted then that The Boar chieftain's hand grasped a cup. She watched his fingers flex upon it as if he wished he was gripping a sword.

Fear slithered down her spine. *We shouldn't have come here.*

But it was too late to run. They stood in the midst of The Boar's lair, trapped on all sides.

"Good evening, Urcal," Donnel dipped his head respectfully. "I know I'm the last man you wish to see tonight."

Urcal grimaced. "Now that isn't strictly true, Battle Eagle. I'd love to see you squirming on the end of a pike. I'd like to ram it up your arse myself."

These words brought a rumble of laughter from the surrounding crowd of kin and warriors seated around the hearth.

Yet none seated at the chieftain's table smiled—and neither did Eithni or Donnel.

"You have a grievance against me," Donnel spoke once more, once the noise had quietened, "and I understand it. I'm here now to acknowledge the wrong I did you ... and to apologize for it."

"Apologize?" Gurth rose to his feet and spat, the offensive matter landing on the rushes a few feet from where Donnel stood. "A few glib words won't make things right."

"Sit down Gurth," Urcal rumbled, his gaze never leaving Donnel. When the warrior obeyed, muttering a foul oath as he did so, The Boar chieftain spoke once more. "My cousin is more hotheaded than me ... although I agree with him. What makes you think coming here and offering a halfhearted apology will make amends for what you did?"

Donnel bowed his head. "I wronged you, Urcal," he said. Listening, Eithni heard how those words cost him. His voice took on a low rasp. "Loxa was for you and Galan to deal with ... I acted rashly, selfishly."

Urcal let out a humorless bark of laughter at this. "Listen to you, the proud warrior attempting to humble himself before me. I see through you, Donnel mac Muin. I heard what Galan said to you—never to darken his door again unless you made amends for what you did. You think a bit of groveling will suffice so you can fly back to your eyrie and join your people again."

Donnel lifted his head, his gaze meeting Urcal's. "That's not it. I know I wronged you ... I knew it two moons ago, but I didn't care. My words are sincere."

Urcal's mouth twisted, while beside him his wife shifted in her seat, her gaze nervous. "What's changed then?"

Donnel reached out and beckoned Eithni to him. She stepped close, and he put a protective arm around her shoulders. "I've changed."

Eithni tensed against him. She was not happy about this at all—this whole scene seemed wrong to her. Loxa mac Wrad had been a brute, just like his brother before him. Donnel had done the world a great favor by cutting him down. She hated that this strong warrior was having to humiliate himself like this before Urcal.

Donnel did not deserve it.

Urcal's gaze narrowed as he noticed Eithni for the first time. His attention till now had been riveted upon Donnel; he had been blind to all else. "What have we here? Is this the woman Loxa rode off with?"

"My name is Eithni," she spoke up. "I'm sister to Tea, wife of Galan mac Muin."

Gurth snorted. "A Wolf bitch then."

"She is my woman," Donnel spoke up, a warning edge in his voice for the first time.

In another time and place a thrill would have gone through Eithni at hearing Donnel stake his claim on her. But not now, not tonight. Urcal and his warriors would only use it against him.

Urcal leaned back in his carven chair. For the first time Eithni noted that the armrests were sculpted in the likeness of boar's heads with long tusks. The Boar chieftain considered Donnel for a moment, scratching his thick beard as he did so, his brow furrowing.

"I don't understand you, Battle Eagle. I never took you for a fool—but coming here you've just put your neck on the chopping block."

"I'm not offering myself up as a sacrifice," Donnel replied, holding Urcal's gaze. "I came because the peace between our tribes is too important to be put at risk over slights and grievances."

"You sound like Galan now," Urcal mocked him. "So noble and fair-minded compared to the rest of us blood-thirsty savages."

"I fought with Galan over his quest for peace—but I understand him now," Donnel countered. "He sees beyond all of this." Donnel swept his arm around the broch. "If we fight amongst ourselves we'll grow weak. I was at the Wall ... I saw the men who threaten this isle. If the Caesars ever cross the water and step upon our shores, we need to stand united."

Urcal's heavy face creased into a scowl. "That's a different matter entirely. Right now, we aren't talking about that ... this is about you making amends for killing my brother.”

“He can’t,” Gurth spat out. The big man lurched to his feet, yanked an axe off the wall, and went to lunge across the table.

Urcal’s meaty arm shot out, and he pulled his cousin back.

Gurth shook him off, turning on Urcal in a rage. “Let me finish him ... for Loxa.”

The Boar chief shook his head, his face thunderous. “I tire of others taking matters into their own hands,” he growled. “I rule here—I decide who lives and dies.”

Gurth glared down at him, but Urcal stared back, his face unyielding. Long moments passed before the bald warrior did as commanded, sinking back down upon the bench with ill grace.

Urcal shifted his attention from his cousin, back to Donnel. “I’m not a merciful man. You made a mistake coming here.”

“My father respected you,” Donnel replied. Eithni was surprised at how steady his voice was, how calm he looked. Both of them were moments away from being attacked, but he appeared utterly unruffled. “He said you were a proud but honorable warrior. A good friend but a formidable enemy.”

Urcal grunted. “Muin was my friend. What of it?”

“Tarl and I have done a lot of damage—but Wurgest and Loxa also played their part. I’m here to see if we can bury the past.”

Urcal watched him. It was a predatory stare that made the hair on the back of Eithni’s forearms prickle. She could see The Boar chieftain was thinking, calculating.

“You want to make amends, Battle Eagle?”

Donnel nodded, although Eithni could feel the tension rippling through him. He too would have noticed the shrewd look on Urcal’s face. Neither of them would like what was coming next. “Then show yourself worthy of that name.”

A muscle ticked in Donnel’s cheek. “How?”

"Tomorrow at dawn you'll fight four of my fiercest warriors—one at a time. Four to represent all of the tribes you dishonored at The Gathering." Urcal's face twisted as he spoke these words. "If none of them succeed in killing you, I'll spare your life and make peace with The Eagle."

Donnel watched him. "And if not?"

Urcal's gaze gleamed. "I'll throw your body to the pigs," he growled. "Then I'll whore your woman to my men, and consider your people my enemy."

Eithni's heart started hammering. Nausea rose within her, and bile bit at the back of her throat. She squeezed Donnel's arm hard. "No," she whispered. "Don't—"

"Agreed," Donnel cut her off. He released Eithni's arm and stepped forward, his gaze locking with Urcal's. "Do I have your word you will honor this?"

"Aye," Urcal replied, a grin spreading across his hairy face, "you do."

Chapter Twenty-seven

Widow's Lament

"WHY DID YOU agree to it?" Eithni choked out the words. "Can't you see Urcal's toying with you?"

They were alone, seated on straw in a stall in the stables. Urcal had put them there for the night, with a group of warriors guarding the entrance to the building in case they tried to flee. There was no light in here; Eithni could only see Donnel's silhouette against the deeper darkness surrounding him.

"I had to," he replied, his voice low. "You can see how angry Urcal is. I need to do this his way."

"He'll have you butchered."

Donnel snorted. "Your confidence in me is flattering."

Eithni balled up her fists at her side. "This isn't about your male pride. You know what will happen if you fall."

Donnel shifted across to her, and she felt his arms go around her. "Listen to me, mo ghràdh," he whispered into her hair. "I swear to you I will not fall tomorrow. I'll not risk any harm coming to you."

Eithni's breathing hitched. *My love.* Did he really mean that? "You shouldn't make such promises," she whispered, all the anger draining from her voice. "You aren't immortal."

"You haven't seen me fight," he replied.

His arrogance—his confidence in his ability as a warrior—was breathtaking. There really was no doubt in him. Eithni wanted to believe him, but she had seen men and women—all formidable fighters—cut down by one well-timed blade. Alpia had been one. No one could cheat death, not even Donnel.

Eithni closed her eyes, glad he could not see her expression. She reached up and traced the lines of his face with her fingertips. "I trust in your skill," she whispered back. "I just don't trust Urcal. Watch yourself tomorrow."

A chill, clear morning dawned, and a crowd gathered at the base of the broch of An Teanga to see Donnel fight.

There was a wide space, bounded by rocks and water on each side, which led down to the stables and the gate into the village beyond. News of the challenge had spread, and a large crowd of men, women, and children jostled for position around the fighting ring.

Donnel stood in the center of it, stripped to the waist and barefoot. He wore a sword at his hip and a fighting knife strapped to his right thigh.

Eithni stood at the edge of the ring, heckled and shoved by villagers. Wrapping her cloak around her, she ignored them, her gaze fixed upon Donnel. She had barely slept overnight, and now her belly felt twisted up in knots.

Cheers went up as Urcal appeared above, emerging from the broch. He lumbered down the steps, his wife and daughter following. Modwen looked peaky this morning, and her daughter wore a strained expression. Watching them, Eithni wondered if there had been an argument in the broch, for even Urcal looked unsettled.

His craggy face was set in grim lines, his dark blue gaze uneasy.

The Boar chief reached the bottom of the steps and strode up to where Gurth stood at the far side of the ring. Eithni had made sure to stand as far as possible from the chief and his cousin.

Urcal's gaze swept over the crowd, and his uneasy expression changed to one of shrewd calculation. He lifted a hand to greet them, and the folk of An Teanga called out to him, their voices ringing out over the water.

Grinning now, Urcal shifted his attention to Donnel, who stood calmly in the center of the ring watching him.

"Morning, Battle Eagle," Urcal boomed. "Sleep well?"

"Aye, like a bairn," Donnel replied. "Thanks for your concern."

The crowd rumbled at this—a mix of laughter and muttering. However, Urcal's expression did not change as he watched Donnel. "A blade and a dagger, eh? Surely a warrior of your skill doesn't need them?"

Donnel raised a dark eyebrow. "You'd go into battle with only your fists as weapons?"

Urcal gave a soft laugh that caused the crowd around them to grow still. "I have, laddie." He stepped forward while Gurth smirked at his side. "I'll take your weapons." The Boar chieftain walked across the grass and halted before Donnel. "Hand them over."

Donnel held Urcal's gaze for a long moment, before he wordlessly unbuckled his sword and unsheathed his knife, passing them both over to Urcal.

The Boar grinned at him. "That's the spirit."

Urcal turned, swaggered back to where Gurth was glaring at Donnel, and dumped the weapons at his cousin's feet. "Gurth will look after these for you." Urcal then glanced over his shoulder, at where a big man with long brown hair and a short beard stood waiting. "Denoch—you can go first."

Denoch—a man who looked around Donnel's age—strode into the fighting ring. He was huge, his shoulders as broad as an oxen yoke. In his right hand he carried a heavy two-headed axe. Its sharp edges gleamed in the morning light.

"What's this?" Donnel spoke up, ignoring Denoch for a moment as his attention returned to Urcal. "No weapons for me, but my opponents are allowed them?"

"Aye, that's right," Urcal called out, a grin still stretching his face. "My rules here, Battle Eagle."

Eithni clenched her hands, gripping her fur cloak so tightly her fingers began to ache. This was what she had feared. She had known Urcal would not play fair, that he would do his best to rattle Donnel and put him at a disadvantage.

Yet if Donnel had been thrown by Urcal's move, his face did not show it. Instead, he shifted his attention to Denoch. The big man stood around four yards away, watching Donnel with an expressionless face and cold eyes.

Eithni swallowed the panic clawing up her throat. Events were now spiraling out of their control. Donnel's words the night before now seemed foolish and hollow. How could Donnel fight that man without a weapon?

Denoch moved first, lunging at Donnel and bringing his axe down overhead in a savage cut. Donnel moved, ducking out of the way as the blade whistled by, but The Boar warrior kept moving. He struck again with an inside cut aimed at Donnel's belly. Donnel dodged again, dancing back, light on his feet. The crowd around them roared. They wanted blood, not this game of cat and mouse.

Denoch's axe cut again and again—and then the game changed when Donnel stepped inside his guard and grabbed hold of the axe shaft. The fight shifted, and the crowd grew still. Donnel kneed his opponent in the groin, drove an elbow into his belly, and sent Denoch staggering back doubled up in agony.

Ripping the axe from his opponent's hands, Donnel tossed it aside and went after Denoch again. Two punches dropped him, and The Boar lay curled up cradling his injured cods, groaning.

Breathing hard, Donnel straightened up, his gaze swiveling to Urcal.

The Boar chief was not smiling now. "Finish him then," Urcal snarled. "Send him to meet The Reaper."

Donnel shook his head. "I've spilled a loch of blood over the last year—I'll not kill a man who was ordered to fight me." He stepped back from the fallen Denoch. "Send the next one in."

Eithni watched, torn between awe and terror. She loathed violence, and it had sickened her to see that fight. And yet the sight of Donnel, the way he handled himself, was magnificent. He had not lied to her. The man could definitely fight.

A warrior bearing a sword came at him next—a lithe, dangerous female with long braided hair who moved like lightning. It took Donnel longer to disarm her, and she managed to draw blood—scoring his left arm—before he did. After that he knocked her out with a blow to the jaw that sent her sprawling.

The third warrior to enter the ring was a man of similar size and build to Donnel. Eithni had seen him at the ringside, watching the previous two fights with interest, looking for a weakness to exploit. He came at Donnel with a fighting knife: a long, wicked blade that flashed in the sunlight as he moved.

After a dance that led them around the perimeter of the ring, right up to the edge of the baying crowd, Donnel managed to grab the man's wrist. After that he made short work of him. He broke his arm, drove him to his knees, and forced him to the ground. Donnel's knee was positioned in the small of the warrior's back.

The man screamed in agony, for Donnel had twisted his broken arm behind him. A moment later he yielded.

"You fight dirty, Battle Eagle," Urcal observed as Donnel's third opponent crawled from the fighting ring.

Donnel straightened up and wiped a forearm over his sweat-slicked brow. "Aye—my father taught me well. He told me to do whatever it takes to win."

Urcal laughed at that, his dark-blue eyes sparkling. "Sounds like something Muin would have said."

"I'll end him," Gurth growled from next to Urcal. The warrior had watched every fight with predatory intensity. "Let me slice the bastard open."

Urcal inclined his head to his cousin. "Are you sure about this, Gurth? I was going to let Elpin go last."

Gurth's face screwed up, and he spat on the ground. "I've had enough of watching our warriors be humiliated. It's time I showed the Battle Eagle how a real man fights."

Urcal raised a heavy eyebrow. "In you go then."

Gurth lumbered into the ring, drawing a heavy double-edged iron blade. "Meet *Widow's Lament*," he said as he circled Donnel. "She sings for your blood, laddie."

Donnel watched the warrior, his handsome face a mask. Sweat gleamed on Donnel's face and torso, and Eithni knew he would be tiring now. He had just fought three warriors, and Urcal had deliberately not allowed him to rest between each fight. Gurth was older than the three that had come before him, but Eithni sensed he was the most dangerous of the lot. He had an intensity about him, a caged savagery that seethed just beneath the surface. His expression was hungry now.

The two men circled each other for a while, and like the other fights, Donnel did not attack first. Instead, he waited for his opponent to strike.

"What's wrong?" Gurth growled. "Don't have the balls to fight me?"

Donnel grinned back, showing Gurth his teeth. "You're the one with the blade. You start this."

Gurth's face turned hard, his heavy brows lowering over glittering eyes. A heartbeat later he lunged.

Eithni watched them, her heart hammering so violently now that she clutched her hands over her breast—afraid it might burst through her rib cage. This fight was different to the other three, and the crowd knew it too. They had stopped baying and heckling, their faces tense as they watched Gurth attack Donnel again and again. He moved swiftly for such a heavy man, each strike wielded with cunning.

Donnel had to work hard to avoid *Widow's Lament*. He was still faster and more agile than his opponent, but he was tired. Eithni could see the energy draining from him.

Gurth saw it too, his mouth a rictus as he chopped, swiped, and stabbed. He had watched the other fights closely, had seen what happened when Donnel got under his opponent's guard. As such, he attacked swiftly, dancing back the moment he had executed his strike so that Donnel could not get too close.

"Getting tired are we?" Gurth mocked as they continued to circle. "You're not invincible after all."

Donnel ignored him. His face was set in harsh lines, his grey eyes dark. Even from yards away, Eithni could feel the anger building in him. She had heard tales of how he had fought in the south—how centurions had fallen screaming under his blade. Fury at the world had turned him savage, although the past two moons they had spent together had changed him.

Fear crushed her ribs. Had she unwittingly robbed him of the ruthless edge he now needed? After watching him fight, she was in no doubt of his ability, but he was now facing a man who lusted for his blood.

Gurth lunged once more, and this time the tip of his blade found its mark—scoring an angry red line down Donnel's left arm. Blood flowed, but Donnel paid it no mind.

Roaring, Gurth came at him again, swinging the blade at Donnel's waist.

Eithni stopped breathing.

Donnel dropped to the ground and rolled, moving in a blur under Gurth's guard. Then he gripped the blade with one hand and kicked the warrior's legs out from under him.

Gurth fell heavily, and the blade spun from his hand. Donnel caught it by the hilt and rolled to his feet.

It all happened in a heartbeat.

Donnel tossed *Widow's Lament* into the sidelines. Folk screeched and jumped back to avoid the blade, but neither men in the fighting ring paid them any attention.

Recovering his footing, Gurth lurched to his feet and reached for his fighting dagger. Donnel was on him before he could draw it.

He drove an elbow into his chest, driving the big man back.

Gurth's meaty fist flew out, grazing the side of Donnel's head, but Donnel kept coming. His face was a rictus of savagery as he punched Gurth in the throat.

The Boar crumpled to the ground and lay choking, grasping his windpipe.

Gasps and mutters reverberated around Eithni. That was a potentially fatal blow.

Eyes blazing, Donnel stood over Gurth, his gaze shifting to where The Boar chieftain stood watching. "Shall I kill your cousin, or is this enough for you?" he rasped.

Urcal held his gaze, his expression thunderous. Eithni saw the war within him, then his attention shifted to where Gurth lay choking. "Leave it," he growled. "We've seen enough."

Chapter Twenty-eight

Urcal's Son

THE CROWD DRIFTED away, many of the men muttering in disappointment. They had come to see the Battle Eagle butchered, and instead had seen their own warriors humiliated.

Eithni watched them go, before she stepped into the fighting ring and crossed to Donnel's side.

"Shall I take a look at him?" she asked, glancing down at Gurth's purple face. Tears of rage and pain streamed down his cheeks.

Donnel nodded, his expression unyielding. The rage had not yet left him either. "Be careful though," he rasped.

Eithni knelt beside Gurth and examined his throat. After a few moments she looked up, meeting Urcal's gaze across the ring. "His wind pipe isn't crushed," she told him coldly. "He'll live ... although he might have problems with his voice for a while."

Urcal held her gaze for a heartbeat before nodding. He then nodded to two men who had remained behind. "Take my cousin back to his alcove."

The warriors obeyed, grabbing the barrel-chested warrior under each armpit and dragging him away. Meanwhile, Eithni rose to her feet and stepped close to Donnel once more.

"So, Urcal," Donnel said after a long pause. "Do you honor your agreement? Will there be peace?"

The Boar chieftain folded his arms over his broad chest and grimaced. "Aye. I'm a man of my word."

"You're a healer?" A woman's voice, interrupted them. Modwen stepped forward, her pale face taut. Eithni saw the desperation in her gaze when Modwen met her eye.

"I am," Eithni replied. "Why?"

"Silence, Modwen," Urcal growled. "This isn't the time."

The chieftain's wife whirled to face Urcal, high spots of color staining her pale cheeks. "Your son is dying. If this woman is a healer, we need her help."

Urcal's face turned thunderous, although despair flared in those midnight blue eyes of his.

Eithni stepped forward, her gaze flicking between the two of them. "Your son is ill?"

Modwen nodded, her eyes gleaming. "Aye, Varar went to his furs with a fever three days ago ... and hasn't risen since. The fever is getting worse."

Eithni did not hesitate. "Can I see him?"

"Aye," Modwen stepped away from her husband and bid Eithni to follow. "Come with me."

The lad lay in a small alcove on the top floor of the broch. His private space sat at the edge of the wide area his parents occupied, next to the one where his elder sister slept.

One look at Varar's flushed face, the way his body twitched under the furs, and Eithni knew she had come not a moment too soon. She ducked into the alcove and knelt next to the boy. He was around three, a handsome lad with a mop of dark hair and a face that reminded Eithni of Loxa's. The warrior would have looked like this boy at the same age.

Shaking off the unwelcome memory of Loxa, Eithni reached out and placed a hand on Varar's brow.

He's burning up.

"Can you help?" Modwen spoke behind her. Eithni glanced over at the woman's worried face.

"I will try," she replied. She hated to give false hope to the loved-ones of those she tended. The truth was that the lad was in a bad way. He was no longer conscious, and the fever was now taking hold of his limbs, making them shiver and jerk.

"I need herbs," Eithni informed the chieftain's wife. "Meadowsweet, Woundwort, Boneknit, or Elderberry—do you have any of these?"

Modwen gave a swift nod. "I will be back soon."

The woman disappeared, leaving Eithni alone with Varar in the alcove. Next to the furs was a bowl of water and a cloth. Eithni wet the cloth, wrung it out, and started to bathe the boy's feverish body. She needed to lower the fever, or it would consume him in no time at all.

Eithni wished she had her healer's basket with her—yet it had been left behind at The Gathering Place. The herbs, powders, and tinctures in it had taken her over a year to gather and prepare. She hoped that the chieftain's wife would be able to find the herbs she needed.

Modwen returned a while later, flushed and sweating, carrying a basket of herbs. "I've found them," she gasped.

Eithni took the basket, her heart lifting when she saw that Modwen had indeed found everything. She got to work, using a pestle and mortar to crush the herbs. She then mixed them with water and drained the juice through a fine cloth into a cup.

With Modwen's help, she raised Varar up into a sitting position and held the cup to his lips. They could only give him a little at a time, otherwise they risked choking him—and Eithni was loath to waste any of the drink. She waited patiently, giving him the contents of the cup bit by bit, knowing that each swallow was doing him good. Eventually, the cup was drained.

"What now?" Modwen asked, hovering anxiously at Eithni's side. "Is there anything else you can do?

Eithni nodded. "I need cold, freshly drawn water and a new cloth. We must continue bathing his body."

Modwen hurried away, returning with cold water she had just drawn from the well outside. Then she took her place opposite Eithni, and together they began to bathe Varar's body.

What followed was a long day and an even longer night. Urcal visited once or twice, a silent, grim-faced figure in the doorway. He said nothing, his gaze riveted upon his son's face, before he eventually left Eithni and his wife to tend Varar.

Exhaustion swept Eithni up in its clutches. Modwen brought her a meal, and at one stage Eithni drifted off to sleep, leaning up against the stacked-stone wall of the alcove.

She did not see Donnel, although she knew he would be nearby, waiting for her.

The night was the worst part of their vigil. In the darkest hour—the time when only owls and wolves are awake—Varar's breathing grew shallow, and his pulse fluttered at the base of his neck.

"The Mother watch over him," Eithni whispered. She could feel The Reaper nearby—as she often did before someone died. A chill settled over the alcove, and the cresset on the wall opposite flickered.

Eithni clenched her jaw. "You will not take him," she whispered.

She leaned forward and wiped a cool cloth over his fevered brow, murmuring the healing charm at the same time.

With my hands I heal
With these herbs
With these words
By the Hag's cauldron
By the power of the night.

Eithni repeated the charm three times before sitting back, her gaze settling upon Varar's pale face.

She worried that she had been brought to the lad too late—that the fever had dug its claws in too deep—but Varar mac Urcal did not die. He was strong, and when the first rays of dawn light filtered in from the tiny window above their head, the boy's eyes fluttered open, fixing upon Eithni.

The eyes were midnight blue, like Urcal's—like Loxa's.

"Who are you?" he croaked. "One of the Fair Folk come to take me away?"

Eithni favored him with a tired smile. "No, my name's Eithni. I'm a healer. We nearly lost you."

"Varar!" Modwen burst into the alcove, joy spreading across her face. "You're awake!" She fell to her knees beside her son, her eyes gleaming with tears.

A shadow fell over them then, and Eithni glanced up to see Urcal standing there, lines of worry etched upon his heavy-featured face. "Welcome back, lad," he rumbled.

A strange sensation settled over Eithni. She had imagined Urcal as a man incapable of tenderness and compassion, yet she now saw that was not so. The four tribes of this isle had more in common than differences; yet because they had all lived in isolation for so long, it was easy to turn your neighbor into your enemy.

Hadn't she thought that the people of The Eagle were her enemies once?

Eithni rose to her feet and gathered her things. She would leave Urcal and Modwen with their son.

Emerging from the alcove, she crossed the rush strewn floor and made her way downstairs. There she found Donnel seated by the great hearth, his fingers wrapped around a bowl of stew. One of the older women was fussing over him like a broody hen. "You'll need that arm seen to," she clucked. "That's a deep cut."

Donnel nodded, his face lined with fatigue and worry. "I will … thank you."

Relief lit in his eyes when he saw Eithni approach. His gaze then searched her face. "Did the boy survive?"

Eithni nodded. "He's awake … the worst is over."

She sat down upon a stool next to Donnel, gratefully accepting the bowl of stew the woman passed her. Around them the inhabitants of the broch were going about their morning chores. Women were kneading bread at the tables and plucking fowl for the noon meal, while warriors broke their fast with bread and stew before going outdoors to work.

Eithni took a mouthful of stew, her belly growling as she did so. It was delicious, and she was starving. When she had devoured half the bowl, she looked up to find Donnel watching her with a half-smile curving his lips.

Eithni froze. "What? Have I got something on my face?"

He shook his head, his smile widening. "No, I was just reflecting on what an incredible woman you are."

Eithni glowed under the compliment, although she tried to mask her pleasure with a scowl. "It would take such a woman to put up with you," she replied. "Coming here was a terrible idea. I can't believe we're still breathing."

He raised an eyebrow. "I told you to trust me."

"Aye, and I did. I just didn't expect you to have to fight four armed warriors with your bare hands."

Donnel huffed. "I'll admit, I was worried for a few moments. I should have realized Urcal wouldn't fight fair."

Eithni shook her head, exasperated. "He did his best to kill you," she reminded him. Her gaze went to Donnel's left arm. The wound had stopped bleeding, but the woman's comment earlier was right. It needed tending. "Let me take a look at that."

"Don't you want to check on Gurth?" Donnel asked. "I think I hurt him badly."

Eithni gave him a narrow look. "The man would have cut you in half with that sword of his," she replied. "I think he can wait."

Chapter Twenty-nine

Homeward Bound

URCAL AND MODWEN led Donnel and Eithni out of the broch later that morning, escorting them down to the stables below. A stiff breeze whistled in from the sound, causing Eithni to shiver. Although the air inside the broch was stale and smoky, it was also warm. The chill outdoors came as a shock after spending over a day within.

Donnel retrieved his pony from his stall and led the grey stallion out into the yard where the chief and his wife waited. There they said their farewells.

Urcal addressed Eithni first. "I owe you a great debt, healer," he rumbled, his voice uncharacteristically subdued, his expression humble. "We thought we'd lost Varar. Your skill is great indeed."

"Do you not have a healer here?" Eithni asked.

Modwen shook her head. "She died nearly four moons ago."

Eithni frowned. That was ill-fortune, for every fort needed an able healer. She felt bad that she had left Dun Ringill so long without anyone to tend the sick.

"If you find someone willing to learn, I'm happy to teach them what I know," she replied. "Just send him, or her, to Dun Ringill."

Modwen smiled. "Thank you, lass. That is kind." The chieftain's wife stepped forward then and hugged Eithni tight. "I will never forget this," she whispered.

"Nor will I," Urcal added. The Boar chieftain's attention shifted to Donnel then, and his expression changed. There was exasperation mixed with respect in his eyes as he watched the younger man.

"My cousin is in a foul temper now," he grumbled. "He wants your guts."

"He had his chance," Donnel said with a grin. "He'll just have to accept defeat."

"Aye," Urcal replied, his thick eyebrows lifting. "Only Gurth isn't the type to forget such things. Lucky for you I rule here. When you see Galan, tell him there is no ill-feeling between our people. The Eagle and The Boar are friends again."

Donnel nodded. "I will."

They rode out of An Teanga with wispy clouds racing overhead across wild blue skies. Once they passed the last of the patchwork of fields, Donnel urged Reothadh into a canter. The stallion surged forward, kicking up dirt behind it, keen for a long run. They rode up the hills north of the fort, threading their way through copses of trees toward the skyline.

The wind was an icy slap on Donnel's face—a reminder that Gateway loomed and that autumn was now upon them—but he did not mind. The cold made him feel alive and reminded him how close he had come to dying back there.

He had said nothing to Eithni, but there had been a number of moments during the fights when he had cursed himself for coming here, for putting Eithni in such danger. However, he had been careful not to let his emotions show—not before or after the fighting.

The Battle Eagle had a reputation to uphold. To those in the crowd he was more than a man—he was a legend.

The folk of An Teanga had hoped to see one of their warriors cut him down. He had seen the awe, and the fear, on their faces as they had sloped away.

He had needed to keep the mask in place while they remained at An Teanga, for he could not risk Urcal changing his mind. However, in the end, it was not Donnel's victory over those warriors that had created goodwill between him and Urcal, but Eithni's miracle.

She had brought the man's son back from the brink of death, saved him from The Reaper's scythe. Donnel had won the challenge, but he had not won these people's hearts.

Only Eithni could have done that.

They crested the hill and rode over wind-seared moors. Reothadh seemed to know the way—there was no need to guide the stallion back to Dun Ringill. An odd blend of excitement and dread warred within Donnel the farther north they rode.

He was going home, back to a place he had spent the last year and a half railing against. He now realized how much he loved it. He was a part of the land, the stones of the great broch, and the briny waters of Loch Slapin that stretched west to the horizon. It was only when his home had become forbidden to him that he had finally realized its worth.

Donnel rode one-handed, his other arm wrapped around Eithni. She leaned back against him, and he felt her melt into his chest as sleep claimed her. The poor lass had barely slept the night before in her effort to save Varar. Despite the pony's jolting gait and the biting wind on their faces, sleep pulled her down into its clutches.

He let her sleep and did not bother to try and talk. There would be plenty of time for that later.

They passed The Valley of the Tors sometime after noon. It had been a late start, and they would not reach Dun Ringill before dark. As such, they made camp for the night west of the Red Hill.

Donnel lit a fire before glancing up at the grass and rock-strewn slopes of Bienn na Caillich. The mountain had always been a point of reference for him. He knew that, once he spied its russet-colored bulk, home was never far away.

Modwen had filled a bag with food for them so there was no need for Donnel to go hunting. Just as well, for he was bone-weary tonight. Seated next to glowing lumps of peat, they shared a supper of bread, butter, boiled eggs, and cold slices of roast venison—a feast indeed after their lean diet of the past two moons.

Eithni sighed as she ate. "I'll never take food for granted again," she mumbled as she took another bite of boiled egg. "Never."

Donnel grinned at her. "You never complained about night after night of dried venison."

She gave him a rueful look. "You wanted to send me away. I didn't want to give you another reason to, did I?"

He huffed. She was right. He held her gaze then, taking in the delicate beauty of her face bathed in firelight. "I'm glad I didn't manage to chase you off," he said after a moment. "I was so rude, no one could have blamed you for leaving."

Eithni gave him a wry smile. "There were times when I wondered what I'd gotten myself into," she admitted, "but I knew I had to stay."

Eithni finished her meal and brushed crumbs off her skirt.

The mood had changed between them, the conversation venturing into shallow waters were they could easily get grounded. Now that they were safe, and far from An Teanga, her thoughts returned to her and Donnel. What did the future hold for them? Nervousness fluttered under her ribcage. Her instincts told her that he cared, yet part of her still doubted him.

She needed to know how he really felt about her.

Eithni's gaze settled upon Donnel. He looked up from poking the fire with a stick. "What is it?"

"Back at the hut, you told me you could never give me your heart," she began hesitantly, forcing herself to hold his gaze. "Do you still feel that way?"

He watched her. His features tightened, and a shadow moved in his eyes. Her belly contracted, and she prepared herself to hear the worst.

"No, I don't," he said after a long pause, "and I'm sorry I said those words ... I know they hurt you." He glanced away then, his expression pained. "There's no real excuse I can give, other than I was scared of what I felt for you. I acted on instinct." His gaze returned to her. "I'm not scared anymore."

Eithni swallowed, her heart now beating furiously. "Back in An Teanga, you said I was your woman ... you called me 'my love'. Do you remember?"

Donnel gave her a slow smile. "Of course I do."

"Did you mean it?"

Donnel slid close to Eithni and cupped her face with his hands. "Yes, I did ... do you not believe me?"

"I don't know," she whispered. "Things have moved so swiftly of late. I'm not sure what to believe."

Donnel's mouth slanted over hers. He did not hold back—he kissed her deeply, passionately—and when they broke apart both of them were gasping for breath.

"I meant it," he said, his gaze snaring hers. "After everything I've done of late, all the blood I've spilled, I thought the gods had forsaken me. But instead they brought me a gift. Eithni ... mo ghràdh ... if you will have me I am yours."

Joy flowered within Eithni, robbing her of breath.

He smiled then, and reached out, caressing her cheek. "I've never met anyone who wears their soul for the whole world to see like you do," he murmured, looking deep into her eyes. "It makes me want to protect you, guard you like a sacred flame ... will you let me?"

Eithni eventually found her voice, although her vision swam as she blinked back tears. "Of course I will," she whispered. "I'm yours, Donnel mac Muin."

With that she threw her arms around his neck and kissed him back.

A misty, wet dawn greeted Donnel and Eithni the following morning. A fine rain fell, causing the embers in the fire pit to smoke and sizzle. A heavy mantle of cloud shrouded the bulk of Bienn na Caillich to the east.

After finishing the last of the food Modwen had given them, Donnel and Eithni packed up and rode west. The closer they got to Dun Ringill, the more settlements they passed—villages ringed by stone walls. Galan had worked hard over the past two years to build defenses for each village, to keep the inhabitants safe from raiders.

Eithni perched before Donnel as Reothadh thundered through the veil of fine misty rain. The weather could not dampen her spirits this morning; a warm sense of well-being enveloped her, as if she sat before a roaring fire.

Last night, after opening their hearts to each other, Donnel had made love to her with heartbreaking tenderness. It had been very different to their urgent coupling in The Valley of the Tors. There had been a wild hunger, a desperation between them *that* afternoon, the moment Donnel had finally given in to his feelings for her.

Donnel had been different ever since that moment in that valley. A sense of purpose emanated from him. He had survived The Boar's lair and with Eithni's help had healed the rift between the two tribes. He was now free to focus on the future.

Images of the night before returned to Eithni, and her lower belly fluttered with excitement. She recalled the things he had done to her and the feel of the cool night air caressing her skin as she arched toward him crying his name. She could not wait to do it all again.

However, despite her own happiness, she could not fail to notice that Donnel grew quieter and tenser as the morning progressed—the closer they drew to Dun Ringill.

He's worried about seeing Galan again.

Donnel had not spoken to Eithni about his brother this morning, yet she knew Galan was never far from his thoughts. She understood Donnel's disquiet, for she had witnessed the final words between them. She had never seen Galan like that before—fury had turned him savage, dangerous. If Donnel had not accepted his exile, had he not walked away, she was not sure what Galan would have done.

What now? Will Galan still be angry? Will he want to listen to anything Donnel has to say?

Up ahead the bulk of Dun Ringill appeared on the western horizon, a broad stacked-stone tower rising out of the mist.

Eithni reached out and placed a hand over Donnel's arm that clasped her firmly around the wait, giving it a gentle squeeze. His tense wait was nearly over. Soon they would know.

"Galan's not here. He rode north with Tea, Tarl, and Lucrezia."

Lutrin's words fell heavily in the damp air. The warrior had come out to meet them, his rugged face creased with joy. He had clasped Donnel in a bear hug, before the other warriors—Namet, Ru, and Cal, who had emerged from the broch behind him—had done the same.

They greeted them with relieved smiles, but Donnel saw the wariness in their eyes. Something was amiss.

The news his brother was away deflated him. "North?" he asked with a frown. "Where?"

"To the Glen of the Stags," Cal spoke up. "Wid sent word that some of his hunters had seen you there. Galan's gone looking for you."

A tense silence fell, and Donnel shared a long look with Eithni. He then turned back to the others. "We left the north five days ago. How long has Galan been away?"

Lutrin's brow furrowed. "Around the same time."

Beside Donnel, Eithni shifted. "They will have found our hut by now. They'll be wondering what has become of us."

Donnel nodded, raking a hand through his hair. Why was nothing in life straightforward? He had been steeling himself for his arrival home, only to discover Galan had gone looking for him. He did not know whether to be pleased or worried by the news.

"I should go north and meet them," he said after a long pause.

Ru huffed, his sharp-featured face tightening. "But you just got here."

"Aye, but I can't wait around while my brothers and their wives scour this isle for me."

Lutrin's frown deepened. "At least stay for the noon meal. Afterward we will saddle up and go with you."

Chapter Thirty

Meeting in the Mist

THEY MET GALAN'S party just south of the Black Cuillins.

It was late in the day, and the mist and rain had grown heavier, converging upon them in a dense milky shroud. The worsening weather worried Donnel, for they risked losing their way in the fog or passing the chieftain and his companions without seeing them.

But as the grey day grew grimmer still, and dusk reached out its shadowy fingers from the west, Donnel spied the outline of four ponies ahead.

Drawing up his stallion, Donnel glanced back over his shoulder at where Lutrin rode a few yards behind him.

"Look ... up ahead. Can you make them out?"

Lutrin's gaze narrowed. The warrior had the best eyesight of any in the tribe, making him a great hunter. "Aye," Lutrin murmured. "It's them."

Donnel inhaled deeply and twisted in the saddle, his gaze sweeping over his companions. The rest of you wait here," he said. "Eithni and I will meet them alone."

Lutrin nodded. Donnel was relieved he did not need to explain anything else. They all knew how difficult this meeting would be."

Donnel urged Reothadh forward and rode toward the advancing riders. Eithni, seated behind him, arms wrapped around his waist, squeezed his torso gently. Placing a hand over hers, Donnel squeezed back. He appreciated her silent support. He had been dreading this moment for a while.

The others had seen them, and as he drew nearer Donnel could make each of them out clearly. Galan rode in front with Tea a few yards behind him. Tarl and Lucrezia brought up the rear, riding side by side.

The sight of his eldest brother shocked Donnel. The past two moons had aged him. He was barely four years older than Donnel, yet his face was set in hard lines, with grooves either side of his mouth that had not been there before the summer. A deep line etched the skin between his dark brows. Galan's harsh expression accentuated his hawkish looks. In the grey gloaming he looked ill-tempered and dangerous.

Their gazes met, and Galan tensed, his broad shoulders drawing back.

His brother did not look pleased to see him. Donnel was not surprised—they had parted on terrible terms. Donnel had brought shame upon his tribe, and he had made Galan look weak—as if he could not control his youngest brother.

Donnel had much to apologize for—and he was not sure where to start.

He drew Reothadh up a few yards from Galan while his brother brought his black stallion to a halt. Tea had also stopped. She watched Donnel, her face suffused with relief. However, she did not speak. Like Eithni, she was waiting for the two brothers to talk.

"I heard you went looking for me," Donnel broke the strained silence first.

"Aye," Galan replied, his voice rough. "It seems we had a wasted trip."

"We left the Glen five days ago."

Galan's gaze narrowed. "And you went back to Dun Ringill?" There was a challenge in his voice and an edge of accusation. Donnel sensed that Galan imagined him and Eithni making themselves comfortable in the broch while the others searched for them. It was time to put his brother right.

"No," he replied evenly. "We traveled south to An Teanga. I went to see Urcal."

Galan's grey eyes widened. "Why?"

Donnel heard the mistrust in Galan's voice, and although it was merited, it stung. After the mess he had made of things, Galan thought he had gone south to stir up more ill-feeling. Although had that been the case, they both knew Donnel would not have left An Teanga alive.

"I remember your last words to me well," Donnel said softly.

Did he imagine it, or did Galan flinch at that? Donnel had just reminded him of his fury that day.

"I was in a black rage," Galan rasped. "I spoke harshly, but you gave me no choice."

"I know," Donnel replied, "and that's why I went to see Urcal. To fix the mess I made."

Galan gave him an incredulous look. "And you're still breathing? Urcal's not a man to forgive easily."

Donnel allowed himself a thin smile. "You're right … he isn't. He took away my weapons and pitted me against four of his best armed warriors. He told me all would be forgiven if I survived."

Galan's mouth twisted. "And you did."

Donnel gave his brother a humorless smile. "Aye, although there would still have been ill-feeling if Eithni hadn't saved the life of Urcal's young son. The lad had succumbed to a fever, and they had prepared themselves for the worst."

Galan's gaze shifted to where Eithni now peeked over Donnel's shoulder, and his expression softened slightly. "We owe you much, lass."

Donnel felt her nod, acknowledging Galan.

The brothers' gazes met once more. "Urcal bid me to tell you that our tribes are now friends," Donnel said quietly. "He bears you no ill-will. However, his cousin Gurth—whom I fought last—won't forget so easily. Fortunately, it's Urcal's word that counts."

He saw the tension release from Galan's shoulders as if a great weight had just been lifted from him. His brother swung down from the saddle and strode toward him. Donnel dismounted and stepped away from his pony.

Galan wore an intense expression, and for a moment Donnel was not sure whether his brother was going to belt him or hug him. Galan did the latter, pulling Donnel into a rough embrace, hugging him tight. When Galan released him, his brother's eyes were shining.

"Don't ever make me do that again," he growled. "It nearly broke me."

Donnel swallowed, suddenly choked up. "I'm sorry," he rasped. "I didn't think about anyone but myself that day. Bitterness and anger turned me cruel ... but Eithni, she healed me."

Galan's gaze widened, before he glanced up at where Eithni still sat upon Reothadh. When he met Donnel's gaze once more, his expression was speculative. "You certainly seem different," he replied. "The bleakness in your eyes is gone ... it's good to have you back."

Eithni leaped down from the pony and raced across the wet grass to her sister. Tea grabbed her, enveloping her in a fierce hug.

"I was so worried," Tea choked, and when Eithni pulled back she saw her sister's face was wet with tears. Fierce, strong Tea was weeping at the sight of her.

Tarl and Lucrezia stepped forward to embrace her too, before Tarl strode across to greet Donnel, leaving Tea and Lucrezia to fuss over Eithni.

Lucrezia scrubbed at the tears running down her face, her eyes alive with joy. "Gods, how I've missed you, Eithni."

"We all have," Tea said huskily. "I've raged at Galan ever since we returned home." She cast a censorious look in her husband's direction. "Not only has Galan been worrying himself sick, but he's had my shrew's tongue flaying him day and night."

Eithni smiled at that. She knew her sister could be vicious when riled.

Galan approached them and put an arm around his wife's shoulders, pulling her close. "I deserved it," he said with a tight smile. "Blood should not turn against blood. I should have defied Urcal."

Donnel stepped up beside him. "I'm glad you didn't," he said, meeting Galan's eye. "It was the only way. I couldn't go on like that ... so full of vengeance and rage." He looked over at Eithni then, and their gazes fused. "And Eithni and I would never have grown close ... if we hadn't been left alone together."

Surprise rippled across the faces of their companions, and Eithni realized that with all eyes on Donnel and Galan, none of them had spotted the obvious.

Tarl gave a low whistle. "Sly dog," he said with a grin, giving Donnel a prod in the ribs with his elbow.

Donnel gave him a withering look in response. "There was nothing sly about it. We're not all like you."

Tarl threw back his head and laughed. "I'd forgotten how much better with women you are than me," he teased, a wicked smile still curving his lips.

"Tarl, stop it," Lucrezia admonished, giving him a playful punch in the arm.

Warmth spread over Eithni as she watched them. How she had missed these people: missed their laughter and teasing, missed their company. They were her family.

The party made camp where they stood for the night, for dusk came upon them swiftly on such a grey day. They erected hide tents to keep the rain off and took refuge around a smoky peat hearth as night settled over the world.

Eithni sat between Tea and Donnel, next to the fire, and ate a simple supper of bread and cheese, listening as the conversation moved around her. She was weary tonight; it seemed as if all the excitement had finally caught up with her. She could have fallen asleep where she sat.

To her left Donnel was talking animatedly with Tarl. It was clear the two—who had always been so close—had missed each other. Donnel was telling his brother of their experiences at An Teanga.

"Eithni, is everything alright?"

Eithni glanced to her right, where she found her sister observing her. She favored Tea with a tired smile. "Aye, just exhausted."

Tea's brow furrowed. "No, I meant between you and Donnel. It's clear you've developed a bond ... but you've both been through a lot."

Eithni's smile widened. Tea was just being protective, but there really was no need. "And that's why we're so well suited. We understand each other." She paused here, struggling to find the words to express herself. "Donnel said I healed him, but he healed me too. I trust him, Tea."

Tea's face softened, and she reached out, placing a hand over Eithni's. "I'm so happy for you," she said huskily. "After Forcus I thought you'd never let a man near you again."

Eithni sighed. "Neither did I, but my time with Donnel changed all that. It's hard to put into words, Tea ... but somehow he set me free."

Later that evening Lucrezia approached Eithni.

The women were laying out furs for them all to sleep on. It was warm and smoky inside the tent, and the air smelled of damp leather and wool. Still, it was far more pleasant than sleeping under the stars, especially in this weather.

"That potion you gave me ..." Lucrezia whispered, leaning close lest anyone else hear her. "It worked."

Eithni stared at her blankly for a moment, before she realized what Lucrezia was talking about: the herbs she had given her friend at The Gathering, to help Lucrezia's womb quicken.

Eithni's eyes widened. "Are you with child?"

"I've missed two moon flows ... and I throw up my oatcakes most mornings," Lucrezia whispered. "It must have happened at The Gathering."

Eithni reached out and hugged Lucrezia tight. Life over the past two years had been hard at times. She had come to live at Dun Ringill and made a new start with Donnel, but it was hard to forget all the darkness. Forcus had been the worst of it, but she had also lost her father and brother. Alpia and Maphan had both been her friends, but they were dead too. It lightened her heart to know that Lucrezia carried Tarl's child. She knew how much it had meant to her friend.

"I'm so happy for you both," Eithni said, her voice husky with emotion. "That is wonderful news."

Chapter Thirty-one

Long Overdue

THE RAIN CLEARED as they rode back into Dun Ringill. A crowd awaited them, for news of Donnel and Eithni's return had spread throughout the fort, and everyone was anxious to see the chief and his brother make peace.

Ruith was among the crowd, full of nervous excitement as she studied the faces of the riders who rode through the gate of the outer wall. She had cast the bones many times ever since they had returned from The Gathering but, strangely, they had not given her any real answers. Each time she had cast the bones and peered down at the symbols carved upon them, she had felt more confused.

Sometimes they spoke of harmony, other times of death and treachery.

It had boded ill, as if the gods themselves had no idea what the future held.

However, when her gaze alighted upon Eithni, seated behind Donnel as they followed Tarl and Lucrezia through the gate, the knot of worry in the pit of her belly eased. Her practiced eye could see at a glance that something monumental had shifted in both of them.

Donnel was smiling again; the hard lines that had turned his handsome face savage were gone. Eithni was radiant: her skin glowing and her unbound walnut-colored hair flying in the wind. That reticence—that reserve—the girl had brought with her from Dun Ardtreck was gone. It was a woman, confident and at ease with herself, that returned home.

Ruith smiled and let the tension that had plagued her ever since returning from The Gathering seep from her. Then she turned, following the riders and the crowd of excited folk up the path back to the broch.

Donnel drained the last of the ale from his cup and pushed himself back from the table. After three huge bowls of boar stew and great slabs of buttered bread, he was now full.

"Where are you going?" Lucrezia, who sat to his right, asked. "We've still got plum and apple pudding. I made it myself."

"I can't eat another mouthful," Donnel replied with a groan, rubbing his belly. "Please save me some."

Next to Lucrezia, Tarl's gaze narrowed. "Hold up ... how about a game of knucklebones and another cup of ale?"

Donnel shook his head. "Later ... there's something I need to do first."

Donnel turned to Eithni, who was seated to his left. "Will you come with me?"

Gaze curious, Eithni nodded before rising to her feet.

Leaving the others to their pudding, the pair of them left the broch, descended the steps to the stable yard, and made their way toward the stone arch leading into the village. Above them the last of the mist had lifted. The sun was warm on their faces.

"Where *are* we going?" Eithni asked, linking her arm through his.

"To make a visit long overdue."

Her face softened in understanding. "To see Talor?"

"Aye—it's time, don't you think?"

Truthfully, Donnel knew he had left this moment far too long. He did not like to think back on how he had shunned his son, for it filled him with shame. Luana would have been furious to see him behave so, but he had been so filled with hate at the world for taking her away from him that he had not cared.

He did now.

He was also nervous and a little embarrassed. Mael had taken his son in and was raising him, along with her daughter, as her own. The woman had her own grief to deal with; she had recently lost her husband and was now bringing two children up without assistance.

Donnel could not let things go on as they had been.

They crossed the village, making their way past clumps of low stone roundhouses built into the ground. Smoke rose from the roofs of many as the inhabitants were indoors having their noon meal—the largest meal of the day.

Mael's dwelling was not far from where her old house had once stood. The roundhouse Maphan had built for her was no more—and in its place was a vegetable plot filled with turnips, kale, and onions.

Mael's new roundhouse was smaller than the one she and her husband had shared. However, one glance at the neat rows of herbs, the clay pots of flowers, and the skins drying outdoors on racks, and Donnel could tell this was Mael's home. She had always been an industrious woman.

They found her feeding the children turnip and onion pottage inside the smoky interior. Talor gnawed on a piece of bread, while Ailene had succeeded in getting food all over her chubby face.

Donnel's heart swelled at the sight of them.

Mael rose to her feet, a wide smile of welcome splitting her tired face. She was thinner than Donnel remembered, her blue eyes hollowed with grief. However, that smile had true warmth in it.

"Donnel! Eithni!"

Donnel stepped forward and embraced Mael before moving aside so that Eithni could greet her.

"How are you?" Eithni shifted back from Mael, her gaze searching her face.

Mael's smile faded just a little. "Well enough." She stepped back, motioning to Talor and Ailene. "The children are thriving as you can see."

Donnel's gaze returned to Talor. The lad, who was now approaching his second winter, stared steadily back at him with wide blue eyes.

Luana's eyes.

Donnel had not spent much time gazing at his own reflection, having only glimpsed it occasionally in the still surface of the lake or the polished curve of a shield, yet he knew the lad looked a lot like him: the same thick black hair and the same shaped face and nose.

"Do you know who this is, Talor?" Mael asked gently.

The boy shook his head, his gaze still fixed upon Donnel.

Donnel's chest constricted at the knowledge his boy did not recognize him, and yet he deserved no better. He had done his best to ignore Talor's existence.

Moving forward, Donnel hunkered down before Talor so their gazes were level. "I'm your da."

Talor's bright blue eyes widened. "My da?"

"Aye, lad."

"Remember, Talor. I said your father was a great warrior?" Mael interceded. Donnel could hear the tension in her voice, the embarrassment. She likely worried that Donnel would think she had never spoken of him to the boy.

Talor nodded, his face growing serious. His gaze took Donnel in, studying him from the crown of his head to the tips of his boots. By the time the lad had finished his inspection, he wore a stunned expression. Donnel had to remind himself that Talor was still very young. He was only just starting to form short sentences, only just beginning to become aware of the world beyond the roundhouse he shared with his cousin and aunt.

A lump rose in Donnel's throat. It was not too late. Talor was not old enough to be angry and hurt by his rejection. They could start again.

He smiled at Talor. "How about a hug for your da then?" he asked, surprised that he was suddenly nervous. What if the boy did not want to go near him?

Talor did hesitate a moment before casting a glance in Mael's direction.

"It's fine," Mael replied gently. "Your da has just gotten back from a long and difficult journey. He'd like a hug."

Talor put down his piece of bread and tottered over to Donnel. The lad's warm, firm body collided with Donnel's, nearly knocking him onto his backside. Even small, the lad had strength to him. Talor's arms encircled his neck. Donnel wrapped his own arms about his son and drew him into a hug.

He squeezed his eyes shut, feeling tears prick his eyelids. He could not believe he had denied himself this, cut himself off from his own flesh and blood. His grief and rage had truly blown him off course, but he had found his way home.

Eithni wiped away a tear as she watched Donnel hug his son. Next to her Mael was also weeping. Wordlessly, Eithni reached out and put an arm around her friend's shoulders. Mael's thinness shocked her; the woman had always been slightly built, but now she felt as if she would snap. She made Eithni feel as if her own lean frame was well-padded.

Finally, Donnel released Talor from his hug and sat the lad back down to finish his meal.

Mael saw Donnel and Eithni outside, leaving the children within so that the three adults could speak privately.

"I'm glad you came today," Mael said huskily. "Talor needs his father."

"I'm sorry I waited so long," Donnel replied, a rasp in his voice.

Mael met Donnel's gaze. "I was happy to take Talor in. He's a sweet-natured lad and good company for Ailene." She broke off here, her blue eyes shadowing. "However, ever since I lost Maphan, I have found it difficult to cope ..."

"We will help you," Eithni said, stepping closer to Mael. "Whatever you need. You know you aren't alone."

Mael nodded, attempting a wobbly smile. Eithni's heart hurt to watch her. Mael had always been so strong, so serene. Losing her husband had changed her. It should not have surprised Eithni, for she knew what grief did to people. She remembered how her father had transformed after her mother died and the fury that had consumed Donnel after losing Luana. They all dealt with it in different ways.

"I don't know how to be a father," Donnel said, casting his gaze back at the shadowed interior of the roundhouse where Talor and Ailene were still eating. "What if I make a mess of it? What if he grows up hating me?"

Mael huffed, wiping away the last of her tears. "None of us know what we're doing ... you just make it up as you go along."

"You will be a great father," Eithni added, meaning every word. "Talor is a lucky boy indeed."

They left Mael to finish her noon meal and begin her afternoon chores, and began the walk back to the broch. However, half-way there, Eithni steered Donnel toward the outer wall—toward her hut. She had not been to visit it since their return, for there had not been time. Yet she wished to see it now.

Her dwelling looked as if Eithni had never been away. Even the garden out front was neat; someone had been tending to it.

She and Donnel walked down the path and let themselves in. The interior was exactly how she had left it over two moons earlier: her dried herbs, and pestle and mortar, still sitting on her work table. Her sleeping furs sat neatly folded in a corner, and the iron griddle where she cooked her morning oatcakes still hung over the fire.

Eithni turned to Donnel, studying his face in the light filtering in from the open doorway. "How I've missed this place."

His mouth quirked. "Would you prefer us to live here then?"

She inclined her head. "Don't you want to live inside the broch? You have your own alcove."

He snorted. "It's tiny ... Tarl and Lucrezia sleep in my old alcove, but I've no wish to have it back. The broch's too noisy anyway. I've gotten used to having space of my own. I'd like to live here."

Eithni glanced around her. The interior of her humble dwelling suddenly seemed shabby and cramped. "Are you sure it's not too small?" she asked.

"Possibly," he admitted with a smile, "but I can extend it to give us some more space." His smile faded then, and he stepped forward. "Would you mind if Talor came to live with us?"

He looked so worried; as if the request was unreasonable, and she would deny him. Eithni moved close, reaching up to stroke his cheek.

"Of course he can," she replied softly, warmth flooding through her. "I don't mind at all."

Epilogue

Blessing

Three months later ...

DONNEL WENT TO Luana's cairn at dawn. He walked alone, carrying a spray of heather, his boots crunching over the frozen ground. It was a still morning. The clear sky promised a fine, if cold, day ahead.

It was not long before Mid-Winter Fire, although at least three more moons of chill weather stretched before them after that.

Donnel climbed the slope to the row of burial mounds and made his way to Luana's cairn. It had been a while since he had visited this place, but it felt right to come here this morning—on the day that marked Luana's death two winters earlier.

The year before he had stood here, in the same spot, filled with black rage and a need to wreak vengeance upon the world. Only twelve moons had passed, and yet he felt completely changed—and as such the world seemed different too.

Last year this row of cairns had been a depressing sight that had filled him with a bleak hopelessness. Now though, he felt just a gentle sadness, mingled with a feeling of peace. His father, Alpia, Maphan, and Luana—he stood here amongst the dead. They had let go of this world. They did not rage, grasp, and bicker like the living did.

Donnel moved close to Luana's tomb and placed a hand on the icy stone. "I don't suppose you thought to see me back here," he murmured to her. "You probably guessed I'd get myself killed before now ... and I almost did." A soft smile curved his lips as he thought of how Luana used to tease him. Yet his memories of her were not quite as sharp as they had been. Her face was slightly out of focus, and he struggled at times to recall the sound of her voice.

His throat bobbed as he swallowed. "I'm happy again, Lu," he whispered, "but I don't want that to mean I'll forget you. I never want to do that."

He clenched his fist against the stone, fighting against the knowledge that, with each passing year, his memories of Luana and their time together would slowly mist and dim. But that was the way of things—you could not hold onto the dead. They wanted you to let them go.

"Talor has your eyes," he said after a long pause, "although I'm unhappy to report the lad has inherited my stubborn nature. I really hoped he was going to take after you."

It was true—with each passing moon, Talor had more and more to say for himself. He now adored Donnel, although he did not like being thwarted. Just a day earlier, Donnel had been forced to reprimand him. Donnel had been about to leave for a day's hunting with his brothers, and Talor had thrown a tantrum because he had wanted to join them. The boy's rage had amused Galan and Tarl, although in the end Donnel had been forced to sling Talor—now screaming with rage—over his shoulder and carry him home.

Donnel glanced down at the heather he still carried. Luana had loved this plant, had worn it in her hair at their handfasting. He stooped down and laid the herbs at the entrance to the cairn. When Talor was old enough to explain things to, he would bring his son here on this day. He had already told the lad much about Luana. He wanted her memory to live on through Talor.

As he straightened up, he could have sworn he felt a light touch on his arm and a gentle caress upon his cheek. He tensed. There was no breeze this morning. What had touched him?

A sense of peace flooded over Donnel then, the sensation so powerful that his breathing stilled. Despite the cold morning and the glittering frost that covered the world, a gentle warmth soaked into his limbs. He knew then—without understanding how—that Luana was with him.

The sensation was fleeting, gone like a butterfly that settles upon a leaf for a moment before fluttering away, and yet he was sure of it.

His wife, who had been so cruelly ripped from him, had just given him her blessing to start afresh.

Donnel kissed the palm of his hand before laying it flat on the rock guarding the entrance to the cairn. "Be at peace in your long sleep," he whispered. "You are remembered, sweet Luana."

He left the burial mounds and made his way down the slope toward the fort. Up ahead, he spied plumes of smoke rising from the roofs of the roundhouses inside the walls and from the great broch itself. As the sun slipped over the edge of the hills to the east, the world around him sparkled, as did the flat surface of Loch Slapin.

Donnel walked home through the village, returning to the dwelling he now shared with Eithni. It looked vastly different to a few months earlier—for he had built another hut next to it and knocked out the wall dividing them. In the past moons, Eithni had extended the garden too, preparing beds for the spring. Donnel had built her a coop for fowl. The birds were already awake, pecking around on the frosty ground as Donnel walked up the path.

He opened the wattle door, his gaze settling upon the scene within.

Eithni sat beside the fire pit, frying oatcakes on the griddle. The sweet, nutty aroma of baking wafted toward Donnel making his belly growl. Next to Eithni sat a small boy, his chubby hands coated with butter and honey as he plowed his way through a dish of oatcakes.

"Slow down, Talor," Donnel greeted his son. "Save some for the rest of us."

Eithni glanced over her shoulder, a smile spreading across her heart-shaped face. "There's plenty for all," she admonished him.

"You spoil the lad," he replied, pretending to look cross when it was difficult not to smile. The sight of them sitting there in such easy companionship warmed his heart. Eithni had welcomed Talor into her life wholeheartedly, and the boy adored her.

Watching them this morning, Donnel reflected on how fickle the gods were. They could be so cruel at times, and yet when you least expected it they could be benevolent. Happiness was fragile and fleeting. You could not take it for granted, not for an instant. With love came the risk of loss. He had not wanted to accept that with Luana, but he did now—and the realization was freeing.

Eithni flipped the oatcakes and glanced back at him once more. "Are you going to stand there for much longer?" she asked, raising an eyebrow. "It's freezing outside—you're letting in a draft. Come in and pull up a stool. These are almost ready."

Donnel smiled. He liked it when she was bossy. Eithni might have looked delicate and sweet, but he had soon learned this woman had a will of iron. It was one of the many things he loved about her.

"Aye, alright then." Donnel stepped down into the living space and pulled the door closed behind him. "Talor, move over and make some space for me."

The End

Historical and background notes for BATTLE EAGLE

Glossary

Aos Sí or Fair Folk: fairies
bandruí: a female druid or seer
Broch: a tall, round, stone-built, hollow-walled Iron Age tower-house
Caesars: the Ancient Romans
Camanachd: the old name for the Scottish game of shinty, a game similar to hockey
Clachneart: the Stone of Strength—an ancient form of shotput

Place names

An t-Eilean Sgitheanach: Gaelic name for the Isle of Skye
Beinn na Caillich: the Red Hill of Skye
Dun Ardtreck: a broch located on the Minginish Peninsula of Skye
Dun Ringill: an Iron Age hill fort on the Strathaird Peninsula of Skye
An Teanga: an Iron age broch located on the southern coast of Skye
Bodach an Stòrr (The Old Man of Storr): a pinnacle of rock on the north-western coast of the Isle of Skye

The four tribes of The Winged Isle*

The People of The Eagle (south-west)
The People of The Wolf (north-west)
The People of The Boar (south-east)
The People of The Stag (north-east)

Gods and Goddesses of The Winged Isle*

The Mother: Goddess of enlightenment and feminine energy—the bringer of change
The Warrior: God of battle, life and growth, of summer
The Maiden: Young goddess of nature and fertility
The Hag: Goddess of the dark—sleep, dreams, death, winter, and the earth
The Reaper: God of death

Festivities on the Isle of Skye*

Earth Fire: Salute to new life and the first signs of spring (February 1)
Bealtunn: Spring Equinox
Mid-Summer Fire: Summer Equinox
Harvest Fire: Festival to salute the harvest (Aug 1)
Gateway: Passage from summer to winter (October 31/November 1)
Mid-Winter Fire: Winter Equinox

* Author's note: I have taken 'artistic license' when it comes to the names of the tribes, festivities, and gods and goddesses upon the Isle of Skye. The historical evidence is very scant, making it a challenge for me to get an accurate picture of what the names of the tribes living upon Skye during the 4th century would have been. Likewise I could not find any references to their gods and festivities. The Picts were an enigmatic people, and we only have their ruins and symbols to cast light on how they lived and whom they worshipped. To make my setting as authentic as possible, I have studied the rituals and religions of the Celtic peoples of Scotland, Ireland, and Wales of a similar period and have created a culture I feel could have existed.

The culture, language, and religion of the Picts is one largely shrouded in mystery. Unlike my novels set in 7th Century Anglo-Saxon England, which is a reasonably well-documented period, researching 4th Century Isle of Skye proved to be a challenge. Pictish culture is largely an enigma to us. However, they did leave behind a number of fascinating stone ruins, standing stones, and artifacts, as well as a detailed collection of symbolic art.

I created the four tribes of The Winged Isle from Pictish animal symbols. This is not a far-fetched idea; many Iron and Bronze-age peoples identified themselves with animal symbols. The clans we identify with Scotland did not appear until a few centuries later.

Cast of characters (in alphabetical order)

Ailene: daughter of Mael and Maphon
Cal, Namet, Lutrin, and Ru: Galan's four most trusted warriors
Deri: young woman married to Cal, one of Galan's warriors
Donnel mac Muin: youngest brother of The Eagle chieftain
Eithni: Healer at Dun Ringill, sister to Tea
Galan mac Muin: Eagle chieftain
Loxa mac Wrad: Urcal's brother
Luana: Donnel's wife (deceased)
Lucrezia: Tarl's wife
Mael: Luana's sister (married to Maphan)
Ruith: the seer at Dun Ringill
Talor: Luana and Donnel's infant son
Tarl mac Muin: younger brother of The Eagle chieftain
Tea: Galan's wife
Urcal mac Wrad: Wurgest's elder brother, the Boar chieftain
Wurgest mac Wrad: Urcal's brother (deceased)
Gurth mac Bolc: Urcal's cousin
Modwen: Urcal's wife
Varar: Urcal's young son
Fortrenn: chieftain of The Stag

Acknowledgements

None of these books would have been written without the support of my readers. Your emails, positive reviews, and support have allowed me to make a living doing what I love. I can't thank you enough!

Thanks to my wonderful sister, Katie. She doesn't just read my books to support me—she loves them too!

I'm also hugely grateful to my husband, Tim. He's been my supporter right from the beginning, and has encouraged me every step of the way. Thank you, babe.

About the Author

Award-winning author Jayne Castel writes epic Historical and Fantasy Romance. Her vibrant characters, richly researched historical settings and action-packed adventure romance transport readers to forgotten times and imaginary worlds.

Jayne is the author of the Amazon bestselling BRIDES OF SKYE series—a Medieval Scottish Romance trilogy about three strong-willed sisters and the men who love them. An exciting spin-off series set in the same story-world, THE SISTERS OF KILBRIDE, is now available as well. In love with all things Scottish, Jayne also writes romances set in Dark Ages Scotland ... sexy Pict warriors anyone?

When she's not writing, Jayne is reading (and re-reading) her favorite authors, cooking Italian feasts, and taking her dog, Juno, for walks. She lives in New Zealand's beautiful South Island.

Connect with Jayne online:
www.jaynecastel.com
www.facebook.com/JayneCastelRomance/
Email: contact@jaynecastel.com